continued . . .

"Presley is a creative, energetic young woman with a wry sense of humor." —The Mystery Reader

How to Crash a Killer Bash

"If you're looking for a lighthearted, fast-moving story with enough polish and pizzazz to keep your interest popping to the very last page, look no further than this party-hearty book."
—Fresh Fiction

"Exactly what a modern cozy should be: light and playful, a little romance mixed with a little mystery, and thoroughly enjoyable start to finish." —Mysterious Reviews

"The mystery is well plotted [and] there are plenty of clues and plenty of suspects, letting readers guess along with Presley." —The Mystery Reader

"I highly recommend this book to all mystery readers, cozy or not. This is a party that you don't want to miss."
—Once Upon a Romance Reviews

"With plenty of action on her investigation and several poignant moments, readers will enjoy the perils of Presley Parker."
—Genre Go Round Reviews

"The second Party-Planner mystery is a delightful whodunit due to a strong lead and the eccentric cast who bring a flavor of San Francisco to life." —The Best Reviews

"Plenty of motives and suspects . . . a cast of lively characters." —Gumshoe

How to Host a Killer Party

"Penny Warner's scintillating *How to Host a Killer Party* introduces an appealing heroine whose event skills include utilizing party favors in self-defense in a fun, fast-paced new series guaranteed to please."
—Carolyn Hart, Agatha, Anthony, and Macavity award–winning author of *Death Comes Silently*

"A party you don't want to miss."
—Denise Swanson, national bestselling author of *Little Shop of Homicide*

The Party-Planning Mystery Series

HOW TO DINE ON
Killer Wine

A Party-Planning Mystery

PENNY WARNER

AN OBSIDIAN MYSTERY

OBSIDIAN
Published by New American Library, a division of
Penguin Group (USA) Inc., 375 Hudson Street,
New York, New York 10014, USA
Penguin Group (Canada), 90 Eglinton Avenue East, Suite 700, Toronto,
Ontario M4P 2Y3, Canada (a division of Pearson Penguin Canada Inc.)
Penguin Books Ltd., 80 Strand, London WC2R 0RL, England
Penguin Ireland, 25 St. Stephen's Green, Dublin 2,
Ireland (a division of Penguin Books Ltd.)
Penguin Group (Australia), 250 Camberwell Road, Camberwell, Victoria 3124,
Australia (a division of Pearson Australia Group Pty. Ltd.)
Penguin Books India Pvt. Ltd., 11 Community Centre, Panchsheel Park,
New Delhi - 110 017, India
Penguin Group (NZ), 67 Apollo Drive, Rosedale, Auckland 0632,
New Zealand (a division of Pearson New Zealand Ltd.)
Penguin Books (South Africa) (Pty.) Ltd., 24 Sturdee Avenue,
Rosebank, Johannesburg 2196, South Africa

Penguin Books Ltd., Registered Offices:
80 Strand, London WC2R 0RL, England

First published by Obsidian, an imprint of New American Library,
a division of Penguin Group (USA) Inc.

First Printing, July 2012
10   9   8   7   6   5   4   3   2   1

PUBLISHER'S NOTE
This is a work of fiction. Names, characters, places, and incidents either are the
product of the author's imagination or are used fictitiously, and any resemblance to actual persons, living or dead, business establishments, events, or
locales is entirely coincidental.
    The publisher does not have any control over and does not assume any re-
sponsibility for author or third-party Web sites or their content.

ALWAYS LEARNING   PEARSON

To my mother, who taught me how to write. To my kids, who taught me how to party. To my husband, who taught me everything else.

ACKNOWLEDGMENTS

Thanks to everyone who helped with this fun series—Colleen Casey, Janet Finsilver, Staci McLaughlin, Mike Melvin, Rebecca Melvin, Ann Parker, Connie Pike, Carole Price, Vicki Stadelhofer, Matt Warner, Susan Warner, Tom Warner. And to my wonderful agents, Andrea Hurst and Amberly Finarelli, and my astute editor, Sandy Harding. Thanks so much!

Here's to the corkscrew—a useful key to unlock the storehouse of wit, the treasury of laughter, the front door of fellowship, and the gate of pleasant folly.

—W. E. P. French

Chapter 1

PARTY-PLANNING TIP #1

When hosting a wine-tasting party, remind guests to use all five senses—eyes for clarity and color, nose for intensity of bouquet, palate for taste, tongue for texture, and ears for the sound of "Mmmmm . . ."

"I'll drink to that!" my office mate on Treasure Island, Delicia Jackson, said after my work-for-hire chef Rocco Ghirenghelli set down a freshly decanted bottle of the Purple Grape Winery's two-year-old merlot.

"You'll drink to what?" I asked her as I watched Rocco pour the maroon liquid into a glass etched with the words "California Culinary College." The wine licked the inside of the glass as it spiraled like a whirlpool to the bottom.

"Ignore her, Presley," Rocco said, raising an eyebrow at Dee. "She'll drink to anything."

Delicia stuck her tongue out at him. That was the kind of relationship my two event-planning assistants shared.

Rocco, rarely out of his chef whites, was dressed in khaki slacks and a brown button-down shirt. He handed the glass to me. "Don't chug it like you usually do."

"I don't chug my wine!" I said. "I'm just not pretentious, like some of those wine snobs."

"There's a big difference between gulping and tasting," Rocco said. "I want you to really *taste* this wine. You have to know these things when you host that upcoming winery event."

"I know," I said defensively. As I reached for the glass, I had a sudden flashback to my college days, those days of wine and chugging. Admittedly I could use a few pointers if I wanted to carry off this prestigious party Rocco had snagged for me. I lifted the glass by the stem, like I'd been taught by the *Wine Goddess* cable TV show, then swirled the contents as if I knew what I was doing. Bringing it to my lips, I inhaled the "bouquet."

It smelled like grape juice. Really good grape juice.

"Okay, now savor it as you take it in," Rocco said, as Dee looked on, frowning.

"I love it when you talk dirty to me." I grinned mischievously. Rocco blushed the color of the red wine. Even his balding pate turned rosy.

I took a sip, swishing the liquid over my tongue and palate.

Dee giggled. "You look like a fish."

"Don't swish it," Rocco demanded. "It's not mouthwash. *Taste* it."

I swallowed.

"So. What did it taste like?" Rocco asked, both eyebrows raised in anticipation.

"Uh . . . kinda fruity, kinda spicy. A bit of a woody aftertaste." I'd learned some of the lingo from the TV show.

"Excellent! You've got a good palate, in spite of your tendency to guzzle wine like it was tap water. All right, now hold your glass up to the light. What color do you see?"

I studied it a moment. "Dark maroon."

Rocco nodded. "Good. Now inhale it and tell me about the aroma."

I took a quick whiff, then a deeper inhale. "Definitely fruity. Like grapes."

Rocco sighed and ran a hand through his thinning hair. Apparently "fruity" and "grapes" weren't the descriptive words he was looking for. "Okay, this time, take a sip and let it rest in your mouth for a few seconds. Notice if it's tart or sweet."

I took a second mini-mouthful, let it "play" over my palate, and said, "Both."

Out of the corner of my eye, I saw Dee pulling the bottle of wine toward her.

"Is it rich or lean?" Rocco asked. "Velvety or smooth? Silky or sticky?"

I set the glass down, causing it to clink against the desktop. "I don't know, Rocco. It tastes like wine. Red wine. How am I supposed to enjoy it if I have to think about it?"

Rocco rolled his eyes, exasperated with his wine-disabled student.

Behind his back, Dee was about to pour wine into her empty coffee cup.

He snatched the bottle from her hand. "That's a sixty-dollar bottle of wine!"

"Come on!" Delicia said, holding her cup out like a street beggar. "Pour a couple of dollars' worth in here. I want to get my *drink* on."

Rocco ignored her. To me he said, "Well? Do you want this job or don't you?"

"Of course I want it! A wine-tasting event in Napa with a food pairing from the California Culinary College? Anyone would kill to do an event like that. I promise I'll study up on wines before the event."

Rocco's face softened. He looked somewhat satisfied, until he no doubt realized that my definition of "studying wine" was essentially the same as "drinking wine." "All right, I'll let my sister Gina know. I've really talked you up, so don't let me down."

"I won't, Rocco. I swear. Thank you. I owe you."

With the wine bottle in hand, Rocco walked out of the office, leaving me to drool over the plum job he'd risked his palate and reputation for. His sister Gina was an instructor at the CCC in Napa and had been asked to cater some *amuse-bouches*—from her bestselling cookbook of the same name at a wine-tasting party. Her longtime friends Rob and Marie Christopher were hosting the event at their up-and-coming boutique winery, the Purple Grape, to announce their newest merlot. They were hoping to make a splash with this inexpensive but hearty wine and thought presenting it at a special tasting would be the best way to launch it.

And I was the lucky party planner who got to put it all together.

Not only was I looking forward to planning the event; I was also excited about spending a few extra days in the world-famous California wine country. I planned to indulge in a spa treatment, maybe take a balloon ride, and hopefully enjoy some personal time with my boyfriend, Brad Matthews—if he could get the time off. As a crime scene cleaner, he never knew when he'd be called to clean up after a messy homicide, suicide, or accidental demise. Unlike a party, death had a way of arriving unplanned.

I'd also decided to take my mother along. She could always use a getaway from her care facility and had mentioned that she had an "old paramour" who lived in the Napa area. I just hoped her early-onset Alzheimer's wasn't playing tricks with her mind again.

"So, Dee," I said to my friend, who was still holding an empty coffee cup. Even pouting, she looked adorable in a ruffly white blouse, short black skirt, and red peep-toe platform heels that raised her from a short five feet to a towering five-three. "How'd you like to play the wine goddess at the party, like that girl on TV?"

She sat up, grinning. "Sweet! I'll wear a big flowered skirt and puffy peasant top and put on a crown made from grapes and—"

I nodded as she continued the seemingly endless description of her planned costume. It sounded like something out of that old *I Love Lucy* episode where Lucy stomped grapes for a laugh. My mind wandered further as I thought about how I might use my other part-time crew members for the wine-tasting event. Gamer/computer whiz Duncan Grant could DJ and help out with the entertainment I'd planned, which included grape stomping, barrel rolling, and of course wine-tasting contests. Berkeley Wong, rising indie filmmaker, would videotape the event for my Web site. And I could always use Treasure Island, or TI as we liked to say, security guard Raj Reddy. You never knew when you might be dealing with intoxicated guests who became obnoxious, especially at an event like this.

As for Brad, I'd bring him along for personal use.

The six of us, all with offices on TI, had become friends over the past year. Everyone seemed to enjoy helping out at my bigger events—but then, who wouldn't want to go to a cool party *and* get paid? Amazingly, after several recent headlining functions, my Killer Parties event-planning business was growing like a well-tended grapevine. Good thing, since the rent was rising on my office space, my condo, and my mother's care facility.

When Delicia's motor finally ran down, I asked her to book a few rooms for the crew at a bed-and-breakfast near the Purple Grape.

"Seriously?" she asked, lighting up again. "You're comping our weekend?"

"Of course," I said, feeling magnanimous. "That's one of the perks you get when you work for an event planner like me. Besides, the Christophers have offered my mother and me a room at their 'villa,' but I'd like to find a place nearby for you, Duncan, Berk, and Raj."

"What about Brad? You shacking up with him at the winery—in front of your mother?"

My mother was no prude. She'd had a series of love

affairs in between marrying five husbands. In fact, even now as her Alzheimer's had slowly progressed, she seemed to be getting more . . . amorous. Apparently she had an endless supply of paramours.

I wasn't a thing like my mother in that department. I'd had one long relationship with one of the professors at San Francisco State, where I'd taught abnormal psychology. But I dumped him when I found out he'd been cheating on me with a cliché—one of his students. When the university dumped me—budget cuts—and I moved to the island, I met Brad. He was the only other guy I'd really been with since then. And I was taking that relationship very slowly.

"Hmm," I said. "That could be awkward. I was planning to sneak him into my room. But maybe you should get him a room too, just in case."

"I'm on it!" As an underemployed actress, Dee spoke mostly in exclamation points. "This is going to be so off the hook!"

With the party only a month away, much of the preliminary work had been done, but I still had lots to do. I pulled out the Killer Parties planning sheet I'd been working on and read over the entries under the who, what, when, where, and why sections. That was the fun part—brainstorming ideas to match the theme and then watching it all come to life.

Ahhh, a wine-tasting party in Napa, an "adventure" for my mother, and a romantic weekend with Brad. I couldn't wait to get my party on.

I spent the next few weeks juggling the wine-tasting plans with several other parties I'd been hired to do, including a Come as Your Favorite Author party—a fund-raiser for the San Francisco Library—and a Red Hat Funvention for a group of women who wore red hats and purple outfits and liked to party. By the end of the month I was more than ready for a peaceful break in the serene wine country.

Early Friday morning I picked up my mother at her care facility. Although the party wasn't until Saturday, I'd been invited to join the Christophers and Rocco and Gina for a pre-party thank-you dinner at the California Culinary College and meet a couple of their neighbors. Brad couldn't make it, so I'd asked if my mother could join us.

"Oh, Presley dear, I'm so looking forward to this," she said after I stuffed her large designer suitcase into the mini-backseat of my MINI Cooper. I pulled up the directions on my iPhone GPS, we fastened our seat belts, and off we went for what I hoped would be a tasty and relaxing evening, with lots and lots of wine.

The forty-plus-mile drive passed quickly, thanks to my mother's tour-guide lecture about the Napa Valley. As a native San Franciscan, she knew the history of nearly every place within a three-hour radius. The breathtaking view of mustard fields and perfectly aligned vineyards offered eye candy, along with rolling hills, fields of wildflowers, and wineries in every style of architecture, from modern to medieval. My mouth watered just thinking about the bottles of wine those vineyards produced.

"Presley?" I heard my mother say, and retreated from the recesses of my brain. "Are you listening to

me? You were such a distractible child with your
ADHD, and you haven't changed."

"I was listening, Mother," I lied. "You were talking
about the history of Napa." I'd heard the speech before
during the several trips we'd made over the years
when she hosted her own parties there. My mother, the
grande dame of San Francisco café society, had planned
events for such resident luminaries as the Smothers
Brothers, Pat Paulsen, and Francis Ford Coppola.

"So as I was saying," she continued, "when Prohibi-
tion came along, it hurt the industry terribly."

While she talked on, I thought about the evening
ahead. Although Rob and Marie had meant for it to be
a thank-you evening, I figured it would give me a
chance to go over last-minute changes and nail down
final details, as well as make sure they'd be donating a
percentage of the money they raised selling wine at the
event. I'd chosen Alcoholics Anonymous, since my second stepfather had died of the disease and it seemed
appropriate.

But most of all, I looked forward to another preview
of Gina's *amuse-bouches*. Everything sounded better in
French. Merlot, cabernet, chardonnay . . .

". . . then many of the wineries shut down," I caught
Mother saying. "But after the Second World War, they
picked up again, and that was the beginning of those
big monopolies like Napology that now churn out
huge quantities for less money."

Rocco had mentioned something about how the
large wineries were changing the valley, causing rumblings from the smaller boutique wineries as well as
environmental groups. "Rob said there have been pro-

tests," Rocco had told me, "from a group called the Green Grape Association. They've been complaining about all the special events, the noise and traffic, the crowds and litter. They claim these events are harming the environment."

"Are they protesting smaller wineries like Rob's?" I'd asked, thinking of the Purple Grape.

"They're going after any winery that isn't green enough to suit them."

Rocco had mentioned a woman named JoAnne Douglas, president of the Green Grape Association. He said Rob had called her a "fanatic for her radical methods" in trying to stem growth in the valley. Needless to say, although she owned a neighboring winery, she had not been invited to the party like the other neighbors.

". . . and today," Mother said, interrupting my thoughts again, "more than five million people visit the three hundred wineries here."

The personal audio tour stopped when we pulled up to the Purple Grape estate. Mother was finally speechless—thank God—as she gazed at the Tuscan-style mansion nestled in the Napa hills and surrounded by rows of vineyards.

"My goodness," she whispered. "We're staying here? I feel like I'm in Italy."

Before I could comment, a tall, good-looking man in jeans and a blue madras camp shirt appeared at the double front doors a few yards from the circular driveway. His casual attire didn't fit the setting, but I was relieved, since I'd also worn jeans—black—with a red Killer Parties logo T-shirt and my favorite black Mary Janes. Mother, of course, had dressed as if a trip to the country were a formal affair, in a yellow pantsuit, matching pumps, and a lacy wrap.

The man smiled pleasantly and waved, then started toward us, following a stone path that wound through an impeccably landscaped flower garden. Noting his graying temples and his lean but muscular physical shape, I guessed him to be a young fortysomething. Out of habit, I checked his shoes as he reached the car. Brown leather Ferragamo loafers. Italian to match the villa?

"Welcome to the Purple Grape!" he said, opening my mother's car door. "You must be Presley," he said to me, "and this must be your charming mother, Veronica."

He lent her a hand to help her out. She blushed—I thought she might swoon—and fell instantly in love. I recognized the symptoms.

"Yes, you must be Rob. Thanks so much for putting us up at your beautiful home." I took in the sprawling single-level house, from the red-tiled roof and wrought-iron fence to the circular fountain surrounded by four marble statues of children wearing crowns of grapes and holding goblets. The place was breathtaking—the perfect party setting. I almost swooned myself at the thought that we'd be staying in such an incredible home. As I started to open the trunk to retrieve my small suitcase, I heard someone call, "Rob!"

A woman came running toward us from the home. She also wore jeans, and a champagne-colored knit top. Her dark hair was swept up and caught by clips. On her feet were slip-on black leather flats—Clarks or

Rockports—simple, practical, comfortable. But unlike
Rob, the look on her face wasn't at all pleasant.

"Oh, here comes my wife now," Rob said. "I'll intro-
duce you." But his smile turned to a frown as she approached. "Marie? What's wrong?"

Marie's flushed cheeks and her wild brown eyes
made me tense up. Uh-oh. All was not well in Napa's
Camelot. It probably had something to do with the upcoming event. Such was my party karma.

"It's that witch JoAnne," she said, breathless from
the short run to my car. Even in her early forties, I
doubted this trim, attractive woman was out of shape.
No doubt stress was causing her to hyperventilate.

Rob sighed; his shoulders drooped. "What's she
done now?"

Out of the corner of my eye, I saw two other people
appear in the doorway of the house. A woman—blond,
younger looking, in tan shorts, a tight tank top, and
leather sandals—was leaning against the doorjamb, her
arms crossed in front of her midriff. I wondered if this
was the JoAnne they were talking about. Next to her
stood a man, nice looking, thirtysomething, dressed in
a black suit in spite of the warm spring weather. I
couldn't make out his shoes from this distance, only
that they were black and probably expensive, judging
by the suit.

I thought I saw a look pass between the two of them.

"She says we have to cancel the party!" Marie cried.
"God, I hate that woman!"

"What?" Rob said, shaking his head. "She can't do
that. There's no way—"

"Yes, she can!" Marie said, cutting him off. "She's

threatening to call the police! After all the work we've done to make this place a success, she's doing her best to ruin us!"

Great. The party hadn't started and already the cops were involved. I had a feeling the fizz in this event was already starting to go flat.

Chapter 2

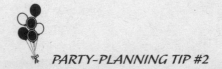

PARTY-PLANNING TIP #2

You can fake your way through a wine tasting and look like a connoisseur if you know just a few secrets. For example, when pouring wine, fill the glass one-third full, but when pouring champagne, the glass should be two-thirds full. This will make you look like an expert.

"Can she do that?" I asked Rob, alarmed at the possibility of having planned a party for nothing. It wasn't so much the money—I was sure he'd pay me my customary party-cancellation fee. It was more the event itself. I'd hoped to make a big splash in Napa and branch out, with more parties in the world-famous wine country.

Rob ran a hand through his graying hair. "I highly doubt it. She's called the police so many times, she's become the witch who cried wolf. Don't worry," he added in an ominous tone. "I'll handle her."

Although Rob looked the part of the genteel lord of the manor, I sensed a fire underneath that cool exterior.

"Marie," Rob said, taking charge, "go back in the house. Make sure Allison is finished preparing the extra rooms for our guests." I looked over at the thin blond woman in the doorway, who must have been Allison, not the JoAnne they'd been speaking about. Marie bit her lip and headed back to the house. When she reached Allison, she said something to her before they stepped back and closed the door, leaving the man alone on the porch. He headed our way.

I looked at Rob, who'd been watching the women, his brow furrowed. After they disappeared, he turned to me, assuming his previously pleasant expression. "Well, let's get you two ladies settled, shall we? Then we can begin working on the finishing touches for our big event tomorrow."

The suited man approached. "Need any help?" he said to Rob, but he was grinning at me.

"No thanks, Kyle. Javier will take care of things. I'll talk to you later."

The man named Kyle nodded, shook hands with Rob, and walked to his silver BMW parked nearby. He gave me a last, almost leering look before he opened the door and entered his car.

What was up with this guy?

Rob signaled a short Hispanic man standing near the three-car garage, next to two large buildings. I hadn't noticed him when we'd arrived, distracted by the picturesque winery. Dressed in baggy jeans, a plaid shirt, and a wide-brimmed straw hat, the man set down the sprayer he'd been holding and walked over.

"Javier, would you take the bags for these lovely ladies and put them in the guest rooms, please?"

Javier, his leathery skin tanned to a deep russet color, nodded silently. He picked up my mother's oversized, expensive YSL suitcase and my compact, sale-priced Target bag and toted them toward the side of the house, where I guessed there was another, less grand entrance.

I checked my Mickey Mouse watch: a little after ten o'clock. I looked forward to working on decorating the garden area, setting up the games, arranging the serving tables, and generally planning the logistics of the party. I'd been out to the Purple Grape only once before, more than a month ago, and although I'd taken pictures and made sketches, I knew I'd find things I'd overlooked that could cause a wrinkle in the final plans.

"Follow me," Rob said, no sign of the problem with JoAnne in his happy expression. He motioned us toward the front entrance. "You can both freshen up, if you like, and then I'd be happy to give your mother a tour of the place."

"I'd love that," Mother said as she followed Rob along the garden path.

I eyed the area as we passed through, trying to picture the setup. Serving tables on the mosaic slate patio. Lights strung across the grape arbor that shaded the entryway. Real and fake grapes decorating the fountain, the front door, and the outdoor furniture.

"You might enjoy a mud bath or spa treatment this afternoon," Rob said as we followed him through the door into the tiled entrance, "before we head over to the culinary college. I'm sure there will be plenty of time to relax."

The Christophers had created a house suitable for

an issue of *Tuscany Home Digest*. Rob led us past the main living area, which featured two large brown leather couches separated by a stone coffee table that was covered with a sheet of glass. Chunky leather chairs decorated with plush pillows in warm shades of red, orange, and brown filled in the large space by the fireplace. Everything was so pristine, I felt as if I were in the lobby of an exclusive hotel rather than someone's home.

Rob led us down the tiled hallway, which was flanked by cream-colored walls and lined with wrought-iron lighting fixtures interspersed with glass display cases. Inside the cases were wine-related memorabilia, everything from vintage wine corks neatly set in rows, to prestigious wine labels from around the world, including a Rothschild—the only one I recognized in my limited upscale wine experience.

I stopped in front of the last display in the hallway. "These are amazing!" I said to Rob, who was a few steps ahead of me. He and Mother turned back.

"Ah, yes. My antique wine screws. Aren't they interesting? These are from the Old West."

I studied the memorabilia through the glass, marveling at the intricate details of the handles. Several, large enough for big cowboy hands, were made from gnarled wood that had been polished to a sheen. Others sported ornate keys and western ranch symbols and horns from bulls and steers.

"They drank wine in the Old West?" I asked, remembering the western movies I'd watched as a kid with one of my dads. "I thought they only drank whiskey."

"Oh, sure they did. Back then people took pride in their wine paraphernalia and their ability to open wines. Not like today, where you've got your electric Rabbit wine openers that even a toddler can use. I've got antique levers, screw pulls, twisters, double-prongs, waiter-style—you name it."

"I've never opened a bottle of wine," my mother said. She grinned. "Someone is always there to open it for me. That's what I call a wine opener."

"Funny, Mother," I said to her, rolling my eyes.

"I'm serious, dear," she said, and continued down the hall after Rob.

I had no doubt she was telling the truth.

Rob stopped in front of an open door. "This is your room, Presley. Yours is next door, Veronica. You'll be sharing a bathroom between the rooms. I hope that's all right."

"Of course," Mother said, stepping into the room I'd been assigned. I knew it was mine because my suitcase sat on top of a hope chest next to the window. The room was as impeccably decorated as the rest of the house, but in dark wine hues instead of brown leather. The fluffy comforter, heavy drapes, and woven area rug over the tile floor were all the same deep purple shade.

On the walls were framed prints of the Napa Valley Mustard Festival, featuring bright fields of yellow flowers with multicolored hot-air balloons in the background and glasses of wine in the foreground. The half dozen satin pillows on the bed matched the mustard yellow in the poster exactly, a color scheme I would never have imagined—purple and yellow?—yet it worked perfectly. Back at my Treasure Island condo, not one piece of furniture matched another, let alone shared the same or a complementary color. And the prints on my walls ran to noir movie posters like *The Maltese Falcon*, while my "collections" amounted to random displays of old birthday cards, Nancy Drew books, and cat fur. That's how much I knew about decorating. But I knew money when I saw it. The Christophers had plenty.

Rob stepped inside and opened the door to the shared bathroom. "This is—"

He stopped abruptly, his hand still on the knob. Voices were coming from the other side of the bathroom door that led to Mother's suite.

"You're going to get in trouble!" said a muffled angry male voice.

A female voice countered with something I couldn't make out through the door, but from the tone, she too sounded angry.

Rob rushed through the bathroom and opened the other door leading to Mother's room. "What's going on in here?" he demanded.

I peered in and recognized Allison. She stood facing us, her arms crossed, her face flushed. Javier stood with his back to me, holding his straw hat in his hand.

"Allison!" Rob continued. "You should have been finished preparing the rooms by now. And Javier, why aren't you back at work? What are you doing here?"

"He's helping me," Allison said, glaring at Javier, her jaw set. She shot a look at Rob. "We were just fluffing the pillows, like you asked." Her tone clearly suggested an attitude—it was hardly the way an employee might speak to her boss. At least, I'd assumed she was an employee.

"*Perdóneme, señor* . . . I . . . I was just . . . on my way,"
Javier stammered, gripping his hat in both hands as if
it might shield him from injury. He shuffled out, head
down, passing Allison without giving her a glance.

Allison tossed an odd smile to Rob—more like a
smirk—then spun around and left the room without
shutting the door behind her.

"Sorry about that," Rob said. "We're all under a lot of
stress with this party. I've got the Green Grape people
breathing down my neck, JoAnne threatening to call the
police, and Napology trying to buy me out. And we
haven't had the best harvest the past couple of years. As
for Allison"—he nearly spat out her name—"she hasn't
been with us long. I suppose it's taking her time to learn
everything." Rob shook his head.

"No problem," I said.

"And Javier," Rob went on. "I know he's worried
about work. He was managing several of the boutique
wineries in the area, but many of them have been ab-
sorbed by Napology." He took a deep breath, sighed,
then put on his happy face again. "Anyway, sorry to
vent. Just wanted to explain. Marie and I are both so
glad to have you doing the party. Once we debut our
new, competitively priced merlot, I think business will
really take off."

"Of course," I said. I thought about my own crew
and their occasional squabbles. Dee was a theater
prima donna, happiest in the spotlight, while Berk saw
himself as a cinema artiste. It was a combination that
often created a lot of drama. Duncan and Berk shared
an office, so naturally they had their little spats, mostly
during the competitive computer games they played.

Rocco had his own cooking show on local TV, so calling him a temperamental chef was putting it mildly. Luckily Brad got along with everyone—sometimes too well. Women found him charming—especially Marianne, the director of the Treasure Island Development Association, to name one. She seemed to find ample opportunities to flirt with him. As for me, my only beef was an occasional sarcastic interchange with Lieutenant Luke Melvin, a detective with the San Francisco Police Department—who also happened to be Brad's best friend.

"The party is going to be wonderful," I said. I glanced around my mother's room, a mirror image of mine, right down to the pillows. She headed for her suitcase, while I made my way back to my own room, via the bathroom, which I noticed had a shower and Jacuzzi, two sinks, and a toilet that included an actual bidet.

Great for rinsing my feet, I thought, *should I be stomping any grapes . . . or putting out party fires.*

After setting up a few things for tomorrow's party—tables and chairs, strings of lights, wine barrel halves—and after much pleading by my mother, we drove up to Calistoga for a mud bath, something she'd been wanting to do. Personally, I prefer clean water and a bunch of bubbles, but she insisted we subject our bodies to steaming hot mud—and even pay for the privilege. I'd hoped to have talked her out of it by the time we finished the half-hour drive, but no such luck. We were headed for muck.

"Wilkinson's Hot Springs Resort should be just

ahead," Mother said, craning her neck trying to spot the place after we turned onto Main Street in Calistoga, a town famous for its hot springs. We'd already passed several places advertising the healing powers of hot springs, mineral waters, spa treatments, and mud baths, but Mother had insisted on Wilkinson's.

"I remember going there years ago—sometime in the fifties or sixties—when this one first opened up," Mother said. "The place was packed with celebrities. I read once that Robert Louis Stevenson and P. T. Barnum used to go to the hot springs, back in the eighteen hundreds."

P. T. Barnum? He'd probably opened his own place, thinking there was a mud sucker born every minute.

"What's so great about mud?" I asked, less than enthusiastically. The thought of ooey-gooey sludge swirling around my lady parts really didn't appeal to me.

"It's not just the mud," Mother said. "It's the mixture of volcanic ash and hot mineral water that's so good for you. The ash cleanses and smooths your skin and the mineral water is so soothing. They say mud baths not only relax your tired muscles, but they also dissolve your aches and pains, improve your circulation, and even treat arthritis."

I knew the claim about treating arthritis had been disproved, but I could always use a little help with tension and stress. With the party coming up—and the threats from this JoAnne character—I needed all the mud I could get.

I spotted the classic, three-tiered Wilkinson's sign, a relic from the fifties that looked like something from *The Jetsons* TV show. The top one announced "Dr.

Wilkinson's Hot Spring Mud Baths." Underneath it said "Motel, Vacancy." And beneath that, "TV. Indoor pool." I felt like I was on the old Route 66.

A girl in a "Got Mud?" T-shirt greeted us as we entered the small pink-painted lobby. "Here for just a mud bath or do you want the works?"

I answered before Mother could speak. "Just the mud bath, please." The works—a massage, a facial, and who knew what else—would have cost more than I could afford.

"Great. Well, let me tell you a little about the experience," the girl said as she began her memorized spiel. "After you change into robes, you'll get into the mud bath and stay about ten minutes. The mud is pumped through a-hundred-and-twelve-degree water, so it's going to be hot."

"Is it cleaned between customers?" my mother asked.

"Oh yes, it's raked," the girl said.

Raked? I thought, but didn't say aloud. What was there to rake? I didn't want to think about it.

The girl continued explaining the procedure, mostly stuff I'd already learned from Mother about the volcanic ash mixture, the healing powers, blah, blah, blah. Finally she led us to a changing room with curtained cubicles, where we twisted up our hair with clips and wrapped it with a towel, then exchanged our clothes for fluffy white robes—and nothing underneath. Moments later we were led into a private room containing two tubs, side by side, filled with mud. I dropped my robe and modestly stepped into the steaming hot pile of . . . mud. I made a face as I felt it squish between my toes. Meanwhile Mother entered the sludge, sinking her body down into the oozing primordial mass.

Inch by inch I eased in, inhaling the scent of lavender that filled the steamy room. I felt my muscles let go as the heat enveloped me. After I finally lay back, the girl placed cool cucumber slices on my eyes, then gave me a cup of chilled mineral water to sip while I melted into the mud. After ten soothing minutes, it was time to head for the showers, then into a bubbling mineral tub that felt like a sparkling Jacuzzi.

"Don't you feel refreshed?" Mother said as we finished toweling off and began redressing in our tiny stalls.

"I'm so relaxed, I feel like a zombie," I said. I wondered if I could fill my condo bathtub with a bunch of mud and get the same effect. Then again, a glass of wine would probably do the trick.

"I told you you'd love it," she said, pushing back the curtain. "I'm dressed. I'll wait for you out in the waiting room."

"Okay, I'll be right there," I said, fastening one of my Mary Janes.

Two women entered the dressing area as I slipped on my other shoe. I heard one of them say something about a party tomorrow night and I stopped for a moment to listen in, wondering if they were talking about the event at the Purple Grape.

"Are you going?" a woman with a high-pitched, breathy voice asked.

"Yeah," the other woman said, her voice husky, like a smoker's. "Nick says we have to go, since the Christophers are neighbors."

"Us too," the higher voice said. "And we're going to dinner with them tonight, although I don't know why they invited us to that. I think he's trying to score points for being a sensitive neighbor. He thinks just because Dennis used to be the governor, my husband still has some clout."

"Us too," said Husky. "But Nick thinks if we show our solidarity against JoAnne, we'll have a better chance of beating her. Let's just hope this new wine we're tasting isn't as bad as their last batch. Otherwise, they haven't got a prayer against Napology."

"God, I hope that witch JoAnne doesn't show up tomorrow night," said Breathy. "She threatened to, at the last Winegrowers' Association meeting. I wouldn't be surprised if she brought her green goons and tried to ruin the whole thing."

"Well, that's not our problem. Besides, maybe she'll leave the rest of us alone if she sinks her pointy teeth into her latest adversary."

Still in my cubicle, I heard the curtains pull back and bare feet pad out of the room.

"Presley!" my mother called from the lobby. "Did you fall in?"

As a matter of fact, I was wondering the same thing. But what, exactly, had I fallen into?

Chapter 3

Let your guests know that a wine-tasting party is actually good for their health! Among other things, red wine is beneficial to the cardiovascular system and may even help reduce the chance of getting lung cancer. Of course, too much can lead to alcoholism and liver disease . . .

Mom and I enjoyed a leisurely drive back through the quaint town of St. Helena, taking in the colorful flowers, budding vines, and enticing smells of Gott's burgers along the way. Hungry, we finally stopped for an alfresco lunch at Sattui Winery and arrived back at the Purple Grape around four, with plenty of time left to dress for the California Culinary College dinner at seven. I called to make sure Rocco and Gina were ready with their wine-paired *amuse-bouche* appetizers. From the little French I knew, *amuse-bouche* translated to "happy mouth." Too cute.

Speaking of Happy Mouth, where was Brad? I could

have used an *amuse-bouche* about then. I still hadn't
heard from him and still hoped he might make the dinner this evening, but with his job, it was always iffy.
You never knew when a dead body might turn up. I left
a second message on his cell and promised myself I
wouldn't bother him again.

"Presley dear?" my mother said as she entered from
the bathroom that connected our two rooms. "I know
you're counting on my being at the party this evening,
but I just talked with my friend Larry and he's invited
me to join him at bingo. Would you be terribly disappointed if I missed your little do? I promise to be there
tomorrow night for the big event."

Disappointed, no. Surprised, yes. My mother rarely
missed a dinner party, even for a man. Who was this
Larry character and what were his intentions toward
my mother?

"What about dinner?" I asked. "You haven't had
anything since lunch." We'd had fresh French bread,
Sonoma Jack cheese, sliced prosciutto, and spicy mustard sandwiches at Sattui and had wolfed them down
with a glass of sauvignon blanc for me and mineral water for my mom, who no longer drank alcohol.

"Larry said he'd buy me a hot dog. Isn't that sweet?
Apparently the high school students sell food there to
raise money for their band."

A hot dog? Since when did Mother eat hot dogs?
This relationship was beginning to worry me. Mom
had become a little naive since developing Alzheimer's and wasn't quite as savvy as she used to be. Or
maybe I'd become a little overprotective, worried she
might wander away or be caught up in a scam. The

fact was, we were both still figuring out this puzzling disease.

"Okay, sure, Mom," I said reluctantly. "But I want Larry's number. What time do you need to be there?"

"Six. The bingo hall is at the Napa County Fairgrounds. I got directions from Larry. I thought you could drop me off on the way to your dinner at the culinary school."

Mother gave me a hug and excused herself to take a pre-bingo nap. Sleep sounded heavenly, but I still had things to do before my crew arrived. I spent the next hour double-checking delivery times, unpacking more decorations, and calling members of my staff to make sure they were ready to hit the vineyard running when they arrived the next morning. When I called Rocco at the culinary college, he reassured me that the food would be incredible for both the party and tonight's dinner and hung up without a good-bye.

I found Rob in the kitchen, reading a wine industry magazine and sipping coffee.

"Hi, Rob," I said. "How's the count for tomorrow night? Still expecting about sixty people?"

Rob set down his coffee mug. "Hi, Presley. No cancellations yet. You'll get to meet a few of the guests tonight at dinner—our neighbors, the Briens and the Madeiras."

Ah, possibly they were the two women I'd overheard at the mud baths earlier. They seemed less than excited to attend the dinner tonight or the party tomorrow. This would not be fun.

"They own wineries too?" I asked, curious about them.

"Yes, Nick Madeira is a Hollywood producer who prefers producing wine rather than movies these days. He'll be there with his wife, Claudette. They own Castello de Vino—the winery that looks like a medieval castle. Our other neighbors, ex-governor Dennis Brien and his wife, KJ, will be there too. Dennis retired out here after he left office. He owns the Governor's Mansion Winery." I remembered seeing signs for both of the wineries when we'd first arrived.

We chatted a few more minutes; then I returned to my room, where I found a message on my cell phone from Brad. I'd missed his call. He'd explained that another job had come up—no doubt a body—and he wouldn't make it until late in the evening. Now that Mother had accepted another invitation with some guy named Larry, I was left dateless, the only single among a group of couples.

At a quarter to six, I drove my mother to the fairgrounds. I'd changed into a silky black knee-length dress and black Mary Janes for the dinner party. Mother, however, was dressed to the nines in a lavender silk pantsuit (her favorite style), matching pumps (always matching), and makeup heavier than usual for an evening with an old paramour in a bingo hall. The woman didn't own a pair of jeans.

"So who is this Larry guy?" I asked along the way.

"Oh, just someone I met years ago," Mom said, her rouged cheeks turning even pinker. "He used to be in the military—some kind of special forces, I think. He retired up here and works in the tasting room at a big winery. Larry loves his whiskey, but I could always drink him under the table." She smiled proudly at the memory. When her third husband died as a result of alcoholism, she never touched another drop.

"How did you find him?"

"He found me on the Internet," she said. "On one of those classmate sites."

"Well, I want to meet him," I said, pulling into the crowded parking lot at the fairground. I helped Mother out of the MINI and escorted her inside the large rectangular building to make sure she met up with her date and didn't wander over to the homeless shelter nearby.

The auditorium-sized room was bright and cheery, well lit, and filled wall to wall with cafeteria-style tables. Most of the seats were already taken, and the spaces in front of the players were covered with fat, colorful markers, quilted supplies caddies, and giant sheets of paper featuring multiple bingo squares. In addition to the paper spreads, many of the players had what looked like electronic bingo consoles resembling minicomputers. And many of the players, mostly female, had brought along little good-luck charms—trolls, Beanie Babies, photos of grandkids, rabbit-foot key chains—to decorate their spots and hopefully give them the winner's edge.

This was a whole new culture to me. My thoughts quickly began to churn up party ideas with a bingo theme.

Mother scanned the room. "There he is!"

She waved at a large man at a far table who was waving back. He stood and lumbered over to greet her, his potbelly leading the way. Special forces? I found it hard to believe this guy had passed the rigorous physical exam. But age, carbs, and a lot of whiskey certainly challenge the body over time.

"Veronica!" he said, embracing her in a welcoming hug. He pulled her back a stomach's length and looked her over. "You haven't changed a bit! Still as beautiful as ever!"

I looked him over as he gazed at Mother. Red faced—high blood pressure? Gin-blossom nose—the whiskey? Audible breathing—heart problems? Raspy voice—longtime smoker? He wore a festive Hawaiian shirt covered with pineapples and palm trees stretched over his tummy bulge, high-water khaki pants, and what looked like brown leather bedroom slippers on his feet. Circulation problems?

"Oh, Larry, you were always a charmer," my mother said tactfully. "It's good to see you after all these years. I want you to meet my daughter. Presley, this is Larry O'Gara, an old and dear friend."

He gave me a mini-bow, and I almost saluted him.

"Not so old, Ronnie," he said. "Presley, nice to meet you. Your mother's told me all about you."

I wanted to say "You as well," but that would have been a lie—I knew almost nothing about this man. Instead I smiled and asked when bingo would be over so I could pick up my mother.

"I'll bring her home," he said. "No trouble. In fact, it would be my pleasure."

I debated whether to let some stranger—a stranger to me, at least—be responsible for bringing my mother home, or to refuse his offer and embarrass all of us. But my mother often suffered from sundowner syndrome, an added condition in which many Alzheimer's patients feel confused and irritable during the evening hours.

"Maybe next time," I said. "We've got a big day tomorrow with the wine-tasting event."

Larry stood at attention. "Understood. We should be done around nine."

"Bye, Mother," I said, hesitant to leave her, and gave her a hug. I knew that a change in environment could affect her comfort zone and easily disorient her, so I whispered in her ear, "Call me anytime and I'll come get you!" I turned to Larry. "Take good care of her, Mr. O'Gara."

"Will do," he said, offering his arm to Mother. She took it, and he escorted her to his table, where a gaggle of women greeted her cordially while eyeing her cautiously. It appeared Larry O'Gara had a female fan club. No wonder. The women in the bingo hall outnumbered the men something like four to one. Not the best odds for a woman wanting to hook up with a prospective date or future husband. Mother was one of the lucky ones.

Satisfied she would be supervised and safe—I'd noticed a female rent-a-cop patrolling the festivities—I headed for the exit, passing the concession area manned by students from the local high school. The smell of succulent hot dogs reminded me I was getting hungry.

Once in the parking lot, I got in my car and started the engine. A red pickup truck that had obviously picked up a lot of stuff over the years, judging by all the scrapes, dents, and peeling paint, pulled up next to me. The name lettered on the truck was Montoya Management. The doors opened, lighting up the inside. I immediately recognized the driver as Javier, the manager of the Purple Grape Winery. The passenger was none other than Allison, whom I assumed was the Christophers' housemaid.

They climbed out of the truck, not noticing me, slammed their respective doors, and walked into the bingo hall without exchanging a word. They reminded me of a long-married couple with little left to say, yet they seemed so mismatched. Allison was sexy and fashionable, while Javier was worn and rumpled. Tonight she was dressed in black short-shorts, a sparkly white tank top, and red three-inch peep-toe heels. Surely these two weren't together in the romantic sense. Of course, my mother always said opposites attract. Perhaps that was Mom's attraction to Larry O'Gara. She was polished, while he was rough around the edges. She was civilian, while he still looked military. She had kept herself looking healthy and attractive, while he . . . had not.

Recalling the two women gossiping at the mud baths about the party tomorrow and the dinner tonight, I began to wonder if the bingo hall might be more fun. I really didn't look forward to meeting these neighbors. But dinner would be a good chance to go over the details and ensure a smooth event tomorrow night. Once I had this wine-tasting party under my belt—bingo! Who knew how many more winery-related events I'd be asked to plan and host?

Before I could start fantasizing about a possible gala for Francis Ford Coppola, the door to the hall reopened and a woman stepped out.

Allison.

She was with another man, not Javier. Gray haired, thin to the point of being bony, dressed in slacks and a polo shirt, the man escorted Allison to a nearby bench. They sat down and lit up cigarettes. Then Allison proceeded to flirt with the old man, giggling at his words, leaning into him, touching his arm. Fascinated, I watched until the two finished their smokes, then reentered the hall, Allison's arm tucked in his.

My goodness. What was that about?

Chapter 4

PARTY-PLANNING TIP #4

If your dieting guests are worried about getting fat while drinking wine, tell them there are only eighty calories in a four-ounce glass. They can work that off just by walking home from the party. However, it's the accompanying cheese and crackers that may put the weight on over time.

I pulled up to the parking lot of the California Culinary College at the appointed time of seven, just as the sun touched the horizon, and parked in the nearly full parking lot. High on a small hill, the towering pastry-colored brick building looked more like a fortress than a cooking school. The slanting hillside in front was lush with herbs and vegetables, available for the students to plunder for their gourmet experiments in the kitchen. I'd read up on the famous campus, where wannabe chefs came from all over the world to learn how to prepare sauces, use spices, and sauté other salivary stimulants. Wine, naturally, was a large part of the experience, and the college offered patrons a variety of wines in "tasting theaters" and at "flavor discovery bars."

The college also invited diners and food enthusiasts to sample the students' creations. The place was so popular, reservations were required well in advance. Since Rob was friends with Gina, who taught at the school, he was able to snag a small private room for our preparty gathering.

I climbed the steps, stepped through the outdoor patio area, and entered the main building through an arched wooden doorway. The dining area was already full of foodies who were listening to their waiters describe various menu choices or tasting flights of wine or answering trivia questions provided on each table in the form of flash cards. But it was the large, buzzing kitchen, viewable from nearly any spot in the room, that captured my attention immediately . . . Diners at their tables could watch the student chefs prepare menu items with words like "confit," "chicory," "endive," and "duck-fat fingerlings."

I spotted Rocco and Gina through the glass surrounding the kitchen and wound my way to the entry on the far side. Standing on the periphery of the ginormous kitchen, I watched half a dozen chefs, men and women, old and young, all wearing white jackets and toques. They were rushing around their stainless-steel cooking stations, stirring, swishing, and occasionally swearing, all while preparing plates of edible art. Good thing the room was soundproof, I thought, or patrons would get an earful in addition to a mouthful.

Rocco was in his element. Hunched over a plate of

unidentifiable morsels, he was doing what he did best—freaking out.

"They're ruined!" he cried as I approached, throwing his hands in the air.

Next to him stood Gina, busily repairing the ruined globs of Happy Mouths. What appeared to be mini-dough-encrusted baked Brie bites were leaking molten cheese. The puff pastries seemed to be imploding. Gina, in her impeccable whites, was calmly stuffing tiny shrimp into the bottoms of the pastries and setting the repaired bites on round water crackers. I was sure these puffy cheesy shrimpy things would still be wonderful, but Rocco, sporting a Jackson Pollock–stained apron, was a mess.

"They're beyond repair!" he yelled at his sister, who ignored him, something she probably regularly did, knowing his temperament.

Rocco snatched his chef's hat from his balding head and threw it on the counter. "They're hideous! They're a disaster! They're—"

"Rocco!" I interrupted his emo tirade from the sidelines. "Calm down! They'll be fine. Look—Gina is fixing them. And when she's done stuffing them with shrimp, they're going to be even better."

Rocco, near tears, blinked several times as he watched his sister work. Indeed, I felt sure the appetizers would be masterpieces once she was done with them.

Gina shot me a "thank you for shutting him up" look and finished the last of the repairs. I had to admit, she was a genius. So was Rocco, but without his sister's patience and problem-solving skills. When Rocco made a mistake, the world was coming to an end—and so was his career—which of course never happened. Too bad he couldn't be more like Gina when it came to dealing with food flare-ups and flops.

"Rocco," I said, "put your hat back on and go check on the wines and the table settings. Make sure everything is ready. And you might want to wash your face. You've got a little something . . ." I gestured, wiping invisible food from my cheek.

He left the room rubbing his face and holding his toque in his hand.

"You okay, Gina?" I asked.

"I'm fine, Presley. Everything's under control. And thanks for dealing with Rocco. God, he's such a drama queen. Every time I work with him, I swear it will be the last." She stood back from her work. "Okay, these are ready—and they don't look half bad. Bring on the guests."

She was finished not a moment too soon. I caught a glimpse of Rob and Marie entering the restaurant, leading two other couples, whom I assumed were the Madeiras and the Briens. I waved when they spotted me; then they continued toward the private room, chatting along the way. I guessed by looking at the women that the older one was the husky-voiced one I'd heard at the mud baths, who appeared to be with a dark-haired, mustached man. Claudette and Nick Madeira. They had to be in their sixties and were twenty pounds overweight from having enjoyed the good life for those sixty-plus years.

The other two were at least twenty years younger—ex-governor Dennis Brien and his blond-highlighted wife, KJ. They had remained svelte, probably from playing golf, tennis, and whatever else rich people do in their spare time. Both men were in suits, as was Rob, while the women wore cocktail dresses and lots and lots of jewelry. I felt frumpy in my simple black dress, more like I was going to a funeral than a party.

I ducked out the kitchen door and followed them to the private room.

Rob introduced us and we all shook hands. The men's grips were large, firm, and warm, the women's slim, soft, and cool. After the three couples were seated, Rob and Marie between them, me opposite Rob, he stood and made a brief announcement explaining the purpose of our preparty get-together.

"Welcome, everyone," he said. "Thanks for joining us the night before the big event tomorrow. We wanted to thank you for helping with the party and make sure that you're all comfortable with the plans."

The men listened attentively. Claudette, however, frequently looked at her diamond watch, while KJ, Dennis's young wife, kept stealing glances at the distinguished-looking Nick Madeira. I wondered if there was some special meaning behind those glimpses—both were certainly attractive people, and each married to someone else—but I forced myself to stay focused on the topic at hand.

"We're serving the Purple Grape's new merlot tonight, the same one we'll be pouring tomorrow," Rob said, indicating the freshly filled glasses of wine in front of each guest. Everyone lifted their glasses, inhaled the bouquet, and took a sip, swishing it in their mouths. I followed suit, exactly as Rocco had taught me. Tasted good to me.

"Plus, you'll be tasting some of the *amuse-bouches* that chefs Gina and Rocco Ghirenghelli have prepared from Gina's new book. You may recognize Rocco from his own local TV show, *Bay Café*."

The guests stared at Rob blankly, bored, unimpressed, or possibly already intoxicated, the way they were downing the wine. Still, he continued his spiel, offering information on the party food, the activities, parking and traffic control, and the guest list.

"Hear, hear!" Nick Madeira said, ringing his now empty wineglass with his spoon, no doubt hoping Rob was finished.

Rob raised his glass. "Nick, Dennis, thanks for coming," he said, ignoring their arm candy. "You know how important this event is for all of us. We've got to keep our boutique wineries competitive with Napology. Angus McLaughlin is doing his best to take over the entire valley. If we get the word out, market our wines aggressively, and keep the prices reasonable, I'm sure we can continue to compete with him. Otherwise we'll go the way of independent bookstores, coffee shops, and mom-and-pop businesses."

Nick Madeira cleared his throat and said, "Yeah, but now that we've got all these 'green' rules and regulations, we're losing money by the buttload. And if we can't use pesticides, we'll have another invasion of the glassy-winged sharpshooter or European grapevine moth that'll wipe out next harvest."

"Nick's right, Rob," Dennis said after taking more than just a sip of his wine. He leaned back in his chair, assuming an air of fiefdom probably left over from his years as governor. "I sure hope you didn't invite that green witch, JoAnne Douglas, to the party tomorrow. She turns everything into her own environmental agenda. We won't last if we have to meet all her nitpicky demands." He washed down his words with another gulp of wine.

"I didn't invite her," Rob said, "or anyone from Nap-*opoly*."

"Nap-opoly?" I asked, interrupting.

Rob shook his head. "Sorry. That's what we call Angus's venture. He's the CEO of Nap*ology* Corporation, but it's more like a monopoly. He offers large-scale productions of cheap wines that we can't compete with. And he's buying up all the small wineries around here, taking advantage of the economic downturn." To Nick and Dennis he said, "McLaughlin wouldn't come even if I asked him. He's a recluse, hiding away in that cabin behind his winery, making his employees do his dirty work. I wouldn't be surprised if JoAnne Douglas was on his payroll."

Dennis swallowed the wine in his mouth and sputtered, "No way! You know JoAnne and Angus hate each other. One works for green, aka the environment, and the other works for green, aka money." The men chuckled.

Gina brought out the first tray of small bites. "This is Olive Oil and Truffle Tapenade," she explained, pointing to a toasty-looking thing. "This one is Mascarpone Puffs with Ragout. And this is Snow Crab Cocktail Claws." She set the platter on the table. Claudette was the first to serve herself, using a small pair of tongs that had been placed beside her plate.

Rob poured more wine, and the men's talk turned to

wine technology—metal screw tips versus traditional corkage, whimsical versus arty wine labels, the pros and cons of selling their products on Craigslist. Meanwhile the women complained about their mud baths (too hot), their massages (too rough), and their facials (too drying). I had a feeling nothing pleased these indulged trophy wives.

By the time the next course of appetizers was served—Cheddar and Apricot Fritters, Shrimp Cakes with Blood Oranges, and Caramelized Polenta-Stuffed Mushrooms—Claudette and KJ were giggling from all the wine they'd been drinking, and the men were in a heated discussion about different kinds of pesticides. Only Marie Christopher and I were disengaged from the conversations—me thinking about the upcoming party, and Marie gazing into her wineglass, lost in her own world. She seemed to be hypnotized by the spirits in the glass, completely under their spell.

An hour and a half later we'd finished the last of the appetizers. I was stuffed. To my horror, Gina entered with yet another tray, this one filled with bite-sized desserts. In spite of the offer of coffee, Rob poured another round for his guests and raised his glass in a toast.

"To Gina and Rocco, for their outstanding gourmet treats this evening. To my neighbors, the Madeiras and the Briens, for being such great friends. And to Presley Parker, for planning our special event tomorrow. I wish you all great success!"

Before I could bring the wine to my lips, I heard a glass shatter on the floor behind me. Startled, I turned in the direction of the sound. My first thought was that Gina had dropped something. But it wasn't Gina who stood in the doorway with glass shards at her feet. It was a woman I'd not seen before. It was hard to guess her age—maybe somewhere in her late thirties or early forties. She had wild-looking strawberry blond hair that formed an A-frame around her freckly face. She wore no makeup other than a swash of clownish red lipstick along her thin lips. Her outfit was almost grungy—faded, ill-fitting denim jeans, a dirt-streaked lime green T-shirt that read "Drink Green Wine," and dirty, well-worn athletic shoes.

Rob stood, his eyes wide, his hands fisted.

"I'm sorry, JoAnne," he said, his face beginning to flush, "but this is a private party. You need to leave."

JoAnne's freckled face hardened. "I knew you were up to something, Christopher. That's why I followed you here. I've been listening at the door. You're planning to go through with that party tomorrow at your winery!"

The woman might have been petite—she couldn't have been much over five feet tall, but her arms were thick and her hands large. Her curly hair made her angry face look even more intense. So this was the infamous JoAnne Douglas I'd heard about. In spite of the small package, she seemed to pack an explosive personality. No wonder Rob was concerned about her interference.

She narrowed her small green eyes. The lines in her tanned, leathery face deepened. "I know what you're up to," she spat. "You're going to try to convince everyone to vote against Measure W. Well, it won't work, because there isn't going to be a party."

No party? Now *I* was getting concerned.

For a moment, everyone appeared to be frozen to their spots. Then Rob, his face twisted in anger, his jaw tight, said, "I asked you to leave, JoAnne. This is a private party. If you don't go, I'll call the manager and the police. And as for the party tomorrow, there's nothing you can do to stop it. We're quite within our rights to host the event."

"Excuse me . . . ," I said, standing up and moving toward JoAnne with a "we come in peace" outreach of my hand, hoping to dissolve the tension.

"Who the hell are you?" JoAnne said with a sneer.

I hesitated. If I told her the truth—that I was the event planner—I might become the brunt of her tongue-lashing instead of Rob. At last I said, "I'm Presley Parker. I'm working for the Christophers." One revelation at a time, I thought, when dealing with a woman at her breaking point.

"Well, shut your trap, Prissy Parker. This doesn't concern you. And if you work for the Christophers, I pity you. They're not exactly generous when it comes to employee paychecks. Just ask Javier . . . or Allison." She shot Rob an evil grin when she said "Allison," and I wondered what was behind it. Unfortunately I didn't have time to ponder. The war of words between Rob and JoAnne was in full battle mode.

"JoAnne," Rob said. "The event tomorrow has nothing to do with the measure. We're not going to cut down any trees or displace any deer or poison any creeks. We're just celebrating our latest wine and want to publicize it. Presley, here, has planned the event for us, and in fact, a portion of the profits will go to support AA. Now, for the last time, please leave or—"

"You lying pig!" JoAnne was now shouting. "You and your pals here are *ruining* the Napa Valley, spreading your polluted vineyards to the streams and wetlands and destroying the water quality for everyone. I've been fighting for years to protect the wildlife habitat and stop the land erosion, but you newbies have no concern for the environment, as long as you can expand your fences and your fortunes. Your so-called boutique wineries are no better than those jerks at Napology who want to take over the whole county."

Nick Madeira cleared his throat and spoke up. "Listen, JoAnne, we're on your side with the environment. Yes, big wineries like Napology are the ones ruining the valley, but not us little guys. They're the ones buying up and consolidating all the smaller vineyards that are suffering in this lousy economy. They're the ones you should be after, not us."

"He's right, JoAnne," ex-governor Dennis Brien slurred more than said. "Yes, I'll admit, I want to defeat Measure W, but only because it's too extreme and it really won't help wildlife, or improve the water, or stop further erosion." He sounded every bit the politician as he spoke, and I wondered how sincere he was. I glanced at his wife, KJ, who sat wide-eyed, intently listening. Claudette, meanwhile, had a tiny smile on her face and seemed to be enjoying the drama.

"Growth is essential for Napa County, JoAnne," Dennis continued. "We all know this area is the most popular region for domestic wines. If we limit growth, that will only impact the economy in a negative way. Plus it'll hurt our county's eight-billion-dollar industry. You don't want that, do you?"

"You're the biggest liar of all, Governor," JoAnne said. "You've brainwashed these guys into believing your political agenda. Well, it won't work with me— I'm not that stupid. My winery has been here for generations, unlike you idiots who pretend you're vintners when you don't know the first thing about producing quality wines. All you care about are your fancy castles, fancy cars, and fancy parties. Well, just wait until tomorrow night.

"I'm warning you, Christopher, if you host that party, you'll get a taste of JoAnne Douglas's *amuse-bouches*." Pronouncing the words "amuse-bootches" instead of "amooze-boosches," she stepped to the table, picked up one of the chocolate mousse desserts left on the tray, and hurled the soft chocolate glob across the table, directly into Rob's face.

I gasped. The men ducked to the side to avoid being in the line of fire, should she sweep up more ammunition, while the women screamed. As Rob picked up a cloth napkin and wiped the gooey mess from his face, Marie rose with her glass of wine. She stared at JoAnne, utter hatred in her usually serene eyes; then with a backhanded sweep, she tossed the red liquid at JoAnne, dousing her face, hair, and T-shirt.

The other guests recoiled as the residue spattered the tablecloth. The women inspected their cocktail dresses for stains. The men rose, ready to defend or attack, as required.

JoAnne wiped the wine from her face with her sleeve, cocked her jaw at the stunned crowd, and said calmly, "Well, then. I'll see you all tomorrow night."

Chapter 5

PARTY-PLANNING TIP #5

For a theme within a theme at your wine-tasting party, try a "horizontal tasting," with wines that come from the same vintage, or a "vertical tasting," using wines from the same winery. Or make up your own rules and taste wines from a certain location, grape variety, or price range.

There was no need to call the police on JoAnne Douglas. She left of her own accord, after blotting the front of her shirt with a cloth napkin and tossing it on the floor. No one said a word for several moments, until Rob broke the silence.

"Well. We may need to double our security tomorrow night, but there's no way I'm going to let that impossible woman ruin our event."

"Are you sure you want to go through with this?" Marie asked quietly, looking up at him. She looked small and fragile in the soft light of the room, especially compared to the two high-maintenance wives, but there was something dark in her eyes. "That's not the first time she's threatened us. Frankly, she scares me."

Marie wasn't the only one concerned. I was beginning to have serious misgivings as well and wondered what Rocco had gotten me into. This was supposed to be a nice quiet dinner before the party, but it had turned out to be more like a high school food fight. What was in store tomorrow night? And what had I'd dragged my staff, my boyfriend, and my mother into this time?

The thank-you party was pretty much over at that point. After the others left, I stayed behind to reassure Rocco and Gina that the food had been wonderful and everything would be fine at the wine tasting.

As if.

Apparently Gina had witnessed the scene from the doorway. "She's a piece of work," she said, stepping in to collect wineglasses. "A fanatic, still obsessed with the old ways. She thinks progress and expansion are deliberately undermining her beliefs."

With everyone hating JoAnne, I felt for her in a way. I wondered how she'd become such a thorn in everyone's side over the years. Did she truly care about the environment, to the point of incurring such wrath from the community? Or was she just stuck in a time warp, unable to accept change?

Or was it something else?

I reflected on my mom and how she'd also retained the styles and symbols of the past. But I had learned early on that change and growth were inevitable, and I was able to roll with whatever came my way—the loss of my job, the move to Treasure Island, the ups and downs of the event-planning business, the changes in my mother due to her disease. Maybe having an unpredictable mother and five fathers during my childhood had forced me to be flexible.

I left Rocco and Gina behind to finish the cleaning and arrived at the bingo hall to pick up Mom a little after nine p.m. I found her sitting at the table where I'd left her, talking with Larry, while other players were packing up their caddies, markers, and good-luck charms.

"Presley!" she said as I approached. "You're here! How did it go at the . . ." She hesitated, and I knew she'd forgotten where I'd been. Taking her out of her usual surroundings had thrown her off.

"The culinary college? Fine," I said, not wanting to worry her about the threats we'd received from an irate—and possibly dangerous?—winegrower. I glanced at Larry, who stood. "How was your evening?"

"Wonderful, dear!" Mother answered. "You'll never guess what happened!" She patted an envelope that rested under her hand.

Probably not, I thought, knowing all the mischief my mother had gotten into since developing Alzheimer's. "What?"

"I won!" she exclaimed, and glanced at Larry. He grinned and nodded confirmation.

"You did?" I asked, surprised at her good luck.

"Yes! Two hundred and fifty dollars! In cash! I got a bingo on the last game of the evening! It was so exciting. I wish you'd been here."

"That's great, Mother. Congratulations." I looked at Larry. "Did you win anything, Mr. O'Gara?"

"Call me Larry," he said. "I didn't, but hell—it only

costs about ten bucks to play—thirty if you want multiple bingo sheets, and more for the computerized bingo. That's not bad for three hours of entertainment in the company of a beautiful lady—plus the possibility of winning two hundred and fifty bucks."

"One of the women at our table won twice!" Mother added; then she patted Larry's arm. "He's good luck."

"Well, I'm so glad you had a good time. Ready to go, Mom?"

Larry pulled out Mother's chair as she stood. She gave him a hug and a kiss on the cheek, then said good-bye and something about seeing him tomorrow. With a last wave, she let me lead her to my car.

Once we were strapped in, I started the engine. "So you had a good time."

"Oh yes! And Larry was the perfect gentleman. Quite the ladies' man, I must say. The women at our table were flirting outrageously with him. But he let them know he was with me."

I drove out of the parking lot and onto the street. "So what are you going to do with all that money? Buy a new outfit? Something for your room at the care . . . hotel?" My mother referred to her care center as the "hotel," and I tried to do the same.

"Oh no, dear, I'm going to buy one of those cute quilted bingo caddies and some daubers—that's what they call the markers. I'm meeting Larry again tomorrow afternoon."

"Tomorrow?" I said, shooting her a look.

"Yes, but don't worry. I'll be back in plenty of time for the wine-tasting party. Oh, and, Presley, do you mind if I bring Larry along? I'm sure he would enjoy it."

"Uh . . . I'll have to check with Rob and Marie, but I guess they wouldn't mind. Are you sure you want to bring him? You saw him tonight and you're seeing him again tomorrow. Don't you want some time to yourself?"

"Oh no, dear. I really enjoy his company, and we've become close after spending the evening together. I'd like to see as much of him as I can before we have to return to the city."

Her words concerned me. It appeared my mother was falling for a man she hadn't seen in years—until tonight. And even then she'd spent only a few hours with him. A romantic at heart—hence the five husbands and countless paramours—my mother never gave up on finding Mr. Right.

Which reminded me—where was Brad?

I pulled up the driveway of the Purple Grape and parked. Rob had given me a key to the front door and had left the porch light on. I helped my mother out of the car and we headed inside. The hallway was dark, but dim lights from the display cases helped us find the way to our rooms. We said good night, hugged, and closed our respective doors.

I changed into my cat-patterned pajamas, brushed my teeth, washed my face, and climbed into the big puffy guest bed with my iPhone. Checking my messages, I hoped for one from Brad, but he still hadn't called. I sent an e-mail to Treasure Island security guard Raj Reddy, reminding him of the event tomorrow, since I had a feeling there would be some added drama at the party. Finally I answered the most demanding e-mails before switching off the light around ten thirty. Exhausted from the stress of the earlier drama, I fell right to sleep.

I'd been dreaming about Brad—something about a corpse he was removing from a crime scene—when a noise woke me. I sat up straight, listening to be sure the sound hadn't been part of my dream.

I heard it again. The sound of something metal clanging against the ground. It came from outside my window, which faced the front garden.

Sweat broke out all over my body.

I checked my cell phone for the time: half past midnight.

Throwing off the covers, I rushed to the window without turning on the light and bumped my thigh on the window seat. Pain seared through my leg. Ouch. I rubbed the throbbing area as I peered through a crack in the heavy curtains.

A figure stood just beyond the glow of the porch light. He—or she; I couldn't tell which—pulled something from a pocket, knelt down, and stuck a hand into a flowering bush.

At first I thought it might be Javier—who else would be running around the property this time of night?—but it was too dark to see more than a shadowy outline. I continued to watch as the figure stood up, glanced around, then walked over to one of the storage buildings next to the garage and disappeared.

It had to be Javier, I said to myself, about to release the curtain. Then, from the corner of my eye, I caught a glimpse of a light, this one off in the distance. I stared as it became two beams and grew larger and brighter.

Moments later I heard the sound of a car engine as it pulled into the driveway.

Who could it be at this hour?

JoAnne?

Had she arrived to harass Rob and Marie about tomorrow night's party?

The car—it looked like some kind of SUV in the semidarkness—came to a stop. The driver's door opened, then closed quietly.

Brad appeared from around the front!

"Oh my God!" I said to the window, then opened it and softly called his name. I could tell he'd heard me by the way he glanced around, but apparently he didn't know where to look. I rushed to the nightstand lamp and turned it on, and returned to the window and waved.

He waved back, then pulled out a backpack from the passenger side of the SUV. His gear. I pointed toward the front door; he raised a hand in acknowledgment. Tiptoeing down the dimly lit hall, I reached the door and was about to open it when a voice from the darkness on the other side of the hall said, "What are you doing?"

Startled, I jumped a foot.

Allison stood in the hallway entrance, still wearing the outfit she'd worn to bingo. Her arms, as usual, were crossed, her face stern, making her look like an irate parent who's just caught her teenage daughter sneaking out.

"I . . . my boyfriend—uh, co-worker . . ." I gestured toward the door. "He just got here. I came to let him in. What are you doing here?"

"I live here," she said matter-of-factly.

I blinked in surprise. Was this woman live-in help?

"Does Rob know about this . . . additional guest?" she asked.

"Uh, yeah," I lied. Although I'd gotten him his own room at a nearby B and B, I'd planned to sneak him into my room. Now I wondered what I'd been thinking. This looked *so* unprofessional.

I heard a light tap on the door and pulled it open.

Brad's smile drooped when he saw Allison standing behind me. He glanced at me for a cue.

"Come in," I said quietly, hoping not to wake Rob and Marie at the other end of the large house. "Glad you made it." I wanted to give him a hug, but not in front of Allison. For some reason, I didn't trust the woman. The fact that she was young and attractive had nothing to do with it. Mostly.

I turned to her. "Well, good night, Allison. Sorry if we woke you. See you in the morning. Big day tomorrow."

"Good night," she said, not moving from her spot. I felt her eyes on my back as I led Brad down the hallway to my room and shivered in my cat pajamas in spite of their cozy warmth. I hated how this looked.

But once I got into the cloudlike bed with him and snuggled in his muscular arms, I didn't care how it looked. I just closed my eyes.

My last thought returned to the figure lurking around the yard. Who was it? And what was he doing so late at night?

*   *   *

I awoke the next morning around seven, with Brad gently snoring in my ear. The double bed made snuggling all night together mandatory, but I had no complaints. I heard my mother running water in the adjoining bathroom and took a moment to slip out of bed and look out the window to check the day's weather, praying for fair skies.

When I pulled the curtain cord, I gasped. "Oh my God!"

The front garden looked like a tornado with a paint sprayer had hit. All the tables and chairs we'd set up were overturned. The decorative wine barrels had been spray painted with graffiti. And the strings of colorful lights lay tangled on the ground.

Someone had vandalized all the setup work I'd done the previous day.

"What's wrong?" Brad said, leaning on an elbow and rubbing the sleep from his face.

"My party stuff . . . ," I said, staring out in disbelief. "It's . . . it's ruined . . ."

Brad threw the covers back and joined me at the window.

I looked at him and raised an eyebrow. Unlike me, he hadn't worn pajamas.

"What?" he said.

"You might want to put a robe on. My mother's on the other side of that door." I pointed to the bathroom.

He looked down and saw what I saw, then grabbed the comforter. Apparently he didn't have a robe either.

I shook my head and returned my attention to the

disaster in the yard. Javier was already righting the overturned tables and chairs. Allison had a can of paint and a brush in her hands, ready to paint over the graffiti. And Rob and Marie were picking up the lights and trying to untangle them. Rob noticed us at the window and made a disgusted face. I assumed he was referring to the mess and not the half-naked man standing next to me.

"I better get out there and help," I said to Brad.

"Let me get a quick shower and I'll join you," he said.

I thought about how I was going to explain Brad's presence in my room to Rob and Marie—and my mother. Maybe they'd be too distracted by the vandalism to care. "Be sure to lock the door on the other side of the bathroom or you may have a surprise visit from Mom." I sighed.

Brad took me in his arms and kissed me. "Don't worry, Pres. I'll help you fix this. After all, that's what I do best—clean up after messy situations. And your crew will be here soon, right?"

"Yeah." *Thank goodness for my band of misfits*, I thought, hoping they were on their way. After Brad headed for the shower, I pulled on blue jeans, another red Killer Parties T-shirt, and black Vans and headed outside to help repair the damage.

Rob stopped his work replacing a party light as I stepped out the front door.

"Who did this?" I asked, surveying the area openmouthed. "Do you think it was that woman, JoAnne, from last night?"

"I'm sure it was," Rob said. "Did you hear anything

during the night? Our room's way at the other end, but yours is right on the other side here."

"As a matter of fact, I did hear a noise that woke me in the middle of the night. I looked out the window and saw someone in the shadows, but I figured it was your winery manager, Javier. I didn't see anything like this." I waved my arm around at the carnage.

"Javier?" Rob asked, his frown deepening.

"I assumed . . ."

"Javier!" Rob called him over.

Javier righted the small café table he was holding, shuffled over, and removed his straw hat. "Yes, sir?"

"What time did you leave here last night, Javier?"

Javier scratched his head. "Oh, about five, five thirty."

Rob glanced at me, then asked Javier, "Did you come back later?"

"No, sir," Javier said. His grip on his hat tightened. "I went to bingo, then home. As soon as I got here this morning and saw what happened, I rang your bell."

"Thanks, Javier," Rob said, giving him a pat on the shoulder.

"Wait!" I said to the winery manager. "Did you bring Allison back here after bingo?"

Javier looked at me with troubled eyes and bowed his head. "No, ma'am. I only took her there. She went home with someone else."

"Allison was at bingo?" Rob asked, sounding surprised.

Javier shrugged, as if afraid to speak, then mutely returned to his work.

Rob turned to me. "Presley, are you sure you didn't see or hear anything else last night?"

"I don't think so. Brad, my . . . associate . . . he drove up right after I heard the noise—about half past midnight. I let him in, said good night to Allison, and—"

"Allison?" Rob asked.

"Yes, she was in the entry hall when I went to let Brad in."

"What was she doing up at that hour?" Rob asked, his jaw tightening.

"Uh, just standing there. I thought I might have awakened her, but she was still in the clothes I'd seen her in earlier—the ones she wore to bingo. I assumed she was live-in help."

Rob laughed coldly. "Live-in help. That's a good one."

I frowned, puzzled. "I thought she worked here."

"She does. But she's not live-in help. Allison is Marie's younger sister."

"Her sister?" I said, stunned at the news. They were as different as night and day. Marie had dark hair and eyes, while Allison was fair. Marie was slim but sturdy. Allison was model thin. Marie dressed in a sensible-casual style, right down to her black flats, but I'd seen Allison only in sexy outfits and jeweled stiletto heels.

Rob seemed to read my confused look. Dropping his voice to little more than a whisper, he said, "Allison is staying with us because she had nowhere else to go after leaving rehab a few months ago."

"Rehab?"

Rob stared at Allison as she painted over the graffiti. "She had a prescription drug problem, but she's supposedly clean now. I didn't know she was playing bingo. That troubles me."

I looked over at her. She caught us looking at her and smirked.

An addict? With an attitude? Living at a winery?

Sounded like trouble to me.

Chapter 6

PARTY-PLANNING TIP #6

If you're hosting your wine party in the winter, why not serve mulled wine for a twist? Heat a variety of wines, anything from a fruity rioja to a dry riesling; then add cinnamon sticks, cloves, nutmeg, sugar, and orange slices, and simmer until serving time. That should take the chill out of any party!

By the time the tables, chairs, canopies, and wine accessories were back in place two hours later, my crew had arrived, caravan-style. Dee had driven her Smart Car, filled nearly to the brim with decorating supplies—streamers, candles, flowers, tableware, and the like. She had even managed to squeeze in a couple of helium balloon tanks. Berk and Duncan had rented a truck and packed it with the bigger party crap—DJ equipment, lighting, video camera, laptops, signage, game parts, and so on. Rob and Marie had already set out the wineglasses, along with multicolored grapes, leaves, and vines I planned to use for place settings and centerpieces. Brad and I hung signs, grapevines, and lights, while Mother fussed with the tasting tables, adding pewter cheese knives, along with wine openers embossed with my "Killer Parties" company name, which would double as party favors for the guests to take home.

Around one in the afternoon, Mother asked for a ride to the bingo hall, so I took a break and drove her there, then turned her over to Larry again. I gave her instructions not to leave the hall and promised to be there at four to pick her up so she could get a nap in before the party. When I returned to the winery, I found Delicia in my bedroom trying on her costume.

"Wow, you look . . . incredible!" I said.

In front of me stood a clone of Lucille Ball, right down to the curly red wig wrapped in a red plaid scarf. Somehow she'd managed to find a white peasant top that fell off her slim mocha shoulders and a flowing blue skirt with a jagged hem—just like I remembered from the old *I Love Lucy* reruns on TV. That grape-stomping episode was one of my favorites because of the hilarious food fight. If I'd known Dee was going to go all Lucy on me, I'd have ordered some of the collectables that matched the episode—Lucy plates, Lucy wineglasses, Lucy wine stoppers, and Lucy snow globes. Leave it to Dee to take it up a notch.

"Hey, Ethel!" she said, putting her hands on her hips after twirling. "What do you think?"

"Hey, Lucy!" I said in my best Desi Arnaz accent. "You look fab-oo-lous!"

I spent the rest of the afternoon supervising, arranging, checking, and double-checking everything. By a quarter to four we were nearly ready, so I took off for the bingo hall to collect my mother. Once again she'd had a wonderful time, in spite of the fact that she hadn't won anything this time. As we drove back to the winery, she filled me in on some of the bingo lingo—things like "blackout," "coverall," "hardway," "money ball"—which ran through my mind like a sieve, and made me promise to accompany her next time.

While Mother napped, I went out to the party area and reviewed the music selections with Duncan. We'd decided on Italian-themed music, beginning with a CD called *Mob Hits* that featured Dean along with Frank Sinatra, Louis Prima, and Rosemary Clooney, among others. When it was time for the party to wind down, Duncan was scheduled to play something by Andrea Bocelli.

Berkeley had already videotaped the pre-party area and was ready to catch the guests in action as they arrived. I often asked him to videotape my more important parties as a selling tool for my Web site and YouTube—at least the parts where nothing went wrong.

While Duncan and Berk were dressed in black jeans and Killer Parties T-shirts, Raj Reddy looked official in his khaki Treasure Island Security Guard uniform. I'd filled him in on the vandalism we'd discovered that morning and gave him a picture of JoAnne Douglas, downloaded from Rob's computer.

Rocco and Gina had spent the day in Rob and Marie's gorgeous Tuscany kitchen, making fresh versions of the appetizers and desserts we'd had last night, including the mud-slinging mini–mousse cream puffs. After Rocco's outburst the previous night, I was relieved to find him calmer today and hoped he'd remain that way throughout the evening. I didn't have time to deal with another temperamental tantrum.

"Break time!" Rob called, surprising all of us by opening a bottle of his new wine and pouring my staff and me a glass. Everyone gathered quickly at the serving table, ready for the relaxing refreshment—all except Brad, who was still hanging a large sign that read, " 'Wine is bottled poetry'—Robert Louis Stevenson."

"Brad!" I called.

He looked down from his step on the ladder and nodded. "Be right there." He tied the last piece of the sign to a rope he'd strung across the entrance to the party area, climbed down, wiped his hands on his jeans, and took the glass.

"No beer?" he said, teasing.

"I'll buy you a beer when all of this is over," I said, then touched my glass to his and announced, "To Rob and Marie, our hosts!" Everyone took a sip and I immediately felt the alcohol work its magic on my tired muscles.

Brad and I sat down in a couple of lawn chairs next to Rob and Marie. I noticed that Allison and Javier had disappeared after finishing their tasks. The four of us chatted about how stunning the party area looked, how fun the games were going to be, and how wonderful the wine was.

"Any sign of JoAnne?" I asked Rob, glancing around.

"No, thank God. But I'm glad you brought extra security. With him and the guy I hired, we should be okay."

Raj, who had passed on the alcohol, stood reading

the guest list, then gave it to me to look over. I recognized only a few names—the Briens, the Madeiras—and another name I'd seen on several billboards and bus benches: Kyle Bennett. It had taken me a while, but now I recognized him as the same man who had been at the Purple Grape yesterday morning when we'd arrived. According to his ads, he was a self-described "attorney working to preserve the Napa Valley like a fine wine." I didn't much trust lawyers who pasted their faces all over town but would reserve judgment until I got to know him better. Rob explained that the rest of the guests were friends, neighbors, or other local small-scale vintners, as well as a writer from *Wine Connoisseur* magazine.

After the wine break, we headed for our rooms to shower and prepare for the guests, who'd be arriving around seven. I roused my mother from her nap and helped her put on a flowery, ankle-length cocktail dress and do her hair. Meanwhile Brad showered and dressed in black jeans and a plain black T-shirt—no logo. I finally took my turn in the shower, then slipped into a knee-length maroon dress and black Mary Janes, touched up my makeup, and brushed my short bobbed hair.

"Presley?" Mother said, entering my bedroom holding a purple makeup pencil. "I'm having trouble with my eye shadow."

I looked at her and immediately saw the problem. The dark purple color she'd applied to her lids was thick and smudged.

"Let me see." Upon closer inspection, I realized she had used her lipstick pencil instead of her eye-shadow

pencil to create the look. "Let me fix this for you, Mom."
I took her back into her room, wiped off the mess with a
tissue, and found a purple eye-shadow pencil in her cos-
metic bag. Gently I applied a thin swipe to her lids, then
smoothed it in with my fingertip. I wanted to think
she'd just made a simple mistake, but I sensed it was
another sign of her worsening Alzheimer's disease. Being in a new place had upset her sometimes fragile con-
nection to reality. Maybe bringing her here hadn't been
such a good idea after all.

"There. All better," I said, wiping the color from my
finger with a tissue. "You look lovely."

"Thank you, Presley. So do you."

"Well, shall we go?" I offered her my arm and she
took it like a grande dame. Leading her out of her
room, I paused momentarily at my room to tell Brad
we were heading out, but he'd apparently already left.
When we reached the festively decorated garden, lit up
with sparkling lights and glowing swags of fake grapevines, Mom sucked in a breath of air at the sight, which
I took as her approval.

I checked my Mickey Mouse watch: six forty-five.
Almost party time.

When the first guests arrived around seven, spilling
into the garden area in their cocktail finery, everything
looked perfect. The white tablecloths made the dark red
wines pop with color. The sparkling glasses beckoned,
ready to be swirled with wine. And the decorations—
swagged grapevines, purple and green balloons, and
large goblets sporting purple votive candles—all added
to the mellow and intoxicating ambiance.

A few minutes later the Briens and Madeiras arrived

via golf carts from their neighboring wineries and were soon huddled together over glasses of the Purple Grape's new merlot. I ducked into the kitchen to check on the *amuse-bouches*, then returned to find that Kyle Bennett, the attorney, had arrived and was chatting flirtatiously with an attractive blond woman. Larry had also arrived and was charming my mother, who seemed to be laughing at everything he said.

My staff was in place, as was Rob's. Javier had cleaned up nicely in his black suit and western string tie and stood behind one of the serving tables, pouring wine. Allison manned another table strewn with my signature corkscrews and cheese knives, smiling and talking with the guests as she filled their glasses. Rob and Marie stood together behind the third table, he in a dark tieless suit and black loafers, she in an ankle-length plum gown, with black pearls and matching plum Kate Spade flats. Tall, maybe five-eight or nine, Marie would have towered over her five-ten-ish husband if she'd worn heels, I realized. They were shaking hands with guests and talking animatedly about the virtues of their latest harvest.

There was no sign of JoAnne Douglas. So far, so good.

While Duncan filled the air with Dean Martin's velvety "Return to Me," Gina appeared with the first tray of edible masterpieces. The crowd grew and the sound of conversation and laughter increased. Soon everyone was sipping wine, nibbling appetizers, and talking.

"Nice job, Ms. Parker," came a voice from behind me. I turned to see Kyle Bennett wearing a smart suit and shiny Ferragamos and holding a glass of the Purple Grape's merlot. "I feel like I'm in the Garden of Eden, practically swimming in a giant glass of wine. Are you available for other parties here in Napa? My clients are always looking for a good event planner."

Apparently he knew my name already. "Hello, Mr. Bennett. Glad you're having a good time. Sure, feel free to pass my name along to your clients."

"Perhaps we could talk about the specifics over dinner sometime?" He gazed at me with glassy eyes. Drunk already? And hitting on me?

"Um, sure," I said, glancing around for Brad. Not seeing him, I took a sip of my own wine, then said, "Or just e-mail me. I do most of my business online these days, aside from the actual party."

"How about tomorrow night? Are you free?"

Oh my God. Did this guy not get it? That was the trouble with drunk people—they so often became stupid.

"Uh . . . sorry, but I'll be leaving tomorrow." I pulled out one of the Killer Parties business cards from a pocket in my dress. "Here's my contact information. I look forward to hearing from you. Now, if you'll excuse me, it's time to begin the entertainment. Enjoy the party."

He raised his glass, gave a little bow, and let me go. I circled the party, searching for Brad, and found him sitting next to Allison on a bench in a far corner of the garden. He seemed to be studying the party guests, ignoring Allison, who was talking to him, a cigarette in her hand. The smoke overpowered the smell of the flowers that surrounded the two of them.

"There you are!" I said when I reached him.

Brad looked visibly relieved to see me. He grinned and stood up and took my hand. "Great party," he said. "You've done it again, Pres."

Allison dropped her cigarette on the ground, pressed it out with her strappy black high-heeled Prada shoe, and rose. "Break's over. Time to get back to work," she said to me. To Brad she added, "Nice talking to you, Brad. I'll give you the insider's tour of the place tomorrow, if you're still around. Believe me, I can show you things the regular tourists don't get to see." She raised an eyebrow at him, whipped her blond hair around, and headed back to one of the tables to pour more wine.

"What was that about?" I said, feeling myself flush with jealousy.

Brad squeezed my hand. "I have no idea," he said. "I was sitting here watching the party action and she sneaked up behind me, lit her cigarette, and sat down."

"You hate cigarette smoke!"

"I know, but I couldn't just leave the minute she sat down."

"Why not?" I said, half teasing, half meaning it.

"Then I would have missed seeing you with Mr. Slick over there." He pointed to where I'd been talking with Kyle Bennett.

"Oh. You saw that." *Good*, I thought. I wanted him to feel jealous too.

"Yeah. Looked like he was macking on you. You guys make a date?"

I shrugged nonchalantly. "He tried, but I told him I had a big mean boyfriend who didn't let me date other men."

Brad laughed. "Well, next time I see him talking to you, I'll take him out." He slapped his fist in his palm, then leaned in and kissed me. I melted into it until I realized where I was and pulled back abruptly. I glanced around to see if anyone had caught me.

"Brad! I'm working," I said. "And by the way, so are you. It's time for the entertainment. And I could use a big strong man to help me."

"You left out 'mean,'" he said.

I collected Javier, Duncan, and Berkeley and asked them to roll a large wine barrel to the center of the garden. Then I took the microphone and announced the beginning of the entertainment.

"All right, everyone. I hope you're enjoying the Christophers' new merlot. Now it's time for some fun. First up will be the Balancing Barrel Boys, who will battle on top of a sideways wine barrel—blindfolded! Next the Grape-Stomping River Dancers, who will turn grapes into wine to the tune of an Irish folk song. And finally, you'll all get to participate in a wine-tasting game. So without further delay, let's get this party started!"

By the time dessert was served around eleven p.m., the party had gone without a hitch and I finally stopped holding my breath. The cake Rocco and Gina had created was a showstopper. It was shaped like a small wine barrel and covered with sugared grapes and leaves. The guests would be talking about it for months.

Around midnight the last stragglers wandered—more like staggered—out. I had to admit, it was one of the best events I'd hosted. The entertainment had garnered lots of cheers and laughs, and I overheard several guests say the party was "a hoot," "off the hook," and "epic." Even Mother and Larry said it was the best wine-tasting event they've ever been to—and they hadn't had any of the wine.

But like a deflating balloon, I was pooped. It had been a long day and evening, in spite of the fact that the party had been perfect. I sent my crew to their respective bed-and-breakfast rooms with a reminder to be back around nine a.m. for cleanup.

After escorting Mother to her bedroom, I rejoined Brad, who was still collecting party decorations and putting them in boxes. The guy seemed to have boundless energy. Maybe because he hadn't had as much wine as I'd had during the party.

"Quit!" I said, taking him by the hand. "Bedtime . . ."

I led him through the front door and we'd started down the hall when I heard voices and stopped. Putting a finger to my lips, I shushed Brad before he could say anything. I recognized those voices—Allison and Kyle. Both of them had come on to us at the party. At the time, I'd written them off as "flirting while intoxicated" and essentially forgotten about them. Their conversation now seemed hushed but heated, as if they were discussing something important but didn't want to be overheard.

"I saw you talking to her! You were all over her!" Allison hissed.

"Yeah, well, what about you? You were practically hanging on that guy," Kyle countered in a loud whisper.

"I was not! *He* was flirting with me!"

"Well, *she* was coming on to me. I wasn't doing—"

"Presley?" I heard my name being called from the end of the semi-lit hall.

Mother.

The voices stopped.

I looked at Brad, then started toward Mother. But as I took a step, something crunched under one of my Mary Janes. It sounded like broken glass. Had a party-goer dropped a wineglass on his or her way to the rest-room and not bothered to clean it up?

I continued down the hall to where Mother stood in her nightgown, green stuff all over her face, her hair in rollers. She looked a little like the Swamp Thing emerging from the lagoon.

"Mother, you should be in bed," I whispered.

"That's not my bed," my mother said, her green face pulled back in a grimace as she pointed into her bed-room. "I don't know where my bed is."

Recognizing the symptoms of sundowner syndrome, I guided her back to her room and bed, reminding her about the party and that we were staying overnight with the Christophers. I covered her up, tucked her in like she used to do me, and stroked her hand until she closed her eyes.

When I thought she was asleep, I tiptoed into my room through the bathroom, slipped off my shoes, changed into my PJs, and joined Brad in bed.

"Your mom okay?" he asked groggily, wrapping an arm around me as I nestled next to him.

"She's asleep," I whispered. "Just disoriented. She'll be okay. It's been a long day for her too. Lots of excite-ment." I relaxed into his heaving chest, closed my eyes, then remembered the conversation between Allison and Kyle. My eyelids popped up, my mind suddenly wide-awake.

"Brad, what do you think is going on between those two?" I asked.

No response other than some heavy breathing—and not the kind I had been looking forward to.

Brad was sound asleep.

Brad woke me at seven the next morning and made up for falling asleep on me the previous night. Then we both showered, dressed, and headed outside to clean up the mess. My crew arrived a little after nine. I'd let Mother sleep in and hadn't heard a peep from her since tucking her into bed in the middle of the night. Nor had I seen any sign of Rob, Marie, Allison, or Javier this morning.

"Presley!" Brad called from the other side of the garden, where he'd been removing wine-stained table-cloths from the serving tables. He held an armful of wadded-up cloth and was staring at the table he'd just stripped.

"What is it?" I asked, approaching him. "The cloths are rentals. Don't worry about the stains—"

I stopped midsentence. Brad wasn't looking *at* the table. He was staring *under* the table.

A chill ran down my spine as I leaned in to see what had caught his attention.

I pulled back reflexively, my stomach clenched.

A body lay twisted on the ground underneath the table, a red wine stain circling the front of a once-green T-shirt.

Something protruded from the center of the stain.

I took a second look, immediately regretting it.

That was no wine stain. It was blood.

"Oh my God!" I managed to say as I recoiled. "That's JoAnne Douglas! She's been . . . stabbed. With a corkscrew!"

Chapter 7

PARTY-PLANNING TIP #7

To avoid making an embarrassing faux pas at your wine-tasting party by ruining the sensual experience, follow these basic tips: Don't smoke, eat hard candy or mints, chew gum, or wear perfume or aftershave. You want to keep your palate and nostrils free from taste-altering substances. Chocolate, however, is perfectly acceptable.

"Stand back, everyone," Brad commanded, extending his arms as my crew came running over to view the spectacle.

"JoAnne?" Marie Christopher said, appearing out of nowhere. Pale, eyes wide, Marie stared down at the bloody sight, her hands beginning to tremble.

"Don't touch anything," Brad called out to the gaping crowd. He pulled out his cell phone and dialed 911. "Presley!" he said, yanking me out of my stunned silence. "Get everyone back."

I immediately shifted into delegation mode.

"Delicia, take Marie away from here. Get her some water."

To Raj, I said, "Check the area. See if you find anyone—or anything—suspicious." Raj saluted and marched off to search the grounds.

Glancing around, I noticed Rob wasn't present; nor were Javier or Allison. "Duncan," I said, "find Rob. And let me know if you see Javier or Allison."

"Berkeley," I whispered to my videographer, then waved my hand around the crime scene area. "Would you get your video camera and tape this, please? We may need it later."

I heard the deep sound of a truck engine and saw a small tractor approaching in the distance. Moments later Javier pulled up near the garage, let the tractor motor idle a moment, then switched it off and jumped down. He must have seen the curious gathering because he headed over toward Marie, who now sat on a garden bench next to Dee, several yards away from the body. Her head was bent over and she held a wineglass filled with water.

"Javier," I said, intercepting him. "We've got a problem here and I need you to stay back. Dee's taking care of Marie."

"What's wrong?" he said, removing his hat.

"Someone's been killed," I said. "The police will be here soon."

Javier's eyebrows peaked. He shuffled back but strained his neck to see what I was talking about. "I'll go get Mr. Rob."

"No need," I said, spotting Rob and Allison as they

entered the party area from the front door of the house, followed by Duncan. Rob was dressed in his casual jeans, a button-down yellow shirt, and slip-on loafers. He frowned when he saw the crowd—or maybe it was the early-morning sun in his eyes. Meanwhile, Allison, dressed in a short silky bathrobe and pink ostrich-feathered slippers, her hair tousled, had a blank look on her face.

"What's going on?" Rob said, striding over to me. Allison, behind him, held her hand up to shield her face from the bright sunlight.

"Uh . . . ," I said, "I . . . have some bad news."

"What is it? What's happened now?" He glanced around as if checking for clues to the bad news.

"It's JoAnne Douglas . . . ," I began.

Rob ran his hand through his hair. "Not again! What is it this time?" Apparently he'd expected to see more vandalism.

I turned toward the spot where JoAnne lay. With the tablecloth pulled up, she was clearly visible, one ratty tennis shoe–covered foot sticking out from under the table like the Wicked Witch of the Valley. The other shoe appeared to be missing. But this witch had not been killed by a house. It had taken a corkscrew to do that.

Nearby, also hidden under the table, I noticed a gallon can of green paint.

Had JoAnne brought the paint? Was she planning to use it somehow to ruin the party?

I watched Rob for his reaction as he squinted at the body a few feet away, then started to walk over. I held on to his arm.

"Don't," I said. "Brad called the police. They'll be here any minute."

Rob shook his head, mesmerized by the sight of JoAnne's dead body. "What . . . what happened?"

"Looks like somebody killed her," Allison said, stating the obvious. "In fact, it looks like she got screwed." A small smile played at the corner of her mouth.

Rob glared at his sister-in-law. "Allison! Don't be vulgar."

"What? She's dead. You should be glad about that. I'm just saying . . ."

"Have a little consideration for your sister, will you?" he snapped, then rushed over to be with his wife, who seemed to be taking JoAnne's death the hardest. Dee let him have her seat next to a tearful Marie.

"Corkscrew," Allison said to me, having lost Rob as her audience. "Poetic, don't you think?"

I ignored her. The young woman obviously craved attention, but she wasn't going to get it from me.

"Excuse me," I said. The word "corkscrew" had triggered a sudden memory of last night. I walked to the front door of the house and ducked inside.

Pausing in the entryway, I listened for a few moments. Noises came from the kitchen, where I assumed Rocco and Gina were still cleaning up their cooking items. Apparently they hadn't heard the news. I started down the dimly lit hallway, stepping slowly and carefully, until I reached the first of Rob's wall displays. I remembered hearing a crunch as I'd walked down the hall last night—a noise that sounded like broken glass underfoot. Eyeing the display, I studied the framed set of antique corkscrews.

The glass that covered the collection of wine openers was intact.

I moved on to the next one. Nothing unusual there either.

I stepped down to the last one. This time, something was definitely different . . .

I reached up to touch the glass.

Bingo.

No glass.

I peered inside, studying each corkscrew. None appeared to be missing. And there were no jagged glass edges on the inside of the frame.

Hmmm.

And then I saw it, even in the minimal light. The corkscrew on the lower left-hand side of the case looked out of place among the antiques—and oddly familiar. I pulled out my cell phone, touched the flashlight app, and held the light up to the corkscrew. Inscribed in fine print were the words "Killer Parties."

Oh my God! Someone had taken one of Rob's antique wine screws and replaced it with one of my party favors!

I looked at the floor, then knelt down and shined the light on the Italian tile beneath the frame. Scanning the area, I saw nothing out of the ordinary. If there had been any shattered glass on the floor, it had been swept away.

I ran my fingers over the cold tile, along the crevices and where the floor met the wall, wondering why the killer appeared to have stolen Rob's corkscrew and used it to kill JoAnne Douglas. Did he—or she—really think replacing it with one of mine would fool anyone?

I suddenly felt something sting my finger and pulled back my hand. Ouch!

Raising the tip of my middle finger, I saw a dot of blood form on the pad.

I touched on the iPhone light and held it up. A small shard of glass stuck out from the center of the red dot. I pulled out the shard, wincing like a baby stuck by a diaper pin, and pushed my bleeding finger into my mouth.

Outside, I heard the screams of sirens.

"Fire! Fire!"

My mother appeared at her bedroom door and rushed into the hallway, sans robe but still wearing her silk nightgown, thank God, and her green beauty mask.

"Calm down, Mother. It's just the police."

Just the police? What was I saying?

Clearly disoriented, she scanned the area. "No fire?"

"No, Mom. You're safe. Everything's okay."

Except for the dead body in the garden.

"What's happening? Why are the police here?"

I walked Mother back to her room and reassured her as I helped her remove her makeup mask and get dressed. Brad would handle the cops. Right now, my mother needed me.

"There's been an incident," I said, buttoning her floral blouse.

Mom's eyes narrowed. I could tell she had become her old self again. "Oh no. Presley. Not another dead body."

"Mother!"

"Well, you do have a penchant for finding a body or

two after one of your big parties. Who is it this time? Not Larry, I hope."

I almost laughed at her matter-of-fact response to the incident—and the thought that it might have been her paramour. I filled her in as she applied her makeup, correctly this time, and answered her questions as best I could. Of course, at the moment, I had questions too, and not many answers.

"Are you sure you want to go outside?" I asked her. "The police are there and—"

"Oh yes. If you're involved in this—and no doubt you are—I want to be there to help. I am your mother, after all."

I nodded helplessly. I knew there was no stopping her. Perhaps my tenacity was genetic. I had a feeling I might need it with this latest development.

"Presley," Mother said, suddenly staring at my fresh white Killer Parties T-shirt. "You're bleeding."

I looked down. Sure enough, a streak of blood ran diagonally across the bold red letters of my self-promoting T-shirt. I checked my middle fingertip. It had begun to bleed again.

"Oh, that. I must have brushed my finger against my shirt while I was helping you dress. Hope I didn't get any blood on you."

Mother's frown deepened. "Where did the blood come from?"

"I cut my finger on a piece of glass. Long story. Honestly, I'm fine. Let's go on outside. I'd like to see what's happening." I stuck my finger in my mouth again to try to stop the bleeding.

"Don't do that, Presley. It's not ladylike, and very

unsanitary. You need a Band-Aid." She dumped out her Coach bag onto the unmade bed and sifted through a colossal collection of what she called emergency items—traveling makeup, mini-flashlight, address book, mirror, scarf, tissues, medications, chocolate, crossword puzzle book, hand sanitizer, toothbrush, nail file, sunglasses, coupons, mints, nail polish, herbal tea, a picture of me at my first big event—Mayor Davin Green's surprise wedding party—and her medic-alert ID information tag noting her Alzheimer's condition, which she refused to wear. Somehow in the vast pile of stuff, she located a Band-Aid, ripped off the paper, and pressed the thing around my middle finger.

"Thanks, Mom," I said, feeling myself revert back to childhood. I was surprised she didn't just kiss it and give me a cookie. "Now let's go."

I led the way down the hall, shooting a quick glance at the Killer Parties corkscrew inside the broken frame along the way, then outside to the garden area, where we'd held the party. Two cop cars were parked in the driveway, and four uniformed officers were scattered around, talking with Brad, Rob, and Marie. An ambulance with paramedics pulled up moments later and checked the body, then stood back, making no attempt at resuscitation. Finally, a police van drove up and four crime scene techs got out and went to work, taking pictures, investigating the scene, collecting samples, and whatever else they did on *CSI*-type shows.

Mother headed over to comfort Marie, who was still sitting on the bench, looking pale and drawn, while Rob, standing next to her, talked to one of the officers.

Mom had a knack for comforting people, so I left her to it. I made my way over to Brad, who was talking with a beefy, red-faced man in a dark suit that had stopped fitting the man several pounds ago.

He paused as I approached. "Ma'am, could you wait over there until I'm finished here?"

Ma'am?

Brad intervened before I snapped the man's head off and stepped on it like an overinflated balloon. "Presley, this is Detective Kelly. Ken, this is Presley Parker, the party planner I told you about. She's the one who put the event together. You're going to want to talk to her. She may have seen the vic last night, snooping around the premises."

Was that true? Had I possibly seen JoAnne Douglas sneaking around the Purple Grape in the dark?

The detective squinted at me, as if looking at a disturbing X-ray. I realized he wasn't looking at my eyes; he was staring at my chest. Men.

"Ma'am, is that blood?"

I glanced down. Oh, it wasn't my boobs that had attracted his attention. It was the streak of blood on my shirt. I tried to brush the stain off, then gave up and held up my bandaged middle finger.

"Uh, I caught a piece of glass in my finger—," I said, hoping he didn't think I was flipping him off. Which I might have been.

Detective Kelly turned over a page in his notebook and wrote something down. Probably something like, "Presley Parker: murderer. Evidence: blood on shirt."

"When was this?" he asked.

"Uh, just a few minutes ago, actually. I was—"

"I'm going to need your shirt, ma'am" he said, cutting me off again.

"Seriously?" I said, stunned at his request. "Wait a minute. You don't think—"

"I don't think anything, ma'am. Just doing my job."

Again with the interruptions and the "ma'ams." I really wanted to hold up my bandaged middle finger again.

"Well, I assure you, I had nothing to do with the death of that woman—JoAnne Douglas. I only met her once. But if you'll listen for a moment, I might know where the murder weapon came from."

The detective looked up from his notebook in anticipation.

"I've been trying to tell you—that's how I cut my finger. When I went down the hall last night, I heard a crunching sound under my shoe. I forgot about it until this morning, when I saw the corkscrew in JoAnne Douglas's chest. So I went back to the hall and started checking Rob's collection of corkscrews. That's when I noticed that the glass covering one of them was gone, and an antique corkscrew was missing. I think the killer took it and replaced it with one of mine."

"Why didn't you tell us, Pres?" Brad said, frowning at me like an irate father.

The detective didn't give me a chance to respond. He asked, "You say you cut your finger on a piece of glass? Did you break the glass, ma'am?"

"Good heavens, no!" I nearly screeched in defense. I took a deep breath to calm myself. "No. I was feeling around on the floor and that's when I got stabbed with a shard of glass." To Brad I said, "I was on my way to tell you when my mom came out of her room in a panic, after hearing all the sirens. She thought the house was on fire."

My explanation didn't relax Brad's frown. Meanwhile the detective made a note in his little book that was probably not flattering. Before I could explain myself better, a thirtysomething woman in a white coat holding a clipboard approached the detective. Her dark hair was twisted into a spiky knot, her brown eyes were outlined in kohl eyeliner, and one of her eyebrows was pierced. The name tag on her coat read, "Dr. Overholt, Napa County Coroner."

"You got something, PattyJo?" Detective Kelly asked her.

"Not much, not until I get her back to the lab. From her temp, lividity, and lack of rigor, I'm guessing time of death was somewhere between six p.m. and midnight."

"What?" I said. "Are you saying she could have been lying under that table during the entire party?"

"Was the party held between six and midnight?"

"Seven and midnight," I said.

"Then, yes," Dr. Overholt said.

Oh my God. JoAnne Douglas's dead body could have been there the whole time—and no one noticed, thanks to the long white tablecloth.

"What about the weapon?" Detective Kelly asked.

"It's an odd wound. It looks as if she was stabbed with the corkscrew—which wouldn't be easy to do—but after seeing that handle on the thing, I suppose anyone could have gripped it well enough to shove it into the middle of her chest. She also had a head injury, but that may have happened in a fall. I'll know more when I examine her."

What was JoAnne doing at the party, uninvited? Was she hiding under the table? With a can of green paint? Was she planning to sabotage the party like she'd promised the night before? Who had killed her? And why had he—or she—used one of Rob's antique corkscrews instead of one of my Killer Party corkscrews lying right there on the table?

Detective Kelly closed his notebook and looked at me. "Ma'am, don't leave town. I'm going to want you to come down to the station later and give a statement. And I'm going to need your shirt."

The tip of my finger suddenly began to throb. This was shaping up to be a royal pain in the . . . finger.

Chapter 8

"I don't like that guy," I said to Brad, after Detective Kelly turned his metaphoric magnifying glass away from me and back to the crime scene. At the moment he was peering at the murder weapon, which was still poking out of the dead woman's chest.

"Like he said, he's just doing his job, Pres. You should know that by now."

"Yeah? Well, where's Detective Melvin when I need him? At least he knows I'm not a murderer. That Kelly guy actually acts as if I'm a suspect. 'Don't leave town'? Where'd he learn that? Those *Police Academy* movies?"

"Hey, it wasn't too long ago that even Luke thought you might be involved in a murder case. There must be something about you that screams 'I did it!' " Grinning, he gave me a squeeze.

"Very funny. It's not my fault that parties are often emotionally charged events. People drink. People flirt. People do things they wouldn't normally do. Besides, nobody died at the Nerf Challenge Party I hosted last weekend. And there were even weapons there."

"That's because the party was for eleven-year-old boys and the weapons were made of foam rubber. This place is riddled with potential weapons." He swept an arm around the half-cleaned-up party site, indicating numerous corkscrews, cheese knives, empty wine bottles, broken wineglasses, and blunt instruments.

He was right. If a person wanted to kill someone, just about anything would work as a murder weapon. As for suspects, no one present appeared particularly upset about the death of JoAnne Douglas, other than Marie Christopher. The news seemed to have sucked all the energy from her body. Meanwhile, Allison acted as if a dead body in the garden was no big thing. Amazing how two sisters could be so different.

I looked for Rob, wondering how he was coping, and spotted him talking again with Detective Kelly. When the detective asked him a question, Rob frowned and gestured toward the body. I wondered how well the cop and Rob knew each other, living in the same county. If JoAnne Douglas had been a longtime thorn in his grapevine, perhaps he'd had encounters with Detective Kelly before.

Speaking of grapevines, news had apparently spread through the local grapevine like a glassy-eyed sharpshooter—or was it glassy-winged? A small crowd had collected on the periphery of the property. The Madeiras and Briens, the neighbors who had attended the party last night, had arrived via their golf carts, apparently having been alerted by the police sirens. Tourists and rubberneckers were also stopped at the edge of the yellow police line to gawk and speculate. I quickly sent Raj to turn them away from the property, but in spite of my efforts to control the situation, one driver wormed his way through the growing crowd: Kyle Bennett. Talk about your classic ambulance chaser.

Kyle got out of his silver BMW. Dressed in a dark, expensive Armani suit, he looked as if he were about to enter the courtroom. I wondered how he'd heard the news so quickly—police scanner? He approached Rob, patted him on the back as if in support, and spoke to the detective. The detective responded, and Rob stepped away and disappeared into the house. I sidled up near Detective Kelly and Kyle Bennett to listen in. No doubt the flashy attorney had hopes of sharing the limelight—or perhaps taking on a new client.

"Did you see anything suspicious at the party last night, Kyle?" the detective asked.

"No, nothing, Ken. It was a very nice event. Hard to believe the poor lady was lying dead under that table while we were—"

"We don't know that yet," Detective Kelly interrupted. "Were you here all evening?"

"Yes, of course," Kyle said. "Except for a couple of bathroom breaks. That wine goes right through me." He chuckled at his lame joke.

Bathroom breaks would place him in the hallway at some point, I thought.

"What about the others at the party?" the detective asked. "Did you notice anyone missing for any length of time?"

"No, not that I recall. Rob, Marie, Allison, and Javier made regular trips inside for more wine, but nothing unusual. You know how it is, hosting a party. There are a million things to do to make sure your guests are enjoying themselves."

From the blank expression on the detective's face, it was obvious he didn't know how it was. I wondered if he'd ever even had a birthday party when he was a kid.

"So Rob Christopher left the party several times?"

"Well, sure, but I didn't mean to imply ... Look, Ken, talk to Nick Madeira or Dennis Brien. I overheard them at the party, talking about JoAnne showing up at Rob's private event the night before. Maybe they saw her sneak in."

"What did you hear?" the detective asked.

"Well, you'll have to get the details from Nick and Dennis. But apparently JoAnne came bursting into their private room at the culinary college and threatened Rob, saying she was going to ruin his party. Everyone knows those two didn't get along. But Rob wouldn't hurt a fly. A grape moth, maybe. But not a fly."

Kyle looked at me standing nearby, obviously eavesdropping. The detective caught Kyle's look and turned to me. He eyed me a few seconds longer than was comfortable, then closed his notebook and headed to where the neighbors, the Madeiras and the Briens, were talking.

By the time I turned back to Kyle, he had dashed to Marie's side and was sitting next to her, caressing her hand. The glassy-winged sharpshooter had nothing on this pasty-faced wine sucker.

I was about to mosey around the party area when I caught sight of Allison in the front doorway. She was busily thumbing the keyboard of her cell phone. What was she doing—tweeting the news?

I took a circuitous route until I was near enough to listen in on the conversation between Detective Kelly and the two neighboring couples. Dennis Brien was in the midst of lambasting the deceased, calling her and her Green Grape "fanatical do-gooders."

"She was the one who's been harassing Rob and the rest of us," Dennis said. "The other night she came busting into our private room at the culinary college and accused Rob of practically ruining the wine country single-handedly. She thought his wine-tasting event last night had some kind of political agenda to kill her new bill. But that wasn't true. He just wanted to celebrate his latest wine. The woman is—was—a nuisance."

"Why did she single out Christopher?" Detective Kelly asked.

"Who knows? I mean, she had it in for anyone who wanted to expand, which Rob planned to do."

"Maybe she was mad because she wasn't invited to his party," Dennis's wife, KJ, suggested.

"I doubt it," Dennis said. "I think he did something to rub her the wrong way. She was always on his case, from the moment they moved here. But still, it wasn't enough to make him want to kill her, if that's what you're thinking. Whoever did this has to be some kind of mental case. I should know. I was always getting threats while I was governor of California. Luckily nothing ever came of them."

"It was awful how she died," KJ said, wincing. "A corkscrew. How bizarre."

"Did any of you see anything last night at the wine tasting that seemed unusual?" the detective asked the four of them. "Anything that might have been suspicious?"

They all shook their heads. Then Nick Madeira turned to his wife. "Wait a minute. Claudette, when you went to the restroom, you said you stopped to admire Rob's collection and noticed the glass was broken on one of them."

"Yes," Claudette said, "but I didn't think anything of it."

"What time was this?" the detective asked her.

"Oh goodness, I have no idea. I was in and out several times." She blushed, talking about her trips to the bathroom. Or was it something else that caused her to color?

"Was Rob there?"

"I might have passed him in the hallway. But then, I passed several people on their way to use the facilities."

Uh-oh, I thought, a sinking feeling settling in my gut. While I was glad the focus had temporarily been taken off me, I had a sense Rob was quickly becoming a viable suspect. Naturally his fingerprints would be on the frame. That didn't mean anything. But would they also be on the Killer Parties corkscrew inside the frame? And on the one used to kill JoAnne Douglas?

I stood back, taking it all in, and remembered what Brad had taught me about determining who might be a suspect. It had to be someone who had MOM—motive, opportunity, and method. It sounded as if Rob had motive, since he wanted to protect his property from JoAnne's new bill. He certainly had method—the corkscrew—but why would he use the one in the case? It would point directly to him. Why not one of the corkscrews on the serving tables? Weren't they strong enough to do the job?

As for opportunity, everyone at the party had gone down that hallway to the bathroom. And anyone could have stabbed JoAnne under the table. Had she been hiding there all evening? Had she been killed there, or murdered elsewhere and her body dragged to the party table? And when had it happened? Before the party began or after it ended, when fewer people were around? Then again, maybe the killer did it during the party, when everyone was busy drinking, eating, and socializing.

Hopefully the ME would have a more specific time when she finished her exam.

Brad was on the phone when I found him a few minutes later. He held up a finger to let me know he'd be done in a minute, so I waited and watched the EMTs place the body into a body bag and transport it to the ambulance. The officers, including Detective Kelly, looked as if they were packing up. Apparently they were done interrogating the witnesses.

Brad hung up. "What's up? Learn anything eavesdropping on everyone's conversations?"

How well he knew me.

"A little," I said. "What about you? Who were you talking to?"

"Luke."

That would be Detective Luke Melvin from the San Francisco Police Department and Brad's good buddy.

"What about?"

"I asked him if he could do a criminal record search on a few of these people."

"And?"

"He said he'd get back to—"

Brad stopped midsentence. Someone was shouting. I turned to see Rob arguing with Detective Kelly, shaking his head and gesturing with his finger. He kept repeating the words "No! No! I told you!"

"Either you come to the station for questioning on your own," Detective Kelly said, "or I'll take you into custody in handcuffs right now. Is that what you want?"

Rob shot a frantic look at Kyle, who stood hovering nearby. "Fine!" Rob said. "I'll come. But you're wasting your time. I've told you everything I know. And I have no idea how that corkscrew got there, but it wasn't me."

Kyle Bennett put a reassuring hand on Rob's shoulder. "Calm down, buddy. I'll handle this. They're just taking you in for questioning. They can't hold you without cause, and they don't have anything. I'll follow you downtown."

Rob looked disoriented, as if the ground had been pulled out from under him. If he was innocent, why was he so upset about going to the police station to be questioned? I assumed Kyle was his attorney by the way he'd stepped up, so Rob would be protected once there. But still, no one likes being questioned by the police. I knew that from personal experience.

Marie stood up and rushed to Rob's side. She said something to him; then he gave her a kiss on the cheek and got into the back of a police car. Moments later he was gone.

Mother wrapped an arm around Marie and led her into the house.

I called my team over. Dee, Berkeley, Duncan, Rocco, and Raj gathered around, waiting for my orders.

"Guys, sorry about this," I said. "If the detective wants you to stay for more questioning, I'll comp another night at your B and B. As soon as we're packed up here, take the rest of the day off, go enjoy the wine country. Thanks again for all your help. You did a great job, as usual."

I got sympathetic pats and smiles as my crew headed back to finish the last of their cleanup tasks. The guys, including Brad, put the heavy stuff in the rental truck, while Rocco and Gina took care of the kitchen. Mother helped me load the smaller boxes of party fare into Brad's SUV, and Dee collected the party platters and bowls. By lunchtime, with no sign of Rob's return, Rocco and Gina brought out sandwiches and fruit to my hungry and tired crew.

Marie appeared briefly, looking tired, and thanked everyone. She insisted Mother and I stay an extra night until "this mess" was cleared up. "I could use the company," she said wearily, slurring her words slightly. I wondered if she'd taken some medication or started early on the wine. After exchanging a few words with Allison, she returned to the house and disappeared inside.

I marveled at the dissimilarity of the two sisters. Allison, dressed in her tight jeans shorts, purple beaded tank top, and glittery Pedro Garcia sandals, had a bounce in her step and a smile on her face. Marie, wearing khaki capris, a loose-fitting white blouse, and flat Burberry sandals, appeared deflated, drowsy, and worn out. Allison got into one of the cars from Rob's garage—a white Mercedes—and drove off without a word to anyone. I wondered where she was going—and what she was thinking.

After lunch, my crew left to do some touristy stuff. Brad took a call about a cleanup in the city and left before he got a call back from Detective Melvin. "I'll try to be back tonight," he said, giving me a kiss goodbye. "And you try not to get anyone killed while I'm gone."

I gave him a dry smile and the stink eye, then returned his kiss, wishing he could stay and enjoy an afternoon in the wine country with me.

"Presley dear," Mother said, appearing after he'd gone. "I've got a great idea!"

"What's that, Mother?" I said, sighing. "Another mud bath? I don't think I'm up for it this afternoon."

"No, no. Something better that will take your mind off things."

I knew there was no arguing with my mother. Besides, I had promised her a nice relaxing mini-vacation in the wine country. And there was nothing I could do for Rob at the moment.

"All right, Mom. What would you like to do? You don't drink, so wine tasting is out. Go to an art show? Take the wine train? Hot-air balloon?"

"None of those things. I thought we'd do something that I'm sure will help you solve this murder case."

I couldn't help but grin at her. "Oh really? Like what? Search for hidden clues? Interrogate a list of suspects? Put together a sleuth kit with a flashlight, magnifying glass, and notebook?"

"Don't be silly, Presley. You've been reading too many Agatha Christies."

"Agatha's more your style, Mom. I prefer Nancy Drew. So what exactly is your big plan to figure out who done it?"

"Bingo!"

Chapter 9

PARTY-PLANNING TIP #9

Consider hosting your wine-tasting party at a local winery. You'll find everything from casual tastings to educational seminars to formal events. If you're in Napa, treat yourself to a hot-air balloon ride, a mud bath, a trip on the wine train, or a wildlife safari (yes, in Napa!). Just watch out for those pink elephants . . .

"Bingo?" I repeated. "You're kidding, Mother. We found a dead woman at my party and you want to play bingo? I don't think this is an appropriate time—"

"Oh, Presley," Mother said. "You wouldn't believe the way people gossip at that place. Every time Larry left the table to get me a snack, the other women there told me all kinds of stories about some of the more color-ful characters in the valley. When I mentioned I was staying at the Purple Grape, tongues started wagging about the Rob-and-JoAnne feud. You want information, play bingo."

"Why didn't you tell me this earlier?"

"Well, first of all, I'm not one for idle talk . . ."

I nearly laughed out loud at that prevarication.

"And secondly, gossip is just that—gossip. It's not fact until proven. You taught me that with your murder investigating."

"Then why go there now and listen to more gossip?" I asked.

"Because. You know what Barbara Walters says."

"No, actually, I don't."

"'Show me someone who never gossips, and I'll show you someone who isn't interested in people.'" She gave a "so there" nod of her head.

I couldn't argue with that. I checked my watch. Nothing to do here, now that my stuff was packed up and the party area was a crime scene. Plus, that cop had told me not to leave town. Brad most likely wouldn't be back until evening. What the hell. A little bingo might not be a bad idea. And who knew? Maybe I *would* hear some gossip about the people involved in this murder. One of our topics in my abnormal psychology class was on the evolutionary biology of gossip. I'd asked my students to discuss the social-bonding aspects of gossip, which can actually bring people together. Mother had a point. Gossip offered a wealth of additional information—as long as it wasn't misinformation.

The problem was how to sift fact from fiction.

After Mother refreshed her makeup, omitting the lipstick from her eyelids, she followed me down the hall to the living area and kitchen, where I did a quick search for Marie. I found no sign of her, nor of Rocco and Gina, who had packed up their cooking supplies and departed. The place felt empty and cold, more like a model home on display than a lived-in residence. Without Rob's friendly demeanor, Marie's gentle nature, and even Allison's smarmy attitude, it was little more than a shell. A very expensive, beautifully decorated shell.

I helped Mother into the MINI Cooper, and we headed for the bingo hall once again. Most of the games were at night, with the exception of Sunday afternoons. Perhaps bingo was an alternative to church for some of the wine-country residents.

As I drove the short distance, I half listened to my mother explain the rules of the game. I hadn't played since I was a kid, and only once at a friend's unimaginative birthday party. When I'd told my mother about the party, which included pin the tail on the donkey and musical chairs, she'd sworn she'd never host a boring birthday like that for me.

She'd kept her word. Memories of my birthday parties included themes like Princess for a Day, complete with pink prom gowns and tiaras, Own Your Own Zoo, which offered pony rides, and Mickey's Clubhouse, featuring characters straight out of Disneyland. Of course, once I turned thirteen, I hosted my own parties, with party activities along the lines of crank calling, toilet papering, and eventually spin the bottle.

"Mom, I don't think I need a review of the game. I played it one time at Rose Mae Lang's seventh birthday party, remember? Somebody calls out a letter-number combination and if you find it on your bingo card, you cover the space with a bean. Whoever gets five in a row yells 'bingo.' No-brainer."

"That's children's bingo, dear. This is much more

complicated and there are lots of different versions, like Double-Action, U-Pick-'Em, Postage Stamp, Quick-Shot, Bonanza. And we don't use beans to cover the spaces."

"You use those big fat markers, right?" I said.

"They're called daubers, dear, remember?"

"Okay, daubers. Do they still blow Ping-Pong balls out of a rotating cage?"

"Most places do use those, although Larry said some halls prefer those electronic random number generators, whatever those are. He also said that most people play more than one card—as many as thirty at a time."

"Thirty!" I shot a surprised glance at her.

"Well, the more cards you play, the better your chances. Some of the younger people who use the electronic machines can play over sixty games at a time."

Sixty? I'd be lucky to keep track of one, what with my ADHD.

"You'll have to know some of the terms too, dear. For example, when you only need one more number to win, you're considered 'cased' or 'set.' When you're 'breaking the bubble' . . ."

When did bingo get so complicated? I wondered. *Cased? Set? Breaking the bubble?* "So now I have to learn your bingo lingo?"

"Oh, Presley." Mother sighed. "Most of the terms are obvious, like 'jumping the gun' and 'false alarm.' My favorite is 'crying number.' That's the next number that would have been called after someone else wins. If it was the one you were waiting for, it's your 'crying number.' "

"That'll probably be the term I'll need the most," I

said, pulling into the crowded parking lot and taking one of the last spaces in the farthest row. I helped my mother out of the car and we walked to the hall, entered through the double doors, and scanned the auditorium-sized room full of people sitting at long tables covered with bingo sheets and the occasional electronic monitors. Nearly every seat was taken, mostly by older folks, with a sprinkling of young and middle-aged people.

A hand waved to us from across the room.

"It's Larry!" Mother said, waving back. "I told him you were coming. He's saved us some seats. Come along, Presley."

I followed my mom to a far table where Larry stood, grinning like a teenager.

"Ronnie! You made it! I was getting worried." He took her hand, kissed it, and guided her to the seat next to him. After Mother sat down, Larry gestured for me to take the seat across from him. In front of us were two bingo sheets each and two large daubers—green for me, purple for Mother.

"My treat!" he said proudly. "I just hope they bring you luck. May I get you both a soda before the game starts? Coffee? Chips?"

"Diet Coke, please," my mother said.

"Coffee would be great. Thanks," I said.

Larry nodded and left for the alcove where high school students sold hot dogs, drinks, and snacks. Mother immediately started chatting with the person sitting next to her, a woman in her seventies with champagne-colored hair, freshly styled by the salon. She wore an "I Heart Bingo" T-shirt covered with lots of rhinestone bling.

I glanced around the room, searching for familiar faces, and spotted Allison and Javier three tables away. From a distance, it looked as if Allison was texting on her cell phone while waiting for the games to begin. Javier, on the other hand, was hunched over his bingo sheets as if trying to memorize the letter-number combinations.

I wondered if Allison had exchanged one addiction—drugs—for another—gambling. Apparently even a death at the winery couldn't stop her from playing the game. As for Javier, did he have a gambling problem as well?

Would I, after an afternoon of bingo?

Yeah, right.

"Presley," Mother said, interrupting my thoughts. She turned to the "I Heart" woman she'd been chatting with. "This is Constance, a friend of Larry's. Constance, this is my daughter, Presley. She's an event planner. She's the one who found the body at the Purple Grape this morning."

"Mother!" Talk about gossiping.

"Oh, everyone knows about the murder, Presley. Constance, here, knew JoAnne Douglas personally."

Constance nodded. "Poor JoAnne," she said. "Although I'm not surprised. She made a lot of enemies in this town."

"How so?" I asked, curious to hear what the woman had to say.

Mother gave me an "I told you this was a great place for information" look.

"Oh, you know, suing practically every winery that wasn't as green as she thought it should be—although

I doubt any of them could live up to her standards and still survive. So many of the little vineyards have sold out to Napology—around here we call it Nap-*opoly* because they seem to be taking over the entire county. Anyway, I don't like to speak ill of the dead. But talk about her wanting everything to go green—now she'll be enriching the environment personally, if you know what I mean." Constance snort-giggled at her little metaphor. I don't know which surprised me more—her reference to JoAnne turning to mulch or a snort coming out of such an elderly woman.

Curious, I asked Constance, "Did JoAnne play bingo?"

"No, no. She thought it was sacrilegious. Even tried to shut it down because it attracted the 'wrong element.' Ha. I knew her through the garden club."

"Do you come here often, Constance?"

"Too often, I'm afraid," she said, smiling at her own wicked ways. "I'm eighty-six years old and still in the chase, as we call it, after more than twenty years. I love bingo. I surely do." She giggle-snorted again.

Well, if nothing else, bingo must keep you young, I thought. This eighty-six-year-old woman didn't look a year over seventy-something.

Larry arrived with our drinks and sat down. He glanced around the room, then said, "You must be one of the youngest people here, Presley. Most who come are our age, although we've recruited some of the younger generation. We don't want bingo to die off with us old folks."

I thought of Javier and Allison, not exactly part of the general demographic either. Had they been "recruited"?

"But for the most part, young people prefer other kinds of games than bingo," Larry continued. "They go to the fancy casinos that offer poker and slots, along with high-stakes bingo. These independent halls can't compete with that."

"Don't those high-tech bingo machines bring in the younger generation?" I asked, nodding toward a middle-aged couple nearby. Each one had a machine.

"Yes," Larry said, "but most of us prefer the old-fashioned sheets. Some of the old-timers think the machines are rigged, so they stick with paper and daubers." He laughed. "Old habits die hard."

"Do they ever have a problem with cheating?" I asked Larry, after eyeing the female security guard who kept watch over the enthusiastic players.

"Every now and then you get someone complaining about cheating, but they've never proved anything—at least not here. A few years ago there was a bingo game over at a Sonoma church. They were using weighted Ping-Pong balls and secret signals with callers in on the fix, so they shut it down. But they've never found anything wrong here. They call this hall 'the least crooked-est.'" Larry laughed. I could see why Mother was attracted to him, with his easy demeanor and friendly smile.

"I've heard about the skulduggery in other halls across the country," Constance added. "Scams, bribes, extortion, fraud, all sanctioned by lobbyists and state officials. Sometimes the charities don't receive the money they are due. There are lots of stories about cheating at the halls."

"How do they keep things regulated?" I asked.

"The state oversees the Bingo Enabling Act," Constance said.

"Bingo Enabling Act?" I asked, surprised there was such a thing. It sounded like some kind of codependency program.

"Oh yes," Larry said. "The state auditors fine operators for infractions, but they're usually minor oversights, not for cheating."

"I had no idea there was so much intrigue associated with a simple bingo game," I said.

"Bingo players are a unique culture," Larry said. "Some of the more serious players are awfully suspicious—and superstitious. They fight over 'lucky' seats or claim their good-luck charms have been stolen off their tables. But they still come to play."

A quiet middle-aged woman sitting next to me spoke up for the first time. She had tiny brown curls, gray at the temples, plump rosy cheeks, and purple mascara on her eyelashes. "I come here because it keeps me out of the bars."

I grinned at her. She didn't smile back. Apparently she was serious.

"Oh, Helen," Larry said, shaking his head. "You do not. You come to see your friends, like me. It's more social than anything. Sometimes the hall holds a barbecue or a special jackpot to bring in people—up to three or four hundred. But usually we get about two hundred for the regular games. I know most of the people here—old and new." I noticed he squeezed Mother's arm. Mother blushed.

"Does all the money from this hall go to charity?" I asked.

"After overhead, it goes to the local schools. You figure, if everyone pays at least thirty dollars for a set of cards, and two hundred people show up, that's six thousand dollars. Per night. That'll buy a few band instruments."

"Nobody wins playing bingo," Helen said, looking at me with rheumy eyes. I suspected this woman had had a hard life. "If you break even, you're lucky. But if I keel over right here, I want people to say, 'She went the way she wanted to go.' Maybe they'll hold my funeral here."

I tried not to laugh at Helen's morbid humor, but it wasn't easy. I glanced at her T-shirt, which featured two colorful daubers that flanked the words "Play Responsibly."

"Cool shirt," I said.

She nodded.

"Is gambling addiction really a problem at a bingo hall?" I asked her.

She shrugged, intent on marking her free squares.

Larry answered, "Can be. That woman over there," he said, pointing to an elderly lady who appeared to be wearing a chenille bathrobe, "lost her house. Went to GA—Gamblers Anonymous. Now she's back. She says she's 'cured.'" He rolled his eyes.

"Wow. I never dreamed the game could become an addiction."

"Some of these people never even gambled until they walked into a bingo hall. And it's perfectly legal."

"Welcome to bingo, everyone!" A disembodied voice came over the loudspeaker. A cheer went up from the crowd. I had a feeling these people couldn't wait to start marking up their sheets. Constance picked up a tiny elephant and kissed it, then replaced it in front of her. Several players fiddled with their lucky charms, arranging them just so, while others, including my mother, decapitated their daubers and began filling in all the free spaces on their bingo sheets. The room suddenly stilled. Voices hushed, heads bent over. Faces turned serious. This was nothing like the bingo game I remembered at Rose Mae's birthday party. These people meant business.

"Our first game will be Straight Lines Bingo," the male caller said. "First player to call bingo with five in a row wins the cash prize of two hundred and fifty dollars. No corners. Are you ready?"

Another ear-piercing cheer went up. Yikes.

Although Mother jumped right into the game as if she'd been playing professional bingo for years, it took me a few minutes to get the hang of it. An image of the first ball appeared on a large electronic screen even before it was called, giving players a head start on filling in their grids—and a head start on calling out bingo if they had a winning card. I barely kept up with the numbers, often missing some. Luckily Larry, sitting across from me, pointed out the ones I overlooked, in addition to covering his own spread of cards. Talk about multitasking—this was not the best game for someone with ADHD.

Ten minutes later a voice called out "Bingo!" Moans and groans filled the room as the rest of us losers realized this first game was over and there would be no cash prize for us this time. I turned to see who'd won the money and was surprised to find Javier with his hand in the air, a big gap-toothed grin on his face. Allison, sitting next to him, was also grinning, and patting him on the back. I made a mental note to go congratulate him at the scheduled break.

Once I had the hang of the next game, I got cocky, until they threw me a curve. This one was called Postage Stamp Bingo, which meant instead of covering five spaces in a row, players had to fill a block of four. Next came Six-Pack Bingo—fill in a six-space rectangle. I almost yelled "Bingo!" when I found one of my sheets had five in a row, until my mother reminded me this was a whole new game. Boo.

An hour and five losing games later, the caller announced a much-needed break. I stood up, stretched out my back, squeezed together my numb buttocks, and took a stroll around the room to get the circulation going in my legs again. I found myself on the other side of the room, where Javier and Allison sat drinking sodas and eating candy bars.

"Hi!" I said, acting as if I was surprised to see them.

They looked up. Javier stiffened; Allison cocked her head.

"What are you doing here?" she said.

"My mother wanted to come and she invited me along. I thought it might be a nice escape from . . ." I didn't finish the sentence.

Allison nodded. "Us too," she said, indicating Javier. "It's so gloomy over there right now. And there's really nothing we can do with that crime scene tape all over the place. Right, Javier?"

He nodded and took a bite of his candy bar.

Allison stood up. "Well, time for a potty break," she said, then dashed off, leaving me alone with Javier, who continued to look uncomfortable.

I sat down in her seat.

"Hey, congratulations on winning the first game! That was exciting."

Javier broke a smile. "Yeah," he said. "Only wish it was enough to pay the bills, you know?"

I nodded. "Rob said you manage several of the smaller wineries but that some of them have closed down."

He frowned. "Yeah, bought out by Nap-opoly, thanks to JoAnne and all her green rules. I'm down to two wineries now. I could definitely use a few more bingos, you know?"

"You think JoAnne is responsible for the loss of the small wineries?"

He said nothing, just took another bite of his candy bar and washed it down with soda.

"Because her requirements are too strict?" I said, pursuing the question.

"The small wineries, they can't compete with the big ones, not with all these rules about restricting expansion and development."

"Do you think any of the owners were upset enough to kill her?" I asked bluntly.

Javier shot me a look. "I don't know. Not Rob. He's a good man. He tried to go along with JoAnne's demands—we all did. But when he found out—" Javier stopped.

"Found out what, Javier?"

"Nothing. It's not my place to speak, you know?"

"Javier, JoAnne Douglas is dead, and your boss—your friend—Rob is down at the police station being questioned. If there's anything you can tell me that would help him . . ."

Javier bit his lip, glanced around, then said quietly, "Okay, but you didn't hear this from me, you know? Rob found out JoAnne was selling bottles of her regular wines as 'new boutique wines,' marking up the prices and using fake labels. He told her it wasn't right, but she said there was nothing illegal about it. He reminded her of the Thomas Jefferson fraud a few years ago, but she just ignored him."

"What fraud?" I asked, puzzled at how our third president could be involved in a wine scandal.

"It was a big scandal. An auction house was selling off limited bordeaux with Thomas Jefferson's label, but the wines inside the bottle turned out to be something different. If something like that happened here in Napa, it could ruin the reputation of everyone who's legitimate."

"Fake wine labels? Wow."

"Yeah, most vintners today use high-tech fraud prevention—invisible markers, tamper-proof seals, ID chips in the corks, microprinted codes. That's how they try to prevent counterfeiters, since there are no 'wine police' to oversee everything. But all that stuff costs money. Lots of money."

No wonder Rob had hired Javier as his manager. This guy knew everything there was to know about wine. "Why would JoAnne do that?"

"To cash in on the boutique trend, I guess. I heard her wines haven't been selling well the past few years. Apparently she just recycled her stock with new labels."

"Javier, do you think Rob—" I stopped midsentence. Javier was looking over my shoulder. I turned and saw Allison standing behind me.

I got up from her seat. "Sorry. I just wanted to congratulate Javier on his win."

Javier also stood. "Excuse me," he said abruptly, and walked away, headed in the direction of the restrooms.

"So, anything new on the murder?" Allison said, taking her seat.

"No. Have you heard from Marie? Or Rob?" I asked.

"I turned my cell phone off during the games," she said. "Too distracting."

Wow. This woman was something else.

"Well, good luck." I started to walk away.

"I don't need it," she said. "I've always had good luck."

I didn't know what to say, so I nodded and made my way back to my seat, tired of trying to find something redeeming in Allison. So far all I could see was a cold, self-centered, wannabe diva.

I wondered if I'd be adding murderer to her list of traits.

Chapter 10

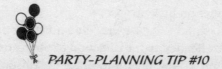

PARTY-PLANNING TIP #10

When serving wines at your wine-tasting party, begin with dry wines first; then serve red wines, and finally sweet wines. If the guests drink sweet wines first, like dessert, that may ruin their taste for the drier wines. Of course, by the end of the tasting, the guests may not care what they're drinking . . .

I returned to my seat to finish the last bingo games. So far, neither Mother nor I had won. Two elderly gentlemen won the next two games, and I noticed that Allison jumped up from her seat and hustled over to congratulate each of the men personally, with a hug and a kiss on the cheek. When a woman won the next game, however, Allison remained at her place.

"Crap," Helen said, after her latest loss. "Deanna Mitchell wins a game almost every week. She's probably cheating somehow."

Surprised at her language and outburst, I turned to

Helen, who up until this moment had been quietly daubing her sheets with yellow ink.

"You really think she might be cheating?" I asked her.

She shrugged, but her tight lips quivered as if eager to say more.

"Larry says it isn't easy to cheat at bingo these days," I said, prompting her.

She leaned over to me and whispered, "Larry is a fool."

That was harsh, I thought. Was this about something else? Maybe jealousy over Larry's interest in my mother? She might have been their same age, in spite of her heavily lined face, graying hair, and formless figure.

I decided to ignore her last comment, but she cursed again when a woman at the front of the hall called out, "Bingo!" after the next game.

"This is all JoAnne Douglas's fault," Helen mumbled, throwing down her dauber.

"What did you say?" I said, not sure I heard her correctly over the loud chatter.

"JoAnne Douglas. She's jinxed the game."

"What do you mean?" I wondered why this woman thought JoAnne could have anything to do with bingo.

Helen harrumphed. "Like I said, she tried to stop our games. She said gambling was contributing to the decay of the Napa Valley. Made a lot of people mad, me included. Then she goes and gets herself killed. Bad omen."

"How did you hear about JoAnne?"

She grunted. "It's all over town. There are no secrets for long around here. Word spreads faster than a vineyard fire." She crossed herself and kissed her fingertips.

Helen appeared to be full of superstition, but I wondered if she had more to say that could be important. I decided to poke the bear. "It seems like quite a few people had a grudge against JoAnne."

"More like who didn't—other than her shyster lawyer. Thinks he's a rock star with all those billboard and bus-bench pictures of his mug around town."

Billboards? "You don't mean Kyle Bennett?"

She nodded. "That bloodsucker made money off everyone, including her."

These were probably the words of an angry, aging woman blowing off steam because she was losing at bingo, I thought. So far she'd spoken in generalities. Did she have something specific to say? I tried a different approach in my questioning.

"So Kyle worked for JoAnne?" It sounded like Kyle, now representing Rob, might have had a conflict of interest.

"Tight as a cork in a bottle, those two," Helen said, pulling at the side of her hair. When one side seemed to hang down farther than the other side, I realized she was wearing a wig, and the gray hair at the temples was her real hair poking out from underneath. "He helped her with all her political crap, and she paid him well for it. Bought himself a fancy car and a fancy suit. Too bad the killer didn't get him too."

Whoa. I hoped there wasn't a gun in her bingo caddy.

"Any idea why JoAnne had it in for the Christophers?" This chatty woman was becoming a gold mine of information.

Helen daubed the free spaces on her next bingo sheet as she talked. "JoAnne never stopped yapping about the Christophers. And his neighbors—that movie guy and the ex-governor. She accused them all of using 'marginal land'—the hillsides, the streams." Helen used stiff finger quotes for the term. "She claimed they were 'ruining the wine country.' " More finger quotes.

The movie guy and the ex-governor? Apparently Nick Madeira's and Dennis Brien's vineyards were also targets of JoAnne's political agenda. And if that was the case, perhaps they should be considered suspects in her death.

"You're talking about the Madeiras and Briens?" I asked to confirm. I didn't want to go around putting random suspects on my list.

Helen set down her dauber and rubbed her hands. Arthritis, I suspected. Maybe this woman was older than I'd originally guessed. "Yep. JoAnne claimed those vineyards would endanger the trees, then the hillsides would erode, and then the streams would be polluted with their pesticides. Yak, yak, yak. I heard she sued all three of them because they weren't 'green enough' for her. Accused them of fouling the streams and reservoirs for their own 'personal gain.' " In spite of her arthritis, she loved using those finger quotes.

"Really?"

She shrugged. "Hell, everyone uses pesticides. There wouldn't be any wine if they didn't. A little pesticide ain't gonna kill you."

I smiled at her attitude toward health. "Did any of them try to stop JoAnne somehow?" *Besides murder,* I thought.

Helen snorted. "I heard they all 'donated' to her cause, which means they paid her off. That's when she supposedly dropped the lawsuits."

The announcer's voice came over the loudspeaker. "The last game of the day will be another Postage Stamp Bingo. Everyone ready?"

Helen focused her attention on her sheets, hovering over them as if they were already winners. I missed hearing the first ball, too busy thinking about what Helen had said. I tried to focus on the next couple, but my mind kept fleeing back to her words. The woman may have been getting on in years, but she was still as bright as her yellow dauber. I wondered if there was some other agenda behind her anger toward JoAnne, other than the fact that the dead woman had tried to interfere with Helen's bingo life.

"Cee-five," the caller said.

"Bingo!" Larry shouted while I was still trying to catch up with the last three numbers called.

Mother clapped and squealed with delight. Constance leaned over and said, "Congratulations," to Larry, while Helen mumbled something—no doubt the word "crap."

A man wearing a waist apron came over to Larry, took his winning bingo sheet, and handed it to a player at a different table. The player confirmed the winning numbers and returned it to the apron man, who pulled out an envelope. He counted out two hundred and fifty dollars and gave it to Larry with a "congratulations."

Larry gave the apron man a five-dollar tip, then turned to Mother and handed her a twenty. She grinned with delight.

I glanced over at Allison and Javier to see their reaction to the win. Javier was eating another candy bar. But Allison had disappeared.

"Do you ever worry about being robbed?" I asked Larry as he escorted us to the parking lot. His arm was around Mother's waist, guiding her along, a big, jovial grin on his face. This man was a happy winner.

He shook his head. "Not here. Karna, the security guard, watches the door and parking lot. She's good about making sure we're all safe in our cars until we drive off. After that, we're on our own."

I looked back at the building. Sure enough, Karna the guard stood watching as the crowd, mostly elderly, dispersed in the lot, entered their cars, and left the premises. I wondered if Larry had tipped her too. Apparently it was protocol to share a little of the wealth, and he'd been very generous.

"Larry," I said, after he helped Mother into my car. "That woman sitting next to me—Helen? Does—did—she have any kind of grudge against JoAnne Douglas? She seemed to imply that JoAnne sued some of the winery owners and then dropped the suit when they 'donated' to her political cause. Do you know anything about this?"

Larry's beaming smile drooped. "Don't listen to Helen. She's a cantankerous old lady who's still angry that JoAnne tried to bust up bingo. Helen takes her game very seriously, in case you didn't notice."

"I sensed that," I said. I opened my car door and got in, then turned to Mother.

She waved to Larry as he headed for his own car, an aging Volvo; then she looked at me blankly, as if she'd forgotten where we were.

I smiled at her and patted her leg. Glancing at the clock on the MINI's dashboard—four p.m.—I asked, "Thirsty?"

She reached over and patted my leg back. "I'm so dry I'm spitting cotton," she said, quoting Marilyn Monroe from *Bus Stop*.

I started the engine.

I found the Douglas Family Winery location using my iPhone GPS app. We pulled up in front of an aging but still charming Victorian house a mile or so from the Purple Grape. The sign that welcomed visitors read, "Open Saturday and Sunday, 10 a.m. to 6 p.m.," but a makeshift sign that had been propped on a sawhorse at the driveway entrance announced, "Closed."

"You know I don't drink, Presley," Mother said. "Not since my third husband died. And you shouldn't either. Besides, this winery is closed. See the sign?"

"I'm not surprised, considering they've had a death in the family." I opened my car door, stepped out, and walked around to my mother's side.

"Presley! Is this that poor woman's place?" she asked when I opened her door.

"It sure is. Shall we have a look around?"

Mother eyed me, then reluctantly stepped out of the car. "I don't like this . . ."

"It'll be okay. Come on. I just want to see if any of

her employees are around. Maybe I can find out more about JoAnne Douglas."

Mother followed me down the stone-paved path to the Victorian's double doors, her heels clicking on the hard surface. A sign overhead read, "Welcome to the Douglas Family Winery, Since 1923." I knocked, then tried one of the ornately carved doors. No response. I stood back, scanning the large, gingerbread-laced house, and spotted a small cottage off to the side that looked like a miniature version of the grand home.

I headed over with Mother in tow, wondering if there might be someone living there. Had JoAnne stayed in the cottage rather than the large house? I knocked on the door. Again, no answer.

"Hey!" I heard a voice call from the double-door entrance where we'd just been. We walked back over.

"Hi," I said, shading my eyes from the late afternoon sun. "Sorry to bother you. I'm Presley Parker and this is my mother—"

"We're closed," the twentysomething woman said, cutting me off. She stood in the doorway wearing a white shirt, black skirt, and low, sensible pumps. The black stitching on the shirt read "Douglas Family Winery." I guessed it to be a uniform. Underneath was a name tag that read "Natalie." "Didn't you see the sign?"

"Yes, but—"

She started to close the door.

"Wait!" I rushed forward and held the door. "I'm not here for wine tasting. I'd like to talk to . . . uh, JoAnne."

Natalie's eyes narrowed. "Who did you say you were?"

I gave her my name again and introduced my mother.

"How did you know Jo?"

I decided not to reveal my hand too soon. "I . . . met her the other night, at the culinary college. She told us to . . . stop by, and she'd show me around her winery."

Mother looked away, no doubt unable to face her lying, conniving daughter. I just hoped she didn't blurt out something and give me away.

"Well, I'm sorry, but Jo . . . she was killed last night. Her lawyer advised us to close the winery until he can review her will and figure out what we need to do."

"Oh my God. What happened?" I asked, trying to look taken aback. I'd learned that feigning ignorance garnered more information that bluntly asking for it. "Was it an accident?"

Natalie shook her head. Her long dark hair rippled and she tucked one side behind her ear. "The police said she was murdered."

"I'm so sorry," I said. "Are you the one who talked to the cops?"

"Yes, they were here. Asking questions. Snooping around. They took our neighbor in for questioning, but I haven't heard anything more." She paused. "You look familiar . . ."

"Presley," Mother interrupted, "I'm feeling a little light-headed . . ."

I glanced at her. She looked fine, especially with that twinkle in her eyes. Apparently she could be just as sneaky and conniving as her daughter.

I turned back to Natalie. "Do you think we could

come in for a glass of water? My mother's not feeling well."

Natalie paused for a moment, then opened the door wide enough to allow us in. I inhaled the intoxicating scent of wine mixed with oak barrels and nearly salivated. The wood-paneled tasting room was large enough to hold at least fifty people and featured a square bar in the middle with room for a dozen tasters along each side. Inside, fresh glasses hung upside-down from a wooden structure overheard, within arm's reach of the pourers.

Mother sat down on a stool at the bar, while Natalie ducked under the bar and pulled out a bottle of water from a small refrigerator in the center. She poured the water into a wineglass and passed it to Mom, looking at her with caring brown eyes.

"Thank you, miss," Mother said, taking the glass. She sipped the water.

"It's Natalie. Natalie Mattos." I guessed her to be about twenty-five or so, well spoken, intelligent, and attractive, with light makeup and full lips.

"You work here?" I asked, taking a seat beside my mother.

"For about a year," she said. "Right out of college. Got my degree in oenology but couldn't find a job as an associate wine maker, so I ended up serving wine. This is a competitive market and tough to get hired."

"Sounds like a fun job," I said, "pouring wine all day, meeting people . . ."

"It's not, believe me," she said, rolling her eyes. "Most of the tourists just want free wine. We're one of the few that doesn't charge for tastings. They don't buy much—at least not here—probably because we don't have cute wine labels with funny sayings on them. The college kids and bachelorette partiers just get drunk, become obnoxious, and throw up in the bushes on their way out."

I remembered those days fondly.

"What was JoAnne like to work for?"

"She was okay. A real stickler for everything being green. The cabernets she produces are certified organic, using only sustainable farming. She's got over a hundred solar panels on the roof, which reduces the greenhouse gases and air pollutants. She never used any synthetic fertilizers or pesticides, just compost and stuff like that. Everything has to be socially responsible and environmentally sound to preserve the ecosystem," she said. Lacking any facial expression as she spoke, she came off like a tour guide spewing a memorized speech.

She must have caught the tiny smile on my face. "We have to tell everyone that stuff. Jo makes us. Made us, I should say. We were even encouraged—I should say highly encouraged—to drive hybrid cars to work or we might find ourselves suddenly laid off."

Wow, JoAnne Douglas really was a fanatic. Remembering something I'd heard at the bingo hall, I asked Natalie, "Did she sell any specialty wines here? I heard she had some boutique wines available."

Natalie's dark eyebrows furrowed. "Not that I know of. Where did you hear that?"

"Oh, just a rumor," I said.

"Well, don't believe everything you hear," she said. "Some people have nothing better to do than to gossip about other people."

Mother pushed her glass toward Natalie and got off

her stool. "Thank you," she said to the young woman; then to me she announced, "I'm feeling better, Presley."

I stood. "Thank goodness, Mom. You had me worried."

Mother rolled her eyes at my acting skills.

"My pleasure," Natalie said. She took the glass, set it in a sink under the counter, and wiped the bar clean of moisture droplets. Ducking out from under the bar, she led us to the double doors. She opened them, letting bright afternoon sunlight into the dark, sensuous tasting room. The aroma of wine was overwhelmed by the scents of spring flowers that lined the walkway.

"Thanks again," I said to Natalie before we headed down the front steps. At the bottom, I turned back.

"Natalie, any idea who might have killed JoAnne?"

"No clue," she said. "It could have been anyone, I suppose. She had more enemies than friends, it seemed. I felt sorry for her. She just wanted to protect the environment, but to most people, she went about it the wrong way. And now I'm out of a job again—with a hybrid car to pay for."

Chapter 11

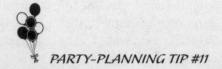

The question of spitting arises when you're hosting a wine-tasting party. Most Americans consider spitting rude, but it's quite acceptable, even necessary, at a tasting event, since spitting helps keep the tasters from becoming intoxicated. However, never spit across another person; spit a jet stream into a spittoon through pursed lips, and make sure there are no drips on the floor, the countertop, or your shirt.

I checked my watch. Too early for dinner—unless you were part of the bingo set, maybe. Not too early for a glass of wine. At least, not today. If I could have started drinking when the body was found this morning, I would have.

"You were great back there, Mom!" I said, giving her arm a squeeze as I drove us out of the Douglas Family Winery drive. "That little fainting spell—brilliant! Thanks to you, I found out a little more about JoAnne Douglas."

My mother actually blushed. "I learned it from watching *Murder, She Wrote*. One time Jessica Fletcher pretended to need a glass of water, and when the suspect left the room to get it, she snooped around and found some valuable evidence."

"Well, instead of getting her *out* of the room, you got us *into* the room. I'll have to try that trick myself sometime."

"Where are we going next?" Mother asked, suddenly full of energy.

I looked at her. "You're not too tired?"

"Not now. This is fun." She pulled down the passenger visor and checked her teeth and lipstick in the small mirror.

"Well, I was thinking we'd drop in on the Purple Grape's two neighbors and see how they're coping with the news. You up for that?"

"Bring it!" Mom said, closing the visor.

Bring it? Where had that come from? Was I creating a monster, dragging my mother around the valley looking for suspects in a murder? What the hell. She'd turned me into a party planner. I could turn her into an amateur sleuth.

The two neighbors' wineries flanked the Purple Grape. The Madeiras' Castello de Vino was on the left and the Briens' Governor's Mansion Winery was on the right. And they were as different from each other as Marie was from her sister, Allison. While the Christophers' home resembled an Italian villa, the Madeiras' place looked like a stone castle, something out of Transylvanian horror films, the kind that Nick Madeira was known for producing. As for the Briens' winery, it stood like a mini-replica of the state capitol building in Sacramento. No surprise there.

I pulled into the stone driveway that led to the medieval castle. My first thought, looking at the sprawling structure, was *Great place for a party!* Medieval theme, obviously, with knights and maidens, bowls of wassail and giant turkey legs, maybe some horses and a little jousting.

Good God. What was I thinking?

We headed for the winery entrance and stepped through arched doorways into the past. Stone walls in the tasting room were lined with costumes of kings and queens, armored knights and fair maidens, along with crossbows and chain mail, swords and shields, and family crests. The dim lighting from the high wrought-iron sconces transported me immediately to the Dark Ages. A long wooden bar—maybe twenty feet—ran from one side of the tasting room to the other, manned by pourers wearing anachronistic Castello de Vino T-shirts. About a dozen people in normal clothing had bellied up to the bar and were enjoying the latest pour. After drinking all that water, my mother excused herself to use the facilities. I squeezed in between a group of young women and an older couple and looked over the printed list of today's samples.

"Would you like to taste our newest sangiovese?" a cute guy in a T-shirt covered with a coat-of-arms-emblazoned vest asked. Blond short hair, lightly freckled face, muscular arms, about thirty, I guessed. His name tag read, "Joe Van Houten."

"Sure," I said.

"It's five dollars for three tastings," he said. "And you get to keep the commemorative glass."

I shelled out five bucks while Joe poured a couple of

ounces into a wineglass inscribed, "Wassail," which he explained was Middle English for "good health." I inhaled the bouquet like Rocco had taught me, then tasted the cool liquid, all the while glancing around for Nick or his wife—what was her name? Claudia? Claudette.

Joe Van Houten looked at me expectantly after I put the glass down.

"Good!" I said, forgetting all the vocabulary words Rocco had tried to implant in my brain. "Uh . . . fruity," I added.

Joe grinned politely. I was sure he saw right through me. I deflected with a question. "Is Nick or Claudette around?"

"You know the owners? I'd be glad to let them know you're here. What's your name?"

I leaned into the bar and turned on the charm. "That would be great. I'm Presley Parker," I said, reaching out a hand. Joe shook it, said, "Nice to meet you," then picked up a phone hidden under the bar. I spotted Mother returning from the restroom, a small bag in her hand.

"Did you buy something?" I asked her.

"They have a delightful little gift shop right near the restrooms!" Mother said. Leave it to her to find a gift shop everywhere she went, including Alcatraz, the de Young Museum, and the Winchester Mystery House. She opened the bag and pulled out a set of wine charms—tiny pewter images of grapes, leaves, a wine bottle, a goblet, a wheel of cheese, and a corkscrew— one for each of six guests to personalize their wineglasses.

"Adorable!" I said. "But you don't drink. And you can't have alcohol at your care facility, even for a party."

"I know," she said. "They're for you. I thought you might be able to use them at one of your future parties."

"Mother! How sweet. Thank you."

I heard someone clear his throat behind me and turned around.

"Nick! I mean, Mr. Madeira. Hi. Presley Parker from the other night. And this is my mother, Veronica."

"Nick is fine," he said, reaching out to shake our hands. Instead of the usual medieval costume, Nick wore slacks, a white button-down shirt, and a tie decorated with grapes. "Good to see you again, Ms. Parker. Any news from the police?"

"Call me Presley. No, nothing. I've tried phoning Marie but my calls go straight to voice mail. We were just on our way to the Purple Grape to check on her and thought we'd stop by, see if you'd heard anything first."

"Unfortunately, no," he said, glancing around at the crowd. There was a moment of silence; then Nick abruptly changed the subject. "Would you like a tour while you're here? My wife and I are thinking of hosting a Renaissance fair party in the summer. Maybe you'd be interested in planning it for us?"

"Sure," I said, thinking perhaps his request was in poor taste, considering the recent events. But I was here to find out any information I could.

Nick began the tour by pointing out the wall decorations. "We bought the winery from a man named Colonel Thomas Allen from Nashville. He modeled the building after a fourteenth-century Tuscan castle. I thought it was spectacular and asked the owner if I could use it for some background shots for one of my horror films. When I learned he was selling, I had to have it."

"It's open to the public?" Mother asked, admiring a portrait of the colonel.

"Yes. We give tours that include barrel tastings, a carriage ride through the vineyard, and a display of vintage winemaking equipment used by the colonel." He looked up at the colonel fondly.

"Fascinating," Mother said. "I can see why the place was hard to resist."

Nick smiled at her compliment. "The site used to be a stagecoach stop, back in the day. People came here from San Francisco to enjoy the hot springs and spend some time in the country. It wasn't long before some of the California emigrants noticed the resemblance to the wine regions of the Mediterranean area and began buying up land."

Nick led us past the gift shop and restrooms, into another spacious room with a full-sized knight-in-armor outfit standing in the corner. "There are over a hundred rooms in the castle, including an honest-to-goodness torture chamber with an antique iron maiden and rack."

Mother gasped. "Oh dear!"

"Don't worry," Nick said, smiling as if he'd heard this reaction many times. "These days we use it just for show. Although sometimes I'm tempted to bring my wife down here and test out some of the equipment." He laughed at his own joke.

Mother shot me a look that said, "Here's your killer,
Presley."

"There are seven levels," Nick continued, leading us
on to the next stone-walled room. "Four underground.
We've got five towers with battlements, a working
drawbridge that leads to the vineyard, and a moat that
runs around the castle. You'll also see frescoes on the
castle walls, and wrought-iron sconces that have been
treated with acid to make them look ancient. Keep your
eyes open and you'll even spot a few gargoyles guarding the place from the towers. And maybe even a ghost
or two."

I shuddered. "Where's the torture chamber?"

"Underground, along with tunnels and wine
chambers—it's a real maze down there, and if you
don't know your way around, you may never be seen
again." He laughed again at his joke. Or was it a joke?
I wondered.

The castle reminded me of the Winchester Mystery
House, where I'd recently held a séance party and
brought the dead Mrs. Winchester back to life. This
place would indeed be a perfect party setting.

"It must cost a fortune to keep this place going,"
Mother said.

"True, but we're lucky to get about a hundred thousand paying visitors a year, so that helps pay the bills.
And we've won a few gold medals for our sangiovese
wines, which are selling well."

"Can we see the torture chamber?" I persisted
ghoulishly, my eyes wide with anticipation.

"Sorry. It's being renovated," Nick said. "We bought
a few more devices at an auction in Europe last year

and they're being installed. But how would you like to taste my newly bottled reserve? It's not available to the public yet."

I nodded, maybe a little too enthusiastically, and we followed Nick back to a private tasting room with a small dark wood bar and stools for eight of his no-doubt closest friends. At the back wall hung an oil portrait of Nick in medieval knight costume, next to a portrait of his wife, Claudette, dressed as a Renaissance lady.

Speak of the devil. Just as Nick finished pouring me a glass of his personal stash, Claudette stuck her head in the door.

"I thought I'd find you here," she said. Recognizing me, she stepped in, wearing white tennis shorts and matching top, and reached out her hand. "Hello, Ms. Parker. What are you doing here?"

"Hello, Claudette. You remember my mother, Veronica?" I said, introducing my mother. "We just stopped by to see if you'd heard anything from Rob or Marie."

She shook her highlighted blond hair. Her diamond drop earrings swayed. "Nothing. We're just devastated for them both."

Funny. Neither one of them looked devastated. Nick was back to business, showing off his castle, and Claudette had apparently been dealing with her devastation by playing tennis.

"I haven't heard from them either. Not since Rob was headed for the police station for questioning. Marie isn't answering her phone."

"Oh dear," Claudette said, checking her diamond

watch absently. "Well, I suppose Kyle is doing what he can to help Rob."

"If you want my opinion, he'd be better off without that jerk," Nick mumbled, then chugged his glass of wine in one swallow.

Surprised at his sudden vehemence, I asked, "You don't think Kyle is a good attorney?"

"Well, *he* thinks he is. And apparently he's doing well," Nick said, "at least, judging by all the money he's been flashing around. I just wonder if he has Rob's best interest at heart."

"Why do you say that?" I asked.

Nick poured himself another glass and took a sip. "He worked for JoAnne for a while, helping her with her lawsuits, threatening to sue the wineries that didn't meet her standards—including ours."

"That does seem like a conflict of interest," I said.

"It would have been, except Kyle suddenly quit working for her and started offering his services to the smaller wineries, saying he'd represent them against the lawsuits. He lost most of the cases, but somehow he still seemed to profit from his so-called efforts."

That was odd. Kyle had worked for JoAnne, then suddenly stopped and began working for the people she'd been suing? Was there more money in defending clients than prosecuting them? Or was there another reason he had jumped the fence?

"The guy's an ambulance chaser," Claudette said. "He follows the money. JoAnne's business had declined over the years and I don't think she could afford to pay him as much as she had in the past. There've been rumors she was selling her wines under new labels to increase her sales, but no one could prove anything."

I'd heard the same rumor at the bingo hall. Does hearing a rumor twice make it a fact? Not necessarily, but it sure makes it a clue.

"Thanks for the wine, Nick," I said, reluctantly finishing off the last sip.

"How did you like it?" he asked.

I'd dreaded the question. "Yummy!" I wanted to say. Instead, I confessed, "I don't know a lot about wine—like all those terms you wine connoisseurs use. I wish I were savvier. My caterer tried to teach me but I flunked Wine 101."

"It's easy, really. Here, I'll teach you some basics—at least enough to fake it. How's that?"

"He's very good at faking it," Claudette said under her breath. Nick didn't seem to hear; nor did Mother. Had she really said that? I wondered.

Nick poured me another half glass of wine. "First, look at it. Is it clear? A nice color?"

I stared at the glass of wine as if it might tell me my future. "Yeah, no floaties," I said. "It's kind of a reddish, purplish brown color." I wanted to say it was the color of dried blood, but that didn't seem appropriate.

"Good. Now smell it. Intense or delicate?"

I inhaled the aroma. "Intense?" I asked rather than said, not sure.

"Excellent. Now the most important part. Take a sip and tell me about the taste."

Remembering Rocco's instructions, I took a small sip, held it on my tongue for a few seconds, and swallowed. "Tastes good. Very smooth."

"Perfect. When you're hosting your next wine-tasting event, here's another secret. Contrary to popular belief, red wines should be chilled and white wines should be served at room temperature."

"I thought it was the opposite," Mother said.

"So do most people," Claudette said. "But Nick loves to prove them wrong—and argue the point. In a minute he'll tell you his wine cures heart disease, reduces lung cancer, lowers cholesterol, and probably prevents leprosy."

Nick shot her a look. "I never said it cured anything, Claudette. And very funny about the leprosy. But there are health benefits. That's been proven."

"What about spitting?" Mother asked out of the blue. I couldn't imagine my mother spitting!

"Believe it or not, spitting is considered proper, as long as you spit into the provided bucket and not on someone next to you." Nick laughed.

I checked my watch. I hoped Brad would be back soon. And I was eager to look in on Marie and find out what was up with Rob. I set my unfinished wineglass down.

"Speaking of Rob, do either of you have any idea who might have killed JoAnne?" I asked.

"No idea," Nick said, swirling his glass of wine. "An ugly way to die," he added.

"I don't know who killed her, but I can't pretend I'll miss her," Claudette said. "Nick and I suspected she'd done something to our crop after we didn't sign her petition, but we can't prove it."

"What do you mean 'did something'?" I asked her.

"Nothing," Nick answered for her after shooting his

wife a daggered look. "Claudette gets these wild ideas. She wanted to have our vines analyzed to see if they'd been tampered with."

"He wouldn't let me do it," Claudette said, pouting. "But we weren't the only ones who didn't get along with her. And it's obvious that someone was trying to send a message."

"You mean like 'hoist on her own petard' kind of thing?" Nick asked, eyeing her.

Claudette shrugged. "I don't know. If I knew what the message was, I might know who killed her. But using a corkscrew to make a point? I'm just saying."

Claudette could be right, I thought, but what was the message—besides "screw you"?

Chapter 12

❧ *PARTY-PLANNING TIP #12*

Swishing the wine around in your mouth before you swallow is another option for your wine-tasting guests. While it seems uncouth, swishing the liquid around your tongue and palate allows your taste buds to detect the subtle flavors of the wine. But try not to make too much noise . . .

The ex-governor's "house," on the other side of the Purple Grape, was a carbon copy of the Sacramento capitol building, except on a smaller scale. The paved circular driveway surrounded a lavish fountain featuring stone carvings of twisted vines and plump grapes. The home itself was framed by towering palm trees, fronted by Roman columns, and topped by a classic dome—just like the capitol. Beyond the mansion I saw acres of precisely planted vineyards, as far as the eye could see. I wondered how many bottles of wine the acreage could produce. That thought made me thirsty again.

I squeezed my MINI into an end spot in the crowded

lot. Apparently the Governor's Mansion Winery was also open for tastings today, in spite of the murder next door. Maybe that had been the draw. I helped Mother out of the car and we climbed the steps of the arched entrance.

"Hmmm," Mother said, staring up at the stunning concrete structure. "A blend of Greek Revival and Roman-Corinthian. See the pilasters, Presley? The columns, the colonnade windows, the cupolas? Simple, classic, and elegant."

I had no idea what pilasters, colonnade windows, and cupolas were but decided not to ask. I wasn't here for a lesson on Greek-Corinthian architecture—or whatever. I led Mother inside, where wine sippers talked and mingled and sipped their wine. We were greeted by a young man and young woman, both wearing black slacks, black loafers, and black shirts emblazoned with the California bear flag and bearing the words "Governor's Mansion Winery." The girl handed us a printed price sheet with today's selections— apparently there's not a lot of free wine in Napa anymore—then indicated the two serving bars on either side of the room.

I took in the presidential room, along with the hearty aroma of wine. Along the marble walls behind the bars hung huge paintings of former governors, including Edmund G. Brown and his son, Jerry, Arnold Schwarzenegger, Ronald Reagan, and, of course, Dennis Brien. At the back wall, a large mural interpreted the wine country's history, with scenes of growers, pickers, stompers, all the way to wine tasters, painted in a Diego Rivera style. A sign over the mural read, "The West

Wing." Did Dennis have aspirations at one time to become president of the United States? Or had he just
declared himself president of his own land?

The ex-governor himself was holding court behind
the bar on the left, while his young, attractive wife, KJ,
hosted the one on the right. Apparently the Briens be-
lieved in mixing with the commoners, I thought, as
Mother and I wormed our way in between a couple of
tasters at Dennis's bar. Unlike his staff, Dennis wore a
white shirt and gray pants. I listened as he gave his
sales pitch to a foursome of tasters.

"Two out of every three bottles sold in the U.S. are
from California," Dennis told a mustached man who
was sniffing his small glass of red wine. "Here in the
Napa Valley, we offer everything from world-famous
mass-market wines to small family-owned boutique
vineyards. It's the temperature here—warm days, cool
nights—that allows the grapes to ripen slowly, matur-
ing the tannins and balancing the acids. Our award-
winning cabernets are handcrafted, organic, and
available at a discount through our wine club."
Sounding like an infomercial, he finally finished his
canned spiel and poured more wine into the empty
glasses.

"Any trouble with wine pests?" I asked, before he
said anything more about tannins and acids and other
terms that made no sense to me.

Dennis's salesman smile drooped when he recognized me.

"Ms. Parker. So nice to see you again." As if by
magic, the smile instantly reappeared.

"Beautiful winery, Dennis," I said. "Please, call me Presley."

Still smiling, he dropped his voice to nearly a whisper as he leaned in and spoke to me. "What are you doing here?"

"Just thought I'd drop by and see the place while Rob's at the police station." The dig was deliberate.

Dennis shot a look around the customers—plastic smile still frozen on his face—and held up a hand as if to quiet me.

"Are you usually this busy?" I asked.

"Not this late on a Sunday, no. But business is business, you know."

"Have you heard from Rob?" I asked. Mother patted my shoulder, then wandered away to look at the wine accessories displayed on tables throughout the tasting room.

"No. Have you?" Dennis picked up a clean wineglass and set it in front of me.

"Not yet. I was on my way to the Christophers' and figured I'd stop by here first."

Dennis pulled a cork out of an opened bottle and poured a third of a glass of red liquid. "Poor guy. Hope he's okay." I didn't see an iota of feeling behind those words.

"I don't suppose you have any idea who might have killed JoAnne?" I asked, holding the stem of the wineglass between two fingers while trying to sound as if I were discussing the clarity of the drink and not a dead body.

Dennis glanced around again, obviously worried about being overheard. He ducked under the bar.

"Josh, take over for me, will you?" he said to a twenty-something guy. "Presley, why don't you come to my office. We can talk there."

I glanced over at KJ, who had stopped in the middle of a pour and was eyeing us. Before I left the tasting room, I swung by Mother, who was at a nearby gift table, and told her I'd be right back and not to leave the premises.

Dennis led me down the hall to a large room that looked like the Oval Office in the White House. A wooden desk was flanked by two flags—one representing the United States, the other the state of California. It sat at the far side of an oval rug, a replica of the original, in red, white, and blue. On the side walls were old wartime political posters that read, "We Can Do It!" and "Uncle Sam Wants You!" I'd always loved the one of the woman in a red polka-dotted headscarf and blue jumpsuit with her biceps curled. Nancy Drew in overalls.

While Dennis commanded the chair behind his desk, I sat down in an Eames chair opposite him. "This is better," he said. "A little more private. I don't like discussing personal things in front of the tasters. Not good for business."

It was all about business for Dennis Brien, I thought. "Sorry about that. I'm just trying to find out who killed JoAnne, since it happened at my party. That's not good for business either. Any ideas?"

"Funny you should ask about wine pests. JoAnne was certain that I had wine pests in my vineyard. Frankly, I considered her more dangerous than that phylloxera louse that wiped out hundreds of acres of grapes years ago."

Dennis opened a side drawer of his massive desk and pulled out a bottle of unlabeled dark red wine. From a side table he extracted two sparkling glasses and set them in front of him. Apparently his office doubled as his own private tasting room. Using a corkscrew, he opened the bottle, poured half a glass of the red wine in each glass, then pushed one over to me.

"Try this. It's the one we're most excited about. A blend of cabernet and merlot. I call it the Governor's Caberlot."

I held up the glass by the stem, trying to remember everything—anything—that Rocco had taught me. First I smelled it—I mean, I inhaled the bouquet. Then I swirled the liquid and examined the clarity. Finally I took a sip, swished it a moment in my mouth, and counted five seconds before swallowing. But after all I'd learned about wine tasting, I simply said, "Yum!" and took in a second, larger mouthful. By my own standards, I would have called it "very drinkable."

Dennis smiled as if I were a child tasting candy for the first time. "Glad you like it. It's going to sell for a hundred and eighty dollars a bottle."

I nearly choked. I'd just downed thirty bucks' worth! What the hell. I took another large swallow, then pushed the glass over, indicating I wanted a refill. Dennis poured another half glass, obliging quickly, and I wondered if he was trying to get me drunk so I'd stop being a wine pest.

Speaking of which, I said, "Back to JoAnne. Any idea who killed her?"

"Heavens, no. KJ and I hardly knew the woman. After all, we're pretty green here at the Governor's

Mansion Winery, in terms of protecting the environment."

"But she thought you had wine pests?" I asked, remembering what he'd said.

"Like I said, she was the pest. Always checking to see if everything was up to her standards. There's a creek on our property that empties into the Napa River. That woman was down there every week checking the water."

"Did she ever find anything?"

"No, of course not. But that didn't stop her from snooping. She said if she found anything, anything at all, she'd sue me and have the winery shut down. She even threatened to have the state auditor come in. But she never caught us . . . I mean, you know . . . there was never anything for her to catch."

His face looked flushed. From the wine? Or the slip of the tongue?

"What I meant to say was, we've all become greener here in the valley. I, personally, use solar panels, biodiesel-fueled tractors, and organic farming. We're working toward going carbon-neutral in the next few years or so. There was really nothing for her to be worried about."

I heard a knock at the door.

"Come in!" Dennis commanded, ever acting the part of governor.

A young woman dressed like the other staff members, in black with the Cal bear shirt, stepped in. Attractive, blond, also in her twenties, she frowned at Dennis with concern.

"What is it, Julie?" Dennis asked, sounding irritated

at the intrusion. His face grew redder—from the wine or the winsome girl's appearance? I'd noticed most of the young women who worked here were blond and attractive. And politicians weren't exactly known for their monogamous behavior.

Julie stepped in and handed a folded piece of paper to Dennis. He took the note, opened it, read it quickly, and then frowned. The blush on his face drained completely, leaving his complexion a pasty white. This man's face was like an open book.

"Thank you, Julie," he said evenly, dismissing her. She backed out and closed the door. Dennis reread the note, pulled open his top desk drawer, put the note inside, and closed the drawer.

"Everything all right?" I asked, probing. Obviously it wasn't.

"Yes, fine. Well, if there isn't anything else, I need to make some phone calls—"

He laid his hands on the desk, preparing to dismiss me, but after seeing his reaction to that note, I wasn't ready to go.

"You've been very helpful, Dennis." I reached over as if to shake his hand and deliberately knocked over his glass of wine with the back of my hand. The "Caberlot" mash-up splattered the front of his white shirt.

He looked as if he'd been shot in the chest.

"Oh my God!" I said, rising. "I'm *so* sorry! I've ruined your shirt!"

He stood up, pulling the front of his shirt out as if to air it. "No problem. I've got others."

Before he could escort me out of the office, I picked up my purse and spilled the contents onto the floor.

"Oh goodness!" I said. "What a klutz I am today. Please, go ahead and change your shirt. I'll just pick up my stuff and get out of your hair."

He hesitated, then said, "You know your way out?" He looked torn between leaving me alone in the office and getting changed into a fresh shirt. I knelt down to retrieve my stuff and waved him on. With a last look, he exited through a door on the other side of the room.

I waited half a second, then tiptoed around the desk and opened the top drawer. If I got caught snooping, I could always say I was under the influence and was looking for a refill . . .

I pulled out the note, opened it, and read the contents:

"Call Allison. Urgent!"

Urgent? Allison? What was up with that?

I put the note back, closed the drawer, dashed back to my purse where it lay on the floor, and finished gathering my stuff.

"You still here?" Dennis said from behind me, startling me. He was tucking in a fresh white shirt.

"That was quick!" I said, cramming the last of my personal things into my purse.

"I have a private bathroom right next door. I keep emergency supplies there. You wouldn't believe how many times I get wine on my shirts."

I stood up, purse intact. "Again, sorry about that." My cell phone ringtone sounded from within my purse. "Excuse me," I said, reaching for it. "It may be something about Rob."

Dennis nodded solemnly as he moved around the

desk and poured himself more wine. He downed it so quickly, I wondered if he even tasted it that time.

"Hello?"

"Presley, this is Rocco."

"Rocco! Are you still in town?"

"Yeah, I stayed with my sister last night. I wanted to hang around and see about Rob and check on Marie."

"Have you heard anything more? I've been trying to call Marie but she isn't picking up. I don't have Allison's phone number, or Javier's. I'd like to know what's going on."

"That's why I'm calling," Rocco said. I felt a heat wave envelope my body that wasn't caused by the wine I'd drunk.

"Uh-oh. What's happened?"

I could feel Dennis's eyes on me as I listened.

"Rob's been officially charged with the murder of JoAnne Douglas."

"Oh my God. On what evidence?"

"They found his fingerprints on the corkscrew. And they discovered JoAnne's missing shoe. It was under his bed. With his fingerprints on it."

"You're kidding! Rocco, do you think he did it?"

"Gina said Rob wouldn't hurt a wine moth."

"Then how does she explain the fingerprints?"

Out of the corner of my eye, I saw Dennis lean forward. He was obviously trying to hear Rocco's end of the conversation. I turned away.

"That's what I was hoping *you* might do," Rocco said. "Help explain all this. You're good at that. And Gina swears he didn't do it."

Unfortunately, I didn't know Rob well, not like

Gina knew him. I had to take her word for his innocence. Rob certainly would have gained by JoAnne's death. No more threats of lawsuits. No more harassment. No more embarrassing appearances. Not to mention no more mousse-in-the-face antics. But was it enough to provoke murder?

To someone, it might have been.

But if not Rob, then who?

"Okay, Rocco. I'm at the Briens' winery, just down the hill from the Purple Grape. I'll be there in a few minutes and we can figure out what to do."

"Actually, I'm not at the Purple Grape. I'm at the hospital."

"Hospital? Why? Are you sick? Did something happen?"

"No, no, I'm fine. It's Marie."

Marie! "Nervous collapse? From all the stress?"

Rocco was silent for a moment, sending another wave of heat through me.

"No, Presley. Marie took an overdose of pills. They think she tried to kill herself."

Was that why Allison had made that urgent call to Dennis?

Chapter 13

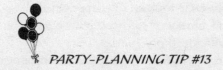

PARTY-PLANNING TIP #13

Decanting the wines for your party is an important part of the tasting experience. Open young wines several hours before the event so they can "breathe," and pour quickly to expose the wine to air. For older wines, open just before serving and pour slowly, so deposits at the bottom won't cloud the color. If it's box wine, you don't have to worry about decanting . . .

I stared at my phone after Rocco hung up, stunned at the news he'd just relayed.

Rob had actually been arrested for the murder of JoAnne Douglas.

And his wife, Marie, was in the hospital after trying to commit suicide.

All this happening while I'd been out playing bingo and tasting wine. Guilt swept over me like a spray of pesticides, and I felt woozy from the shocking news— or was it from all the wine I'd been "tasting"?

"What's wrong?" Dennis said. He reached over and held my arm. "You look as if you're about to faint."

"I'm fine . . . ," I said, waving away his hand. "It's Rob . . . he's been officially arrested."

"Whoa," Dennis said. "The police have enough evidence to charge him?"

I nodded, still numb. "And Marie . . . she's in the hospital."

"What?" he said. "How . . . what happened?"

I met his eyes; his were filled with concern.

"Rocco said she took an overdose of pills."

"God, no." He shook his head in disbelief. "She tried to commit suicide? Poor Marie."

"I have to go," I said, shaking off the numbness, and headed for the open office door.

"Does Allison know?" came Dennis's voice behind me.

Allison? I suddenly remembered the note I'd read that was tucked in his desk drawer. The one that said, "Call Allison. Urgent!" I turned back to Dennis and said, "I don't know. Why don't you ask her?" I left him standing openmouthed in his office and went in search of my mother.

I panicked when I didn't see her perusing the knick-knacks for sale around the tasting room, but thanks to an alert staff member who'd spotted her leaving, I found her outside, looking down into a nearby pond and breaking off bits of a gourmet cracker for the few ducks that floated about.

"Mallards. Aren't they beautiful?" she said when she saw me. "You usually see them in pairs. The male is the prettier one, with the bright green feathers. The female is that plain brown one. They pair up in the fall and stay together until spring, when the female lays her eggs. Then the male takes off and fools around with other females who are unattached. Typical."

Mother could tell you anything you wanted to know about animals, but she couldn't remember the names of my three cats. Such was the insidious disease of Alzheimer's.

"Mother, we have to go. Something has happened and we need to get back to the Purple Grape."

"What is it, Presley?"

She quickly crumbled the rest of her cracker into the pond and brushed off her hands. I filled her in as we walked back to the car, hoping the news wouldn't upset her too much. But to my surprise, she took it matter-of-factly. "Well, we've got to hurry, then, so we can help Marie when she comes home from the hospital."

Ten minutes later we pulled up to the Purple Grape. To my relief, Brad's Crime Scene Cleaners SUV was already there. *Thank God*, I thought as I helped Mother out of the car. We hurried up the path through the garden area and around the crime scene tape to the front door and entered without knocking. I heard voices and followed the sound to the kitchen, where I found Brad talking with Rocco.

Rocco looked disheveled in his jeans and white CCC collared T-shirt. The wisps of hair on either side of his balding head were mussed and part of his shirt was untucked. He held a cup of coffee in both hands.

"Did you tell him?" I asked Rocco, then looked at Brad in his Crime Scene Cleaners jumpsuit, his rubber gloves sticking out of one of the pockets, to see if there was any sign he'd heard the news. I knew by his frown and pressed lips that Rocco had indeed filled him in.

"You all right?" Brad asked me as he came to my side. He glanced at my mother.

"I'm fine. So glad you're here." I would have kissed him, but it just wasn't the time. I turned to Rocco. "Have you heard from Rob? Or Kyle?"

He shook his head. "Not yet."

"What happened?" Mother asked, looking bewildered. Had she forgotten what I'd told her, or was she just asking for details?

Rocco took a deep breath, set down his coffee, and began. "I came back to get one of the platters I left behind. Gina noticed it was missing. When I got here, I thought I heard Marie cry out from down the hall, so I went looking for her. I found her in her bedroom, white as a ghost, still holding her cell phone as she sat on the bed. I asked her what was wrong and she told me Kyle had just called and that Rob was being held for the murder of JoAnne Douglas. I couldn't believe it."

"Poor thing," Mother said, shaking her head and biting her lip.

"How did Marie end up in the hospital?" I asked Rocco, puzzled at how she got from her bedroom to the emergency room.

"After she hung up, she said she wanted to lie down," Rocco said. "I offered her a ride to the police station, but she said Kyle had told her it would be pointless and to wait because she wouldn't get to see him for hours. He promised to call when he could arrange a visit. So she asked for a glass of water and I brought it to her. I watched her take a couple of what I assumed were Valium or sleeping pills that were on the nightstand. Then she lay down on the bed and told me to close the door on my way out. It . . . it never occurred to me that she might . . . take the whole bottle." Rocco grimaced at the thought.

"How did you find her?" I asked.

"By chance," Rocco said. "When I got back to Gina's place, she told me I'd picked up the wrong platter and had brought one of Marie's instead. The ones from the Culinary College are Fiestaware, like Marie's, but they use the burgundy, not the plum. Marie's are plum. So I came back to switch them and thought I'd check on Marie while I was here. I peeked in, and that's when I noticed the overturned bottle. When I picked it up, all the pills inside were gone. I tried to rouse Marie, but she was unresponsive, so I called 911." His hands trembled as he recalled the experience of finding Marie.

Brad brought me a cup of coffee, and one for my mother. He offered Rocco a refill, but Rocco shook his head, then went to the refrigerator and pulled out a bottle of white wine. "I need something more medicinal," he said, pouring the wine into a stemmed glass. Eschewing his usual wine-tasting standards, he essentially gulped it down, then closed his eyes and visibly melted into the effects of the alcohol.

"I needed that," he said, smacking his lips.

"Presley," Mother said. "I'm going to go lie down for a few minutes. I have a bingo game tonight. Will you all excuse me?"

She took her coffee with her and ambled down the hall to her room. After she was gone, Brad took me by the hand. "Come here. I want to show you something I found." We left Rocco sitting on a bar stool, enjoying his "medicine," and went outdoors to the table where

we'd discovered the body of JoAnne Douglas only that
morning.

"What is it?" I asked.

"Normally the police do a thorough job before they
leave the scene of a crime," Brad said. "But I asked to
handle the cleanup since I was already here."

I glanced at the site just beyond the crime scene tape.
"I remember. So what did you find?"

Brad ducked under the tape and pointed to a bed of
bright red geraniums just beyond where the body had
lain. I followed him and knelt down and lifted some of
the ruffled leaves and petals.

"There's nothing here." I stood up.

Brad knelt down and pointed to a metal rod poking
out of the ground.

"A sprinkler head?" I asked. "So?"

"Check again."

I looked closely at the silvery object. While it appeared to be similar in size, color, and material to the
many sprinkler heads that protruded out of the ground,
this one was definitely different. It was shorter and
smoother and there were no openings at the top.

I reached for it.

"Don't touch it!" he said.

"Why not? What is it?"

He leaned over to access one of his pockets and
pulled out a metal object. He held it up for me to see.

"That's one of the Christophers' cheese knives," I
said, recognizing it instantly. I'd seen several on the
serving tables, lying next to the cheeses. A light went
on. I looked down at the metal object poking up from
the dirt. "You mean . . . that's a cheese knife?"

"Yep. Camouflaged by those flowers, it looks like another sprinkler head. Easily missed. I happened to notice it while cleaning up the area."

"You think it's important?" I said, rising to standing.

"Could be. One of Detective Kelly's men is on his way to pick it up."

I thought for a moment, trying to visualize what might have happened. "Are you thinking that someone stabbed JoAnne with the cheese knife first, and then inserted the corkscrew?"

"Possibly. We should know more when the ME's report comes back."

"But why?"

"Good question."

"Can they get fingerprints from it?" I asked, my mind spinning at this new turn of events.

"They should be able to get at least a partial print, maybe more."

"And what if it has Rob's print on it? Won't that just make things worse for him?"

"But what if it doesn't?" Brad suggested. "What if it has someone else's print?"

I looked at the knife stuck in the ground. "Then Rob is off the hook."

"Bingo!" he said.

I shook my head at his play on words. At the moment, I'd had just about all the bingo I could take.

While Brad showed the newly arrived officer where the cheese knife was, I went in and checked on Mother. I found her lying on her bed watching *Cupcake Wars* on the TV provided in her room. Brad had suggested we head to the Napa Police Station to see what we could find out about Rob's arrest. I told her our plans and that if she was hungry, there were plenty of leftovers in the Christopher refrigerator.

"Will you bring me back a cupcake?" she said, not taking her eyes off the screen.

"I'll try," I said, knowing she would forget her request by the time I returned. Still, if I ran into a cupcake along the way, I'd get one for her. And two for me.

Brad drove us downtown in his SUV and pulled into the tree-lined parking lot of 1539 First Street. We got out and headed for the gray concrete building that the police shared with the fire department, located next door to city hall. When we arrived, past five, the office had reduced staff, but Brad had called ahead and he held his ID up to the window for the officer to check. I recognized Detective Ken Kelly immediately.

Once we were let inside, Brad and Ken shook hands, and Detective Kelly led us back to his office behind a set of locked doors. He took a seat behind a cluttered desk and gestured for us to sit opposite him in a couple of metal chairs. I glanced around, curious about the kinds of crimes the detective might be working on, but there were no whiteboards filled with suspect names or "Wanted" posters of dangerous felons visible. Just walls of smoked windows that looked onto the parking lot, a serene view without a hint of criminal activity.

"I'm talking to you as a courtesy," Detective Kelly said to Brad, ignoring me, "because you work with SFPD. But I can't tell you much, other than what you already know. Rob's being held on murder one. He'll be arraigned on Tuesday. Until then, I can't discuss the case."

"I understand," Brad said. "Thanks for seeing us. You say you found fingerprints on the vic's shoe—and the shoe was hidden under Rob and Marie's bed, right?"

The detective nodded, tight-lipped.

"Don't you think that's kind of strange? If Rob killed JoAnne, why would he take her shoe off and then hide it in his own room, under their own bed? Likewise with the corkscrew. Sounds like a setup to me."

"We've considered that," the detective acknowledged. "But after working this job for over twenty years, I've found most criminals don't belong to Mensa. They do stupid things, especially when they commit crimes that are spur-of-the-moment, like this one appears to be."

"You're right about stupid criminals," Brad said, "but Rob seems pretty intelligent. I heard he graduated from UC Davis. So why would he be so careless about something so potentially harmful to himself?"

"Like I said, in states of panic or stress, criminals don't always plan things logically."

"But how could he have planned it? He didn't know she would be at the party. If he killed her, why not just stab her with a cheese knife and leave it at that? Why use the incriminating corkscrew?"

The detective looked down at his desk. He wasn't telling us something.

"What?" I spoke up after listening to all of this. "Is there something else?"

Detective Kelly pressed his lips together, then said, "The ME said she was hit over the head with something blunt and heavy before she was stabbed. I'm guessing it was a wine bottle. My guys are searching the trash bins at the Purple Grape."

"A wine bottle?" I asked.

"I figure Rob killed her sometime during the party," the detective continued, "first by bludgeoning her, then stabbing her with that knife you found, and finally with the corkscrew—to send a message. Her shoe must have fallen off at some point, so after she was dead, Rob grabbed it and hid it, thinking no one would suspect him of being a murderer. Unfortunately, his prints were all over the corkscrew and the shoe. And I'm betting they're all over the cheese knife you found, as well."

He placed his hands on his desk as if he were about to rise. "By the way, I'm only telling you this because you work with Luke Melvin," he said to Brad.

Up until this point, I'd pretty much been ignored. Now that we were about to be excused, I said, "Can we see Rob?"

"I'm afraid not. He's over at the Napa Country Department of Corrections. Right now he can only see his lawyer."

I knew we weren't going to get anything more from this tight-lipped, by-the-book detective. Not even Brad would have much influence on him, since he hadn't worked with the Napa Police Department. I wondered if his friend Detective Luke Melvin of SFPD could find out more.

"Okay, well, thanks," Brad said, standing. He leaned over and shook the detective's hand. I kept my hands to myself.

I had a sinking feeling about the cheese knife. If the

cops found Rob's fingerprints on it, that would only increase his chances of being convicted of this crime. But Brad, having once been a cop himself, would never consider withholding evidence from the police. Then again, what if Rob had actually committed the crime, in spite of what anyone else thought?

The phone rang just as we reached the office door.

"Kelly," the detective said into the phone.

I turned back to listen to the detective's end of the conversation, wondering if it might be something about Rob.

"Yeah . . . ," he said. "You sure? . . . Good work."

He hung up and stared at the phone for a few agonizing seconds, then looked up at us.

"That was the tech. They got a print from the knife."

I blinked. "Well?" I asked, holding my breath.

"It's a match," the detective said. "We've definitely got our killer."

Chapter 14

PARTY-PLANNING TIP #14

Spitting, swishing . . . now swirling! Teach your guests the value of swirling the wine in the glass to see whether it has "legs"—how long it takes the wine to trickle down the inside of the glass after it's been swirled. This also introduces more oxygen into the wine, alters the tastes, and balances out the flavor. Plus it's fun!

Brad held the door of his SUV open for me, but before I hoisted myself in, I turned to him and asked, "Can we go to the hospital and check on Marie?"

He nodded, helped me into the car, and closed the door. There were several things I could count on from Brad, and one of them was the way he listened to me. Sure, he gave me a hard time sometimes, especially when he didn't agree with my requests, but he always supported me when I needed him to.

He pulled out his cell phone and got directions to Queen of the Valley hospital—the "Queen," as Detective Kelly had called it—in downtown Napa. It took only a few minutes to reach the white, flat-topped, fifties-looking structure and find the emergency room entrance. Brad followed me inside and we stepped up to the clerk manning the reception desk just off the waiting room. I asked if we could visit a patient, Marie Christopher, half expecting the woman to say "Relatives only" or "She's still in intensive care," but to my surprise she gave us the room number and directions.

As we made our way down the hall, I couldn't help but peek into the open doors of the patient rooms. It was like being at a car wreck—curious to look but afraid of what I might see. When we reached Room 112, I peered in, then entered quietly in case Marie was sleeping or the doctor was there. I found her in bed, sitting up, her head turned toward the slatted windows that looked onto a lighted courtyard.

She turned when she heard me approach her bed. I was stunned at the paleness of her skin, her unkempt hair, her lack of makeup.

"Presley," she said, her voice sounding hoarse. Her mouth looked dry and red.

I glanced back for Brad, thinking he was right behind me, but he'd hesitated at the door.

I'll wait, he mouthed and pointed down the hall toward the waiting room. I nodded and returned my attention to Marie.

"Hi, Marie," I said. I moved in closer until I was standing right next to her bed. "How are you feeling?"

She shrugged. The shoulder of her loose hospital gown slipped down, revealing more pale skin, and she pulled it up modestly. "Sleepy, but I can't sleep. My throat hurts."

I sensed that the sore throat was a result of having her stomach pumped but decided not to mention it. "Do you need anything?" I mentally cursed myself for not bringing some magazines or flowers.

"No. They're going to let me go home as soon as the doctor finishes rounds and officially releases me. I need to get back to the winery. I can't afford to be away."

I blinked, surprised. "Really? I thought . . ." I shut my mouth when I realized I was about to refer to the seventy-two-hour psychiatric hold that hospitals imposed on suicidal patients so they can do a mental-health workup. Brad called it a 5150.

"This was all a big misunderstanding," Marie said, looking down at the white blanket that covered her and picking at some lint with her non-IVed hand. "I don't know how I ended up taking all those pills. It was just an accident."

"You mean, you didn't try to . . . commit suicide?" I asked bluntly.

"Of course not," she said, still not meeting my eyes. Maybe she was too ashamed to look at me. Or maybe she wasn't telling the full truth. I knew from teaching abnormal psychology that many people who attempt suicide often deny it later out of embarrassment.

"So what happened?"

Marie bit her lip, then said, "I'm not sure. It's still a little fuzzy. When I heard the police were charging Rob with murder, I just wanted to go to sleep, hoping I'd wake up and it was all a bad dream." She sighed.

"But Rocco said you took a whole bottle of pills. He found the empty bottle when he went in to check on you. You weren't responding when he spoke to you."

She shrugged and the gown slipped again. "I remember I took a couple of pills, but not as many as he said I did. I don't know why he found the bottle empty. Maybe there were only a few pills left. Or maybe I woke up and took some more pills without really thinking about it. Or maybe . . ." She paused, frowned, and blinked several times.

"What, Marie? Do you remember something?"

She rubbed her forehead as if she had a headache from trying to sort it all out. "I don't know. All I remember is drinking some tea that someone had put on my nightstand. Maybe there was something in the tea . . ."

Rocco hadn't mentioned finding a cup of tea.

"Marie, are you saying someone might have drugged you?"

She shook her head and readjusted her gown again. "I don't know. I . . . I thought I heard someone come into the room while I was sleeping. I heard my name . . . I woke up, or I thought I did . . . Maybe I drank the tea . . . I just don't remember. I'm sorry."

Tears welled again, and her hands balled into fists. She leaned back on the pillow and closed her eyes, as if forcing herself to relax.

Or maybe I'd upset her and she was shutting down.

"I'm so sorry, Marie. I'll let you rest. Are you sure there isn't anything I can do for you? Do you need a ride home?"

Her moist eyes fluttered open. "No. Allison is coming. She'll take me home."

"Well, then. Mother and I will pack up and be out of there before you get there. I'm sure you'll want your privacy."

Marie reached out and took my hand, squeezing it with an urgency that surprised me. "No, please don't go, Presley. Stay. The house is so big—I'll never know you're there, so you won't be bothering me. And I need you. Rocco says you're quite dogged when it comes to finding out the truth when . . ." She paused. "I know Rob didn't kill JoAnne. I'd be so grateful if you could help find out who did." She gave my hand another squeeze.

"All right. I'll do what I can. Now, you rest. And when you get home, I'll have Rocco whip up some of his wonderful chicken soup for you. He'll have you back on your feet in no time."

She released her grip on my hand, nodded, and closed her eyes again. I still wasn't sure she should be released from the hospital so soon, but if the doctor felt she was well enough to go home and was no threat to herself, who was I to argue? What I could do was make her feel comfortable when she got back home.

And do what I could to find out more about JoAnne Douglas's death.

Like who—if anyone—might have come into Marie's room and spiked her drink.

Brad was on his cell phone in the waiting room. "Thanks, buddy," he said and hung up. "How is she?" he asked, walking over to meet me.

"Apparently fine. She claims she doesn't remember taking extra pills. She says the doctor is releasing her soon."

"What? They're not keeping her on a 5150?"

"I guess not."

"Should we wait around and give her a lift?"

"I offered, but she said her sister would be coming by to take her home." We headed for the hospital exit. "Who were you talking to?"

"Luke."

"Great!" I said, smiling at the thought of my frenemy. I wasn't a big fan of the San Francisco homicide detective, but at the moment he might be of use. "I was going to ask you to call him. Do you think he can find out more about Rob's arrest and what they have on him?"

"He says he'll do his best. He knows Kelly. Doesn't particularly like him—thinks he's a cocky SOB. But he'll try to find out what's going on."

"Cocky?" I said, nearly laughing. "That's the pot calling the kettle black. No one's cockier than Detective Luke Melvin."

"Funny. He thinks the same of you," Brad said as we headed for the SUV.

"Me? You've got to be kidding. Cocky? I don't think so!"

Brad opened the car door, gave me a boost up, then got into the driver's seat and started the engine. I quietly steamed at Luke Melvin's comment about me, until my mind drifted back to the murder.

Brad finally broke the silence after we pulled up the driveway of the Purple Grape. "So have you made one of your party-planning-slash-suspects lists yet?" he asked. I hated it when he read my mind.

"Working on it."

Once inside the house, I checked on Mom and found a note she'd left saying Larry had picked her up and taken her to the evening bingo session. I'd nearly forgotten about it, with all that had happened. I hoped nothing went wrong, but couldn't help worrying, knowing Mom and her increasing eccentricities.

I returned to the kitchen and sat at the tiled table, while Brad pulled some leftover *amuse-bouches* from the refrigerator and set them in the center of the table. I opened my purse and pulled out one of the party forms I kept with me in case of an emergency party-planning request. You never knew when someone might want to throw a Bunco Brunch or a White Trash Bash.

I filled in the blanks, including the latest information I'd learned.

Under "Host" I wrote "Rob and Marie Christopher, winery owners." Then I added another category— "Victim"—and jotted down "JoAnne Douglas, radical environmentalist and winery owner."

Moving down to the guest list, I added the word "Suspects" and wrote down "Allison, Javier, Nick and Claudette Madeira, and Dennis and KJ Brien."

"Not much in the way of a list," Brad said, reading the names upside down.

"Watch out or I'll add your name," I said.

"I'm innocent, I tell ya," he said, then leaned over and kissed me in a not-so-innocent way.

"Stop! You're distracting me." I tried to suppress a smile and look serious, but it wasn't easy after a kiss like that.

Under "Occasion," I scribbled "Wine-tasting to publicize the release of a new wine," then added—"and the murder of JoAnne Douglas." For "Time" I put "7:00 to 10:00 pm Saturday night/AKA Opportunity—before, during, or after the party."

Nothing like nailing down the time frame. I took a soggy crab puff from the plate and amused my *bouche* with it, while I wrote "Crime Scene" next to the word "Place." I added "Garden at the Purple Grape Winery, under a serving table."

I paused for a moment and popped in another small bite of food. Under a serving table? What a strange place to kill someone. Had the murderer moved her there? If so, when? And how, without being caught?

Under "Party Details" I put "JoAnne Douglas sneaked into the party with a can of green paint and was stabbed with a cheese knife and antique corkscrew."

Bizarre. Why? In other words, what was the motive?

That was the Big Question.

"Looking for a motive?" Brad asked, a bit of chocolate mousse at the side of his mouth.

I nodded. "As usual, I've got more questions than answers, but it's a start," I said. Being a linear thinker, I tended to do things in an orderly way. I'd learned from a teacher who helped me with my ADHD that making lists was one way to organize my thoughts.

Thinking of motive, I went on. "JoAnne had a lot of enemies who didn't like the way she was trying to enforce her political and environmental agenda. But was that enough to get her killed?"

Brad shrugged. "Remember what I told you: Look at the victim first, then the crime scene, then the suspects." Distracted by his mouth, I wanted to lick the chocolate off his lips.

He was right, as usual. I'd have to do more research on JoAnne and find out if she might have been killed for reasons other than her green beliefs.

My first thought was: *Question Natalie, JoAnne's employee.*

I'd learned from experience that people behind the scenes often knew more than anyone else. Natalie was definitely behind the scenes.

"Why don't you draw a picture of the crime scene?" Brad suggested.

"Good idea," I said, and turned the form over. I sketched the table, then drew JoAnne's outline underneath. She'd been lying on her back with the corkscrew sticking out of her chest, her legs bent.

"Don't forget the missing shoe," Brad added, looking over the drawing.

I drew one shoe on her foot, and the other one off to the side, with the words, "Found under Rob and Marie's bed." Next I added the cheese-knife handle sticking out of the flower bed. To round out the scene, I drew a couple of bottles of wine, some glasses, a few grapey decorations, and two Killer Parties–embossed wine openers on top of the table.

I sat back and studied the scene.

"Well, now you've got plenty of clues. But what's missing from the picture?" Brad asked.

"What do you mean? I've drawn the shoe and the cheese knife and the paint." I pointed to the two clues on the drawing.

"No, I mean, what can't we see. That's just as important as what you can see."

I frowned at him, completely baffled. "You mean, something's missing? I can't really see what I can't see," I argued.

He smiled.

"Tell me!" I said, growing frustrated.

"I don't know," he said. "I'm just saying, sometimes it's what you don't see that tells you more."

I looked at my drawing again.

A thought came to me. "How about the person standing behind the table pouring the wine?"

Brad raised an eyebrow.

"It could have been Rob. Or Marie. Or Allison. Or Javier. But none of them stayed at one table for long. They kept circulating, getting more bottles of wine, cleaning up used glasses."

"What if you gave each one a motive?" Brad suggested.

"Okay. Rob had apparently been arguing with JoAnne over the direction of his winery. Maybe he'd discovered her sneaking into the party and . . ." I shrugged. "Marie didn't like JoAnne and seemed to think she was a threat to their winery. Her sister Allison just seemed indifferent to everyone. But if she has a gambling problem or she's back on drugs, that could be an issue. I'm not sure how it would relate to JoAnne's death, unless she was being blackmailed or something."

"You think Javier belongs on that list?" Brad asked.

"He and Allison were at the bingo hall together. And

I've seen them talking together several times, arguing, acting kind of weird. But they certainly don't seem like a couple. Javier's been losing management jobs. Maybe JoAnne's threats to the Purple Grape caused him to kill her to protect his job?"

"That seems a bit of a stretch."

I sighed.

"What about the neighbors?" he said.

Ex-governor Dennis Brien and his young wife, KJ. Hollywood mogul Nick and his wife, Claudette. Both couples had had issues with JoAnne. Claudette had suspected she'd done something to her and Nick's crop. And KJ had hinted that JoAnne was jealous of Dennis's political influence.

Claudette seemed to imply that something was not right in Camelot with her shining knight, Nick. Was he cheating on her? Or was it something else? And I'd almost forgotten the note Dennis had received from Allison, urgently asking him to call her. What was that about?

Just when I thought I had a complete list of suspects, I realized I'd left off Kyle Bennett, the attorney. But was he really a suspect? I added his name, even though I couldn't come up with a solid motive for him. He had worked for JoAnne but had left her employment—why?—and gone to work for the smaller vineyards, helping them protect their properties. Now he was representing Rob on a murder rap. Was ambulance chasing the worst of his crimes?

It all led back to the victim: JoAnne Douglas, just like Brad said. Had she annoyed one too many people?

Stepped on one too many toes? Been a pest to someone who wanted to rid the county of her radical agenda?

Or had JoAnne discovered something about the killer and was murdered to keep her quiet?

Whatever it was, I needed to know more about JoAnne Douglas.

Chapter 15

PARTY-PLANNING TIP #15

Hosting a wine-tasting party? Accessorize, accessorize, accessorize! You can shop online for such swag as wine charms (to help guests keep track of their drinks), bottle stoppers (toss away that ill-fitting cork), personalized corkscrews (to honor a special guest), or DIY photo coasters (featuring laminated snapshots of the guests from previous parties). Then send them home with the guests as party favors!

I stood up from the table. "I have to talk to Natalie Mattos."

"Who's Natalie Mattos?" Brad asked.

"JoAnne's assistant. I met her this afternoon when I stopped by JoAnne's winery. She has to know more about JoAnne that will help me understand the woman. I feel like there's a piece missing from all this."

Brad looked at the clock in the kitchen. "It's getting late, Presley. If she works at the winery, she's probably gone. You can see her tomorrow."

He was right. Prodded by my ADHD, I wanted to do

everything *right now*, but chances were that Natalie was gone for the day. I'd have better luck finding her tomorrow—if she returned to JoAnne's winery. If not, then what?

"When is your mother due back?" Brad asked, clearing the leftovers from the table.

"Around nine. Why? You want to play bingo?"

He laughed. "No, I've got a better idea. Hope you're hungry."

I'd been so preoccupied, I didn't realize I wasn't just hungry, but starving.

"Sounds great. What did you have in mind? French Laundry? Tra Vigne? Mustards Grill?" I practically drooled as I listed some of the world-famous gourmet restaurants in the Napa area. I'd always wanted to dine at one but couldn't afford their gourmet prices. Besides, I'd heard the French Laundry was booked months in advance.

"Not quite," Brad said, smiling mysteriously. "Let's take your car. I don't think the place would appreciate a Crime Scene Cleaners truck on the premises."

Intrigued, I led the way to my MINI and offered the keys to Brad. He squeezed into the driver's seat and I took the passenger side. Ten minutes later we pulled up to what looked like a parking lot filled with a dozen aluminum-sided trucks and a couple of Airstream trailers, all parked in a circle like a wagon train on the prairie.

But these weren't covered wagons. These were food trucks.

"Wow," I said, getting out of the car and taking in the sight and the smells. "What's with all the chuck wagons?"

"Time to eat," Brad said, and took my hand. We walked up to the first truck, painted bright green and yellow and sporting a lighted awning. A line of hungry people holding glasses of wine stood waiting in lines at the open windows.

I glanced ahead at the next truck, and the next. The place was jam-packed with food options. "What is this place?"

"Gourmet Food Truck Night," Brad said simply. "It's held next to the Oxbow Public Market on the first Friday of every month, but it's been so popular, they've recently expanded to Sunday nights. It runs from six until midnight."

"Oh my God, it's like a huge block party!" I read the clever names on the trucks—"Who Let the Dog Out?" hot dogs, "What the Duck?" barbecue, "Phat Wraps," and "Creative Cupcakes." People sitting at picnic tables and on portable chairs noshed on fish tacos, dim sum, oysters, Indian food, Vienna sausages—something for every taste. I wished I'd brought Zantac for dessert—I'd need it after chowing down on all the foods I suddenly wanted to try.

"I heard the dumplings from Dim Sum Charlie's are the best," Brad said. "And the ribs at the Flying Pig. Plus the Chocolate Velvet Cupcakes are killer."

We decided to split up and buy different foods to share. Brad headed for the ribs, while I stood in line for the dumplings. He beat me and found two seats at a long table, shared by a friendly group of partiers. I sat down opposite him with an overflowing plate of dim sum. Unable to wait any longer, I took a bite of the dumpling; it melted in my mouth. While enjoying the spicy, sensuous pleasure, I listened to the violin quartet play classical music in the background. In spite of the cool night, I was toasty, thanks to portable heaters nearby.

This place was hog heaven.

I glanced at the woman sitting next to me—middle-aged, brown hair cut short and sensibly—sitting across from a man with graying hair and glasses. She was eating what could only be described as escargot lollipops—snails on sticks covered in puff pastry. They smelled of garlic and actually looked tasty. But no way was I going to find out.

"Come here often?" I asked her, since we were sitting elbow to elbow.

She swallowed the food in her mouth and nodded. "Every chance we get. It's so much fun. We see our neighbors, have something great to eat, listen to the music, and just enjoy the ambiance of Napa. This your first time?"

"Yes, it's wonderful," I said. "I'm Presley Parker, by the way, and this is Brad Matthews." We air-shook hands, thanks to messy fingers.

The woman offered us two glasses of wine in plastic cups. "I'm Julie Obregar."

"Nice to meet you. And thanks for the wine."

"How do you like those dumplings?" she asked, nodding her head toward the lumps on our plates.

"They're to die for," I said, remembering the bite I'd just had.

"Wait till you have a cupcake," she said. "Death by chocolate."

"I've heard." I shot Brad a look. He smiled, his face dotted with barbecue sauce.

"I wish they would do this more often," Julie said, "but the city has been threatening to shut the trucks down. I don't know why. Everything's been cleared by the health department, there's no alcohol sold on the premises, and people dispose of their trash, but so far, the city won't give. This may be the last one."

"That's awful," I said, having now acquired a taste for Food Truck Dumplings. I'd heard we were getting some food trucks in San Francisco and hoped they were as good as these.

"It is when you consider the fact that downtown Napa needs all the help it can get. They put in the Riverwalk and filled the area with restaurants, but meanwhile many of the shops are closing and the outdoor mall looks like a ghost town."

"So why the crackdown on food trucks?" I asked. "You'd think the city would love the business."

"Tell me about it," Julie said, rolling her eyes. "According to the food trucks Facebook page, the city wants them to buy special permits that will cost up to ten thousand dollars. Plus they need to add ramps to the restrooms to comply with the American with Disabilities Act. And the American Beverage Committee says unpermitted BYOB has to stop. It's all because someone complained about these code violations."

"Can't the citizens do something about it?"

"We're trying. We've got our Facebook page—*Save the Napa Food Trucks*. It's really brought our community together. But it only took one annoying party pooper to ruin everything."

My ears pricked up. "What do you mean, one party pooper?" I asked.

Julie took a swallow of her wine. "Oh, there's this local vintner who's been causing all the trouble."

In spite of the outdoor heaters, I shivered.

"But maybe things will change now," she added.

"How so?" I asked.

"The woman was killed last night."

Oh my God. Joanne Douglas.

"Wow," I said, once Brad and I were back in the car. "JoAnne keeps looking worse and worse. She was trying to shut down the food trucks? No wonder Julie called her the most hated woman in the wine country. It's as if she went out of her way to cause friction and annoy people—and get herself killed."

"Sounds like a mental case to me," Brad said.

"I don't know. Something must have caused all that bitterness. I still think there's a piece missing."

"You always want to psychoanalyze everyone, Presley."

"That's because all behavior is motivated," I said. "I taught that in Psych 101. There's got to be something behind all of her anger, and I'm hoping her assistant Natalie will tell me what it is. That is, if Natalie is still working at the winery. If she's not, I'm screwed." I thought for a moment. "Unless . . ."

Brad shot me a look. "Uh-oh. What are you thinking?"

"Bingo!"

"Bingo? No way. Poker's my game, not Ping-Pong balls and oversized markers."

"Think about it, Brad. The bingo hall is the best place to get information around here. If Natalie isn't at the winery anymore, I might be able to find out where to locate her. There's still an hour before the games are over."

Brad raised a suspicious eyebrow.

"Besides, I want to check on Mom, make sure she's all right, what with all that's happened around here. Then we can take her home instead of relying on Larry."

"All right," Brad said, "but if you get a bingo, I get ten percent."

"Deal!"

We pulled into the lot, which was packed, as usual. Entering the hall, I did a quick search for Mother. I spotted her sitting next to Larry, engrossed in the current game. Helen and Constance occupied their usual seats nearby. Brad and I stood on the sidelines to keep from distracting the players—although I had a feeling not even an earthquake would stop these people from marking the next called number—and I spent a few minutes looking for Allison. Not surprisingly, I found her, but she wasn't in her usual place. This time she sat next to an elderly man in the middle of the room.

Odd, I thought. Larry had said most of the players pick a seat and stay with it, thinking it might be bad luck to move. Apparently Allison didn't believe in this superstition.

"You can't stand there," came a voice next to me. I turned to see the female security guard looming beside me. Her name tag read: "Karna."

"What?" I asked.

"No observing," she said, her hands on her big leather belt. I looked for a gun, but there was nothing more threatening than a flashlight. Typical rent-a-cop. "You have to play or you can't stay. Those are the rules."

"Really?" I said, surprised an innocent game like bingo didn't allow onlookers. "You think we're counting Ping-Pong balls or something?"

She pressed her lips together, showing me that she meant business—and that she didn't have a sense of humor.

I looked at Brad. He shrugged, pulled out his wallet, and headed over to the ticket desk to buy us in. I followed him, giving Karna a last glance, and searched for an empty spot where Brad and I could sit. I spied some room next to a gray-haired couple who were munching on corn chips between marking their sheets. Sitting down, I waved to Brad to join me, and he sauntered over with our game sheets and daubers in hand.

"How much did that set you back?" I asked when he squeezed into his seat between two women across from me.

"More than dinner," he grumbled. I knew he didn't want to play and was doing me a favor. I owed him.

"Hey, maybe you'll win," I said, marking all the free spots on the sheet I'd be playing next.

"I'd better," he said.

The gray-haired man next to me sneaked a glance at us, no doubt wondering why we were two hours late and without our own daubers, bingo carriers, or lucky charms. I smiled at him, hoping a little flirtatious look would melt his seeming consternation. He leered back at me, displaying a row of crooked, yellowed teeth. Dirty old man.

"Come here often?" I asked him, thinking I might as well try to make Brad jealous.

"Shhhh!"

The old man had just shushed me!

Brad stifled a grin and shook his head.

After a few more called number-letter combinations, the old guy yelled, "Bingo!"

"Hey," I said to him. "I brought you luck!"

The woman sitting across from him smiled. "Don't pay no attention to Ralph. He takes his bingo a little too seriously. I'm Mary, his long-suffering wife. You're new here, aren'tcha?"

I nodded. "My second time. Brad's a virgin."

The old man shot me another leering look.

"A bingo virgin," I explained to him. He didn't seem to get it.

The roving bingo payoff guy came over, took Ralph's sheet, handed it to another player for verification, then paid the man his two hundred and fifty dollars. A handful of people around him congratulated him. He nodded grumpily.

When the excitement died down, I said to Mary, "Does he often win?"

"About once a month," she said, ripping up her losing bingo sheet and tossing it in the nearby trash. "Considering we're here twice a week, that ain't so good."

Bingo—I'd found a regular. Maybe Mary knew something about JoAnne Douglas. "I suppose you heard about the recent . . . death."

"Murder, you mean," she corrected me. "Everyone's heard about it. Poor thing. I mean, she wasn't the most popular gal in town, but nobody deserves to be tapped like that."

I stifled a grin at her language. "Do you happen to know her assistant? A young woman named Natalie Mattos?"

"Sure, I know Nat. She's a great gal. How she put up with JoAnne, I'll never know."

This place truly was a wealth of information. "Any chance you could tell me how to find her, now that the winery has closed?"

"I heard she's already found another job," Mary said.

That was quick. "Really? Where?"

"She got hired by the Napa Valley Wine Train. She's probably there now, doing the night shift."

Chapter 16

PARTY-PLANNING TIP #16

Selecting the right corkscrew for your party is almost as important as choosing the wine. The lever style is one of the easiest to use. You simply clamp it onto the wine bottle and it does the work for you. However, it can be expensive (thirty to one hundred and fifty dollars) and therefore may not be affordable as a party favor.

"Thanks, Mary!" I said, then pulled out my iPhone. I did a search for the Napa Valley Wine Train and checked the details for the evening event. Sure enough, there was a five thirty p.m. train that was due back around nine thirty. We still had time to meet the train after bingo.

"Brad!" I whispered to him, after realizing I might be able to talk to Natalie soon.

Brad didn't answer, too busy marking up his sheet while playing the current bingo game. I'd lost interest in winning. I had other things on my mind. Like finding out who murdered JoAnne Douglas—and talking to Natalie.

Brad reached over and daubed several of my squares for me. After a few minutes, someone called "Bingo!"

"Presley!" I heard my name called. Mother. Uh-oh. She'd spotted me. "Hi, Mom."

"What are you doing here?" she asked, her eyes wide as I walked over to her table. I didn't know if that meant she was surprised, delighted, or horrified that I'd shown up unexpectedly.

"Brad and I were in the neighborhood and thought we'd play a few games, then take you home. How's it going? Won anything yet?"

"No, but Larry won again!" She beamed as she patted his arm.

Larry grinned and blushed. "She's my lucky charm," he said, placing his other hand on hers.

This time she grinned and blushed. These two were acting like a pair of teenagers.

"I'd better get back," I said. "Another game is about to start."

"Good luck, honey!" Mom said.

Larry whipped out a five-dollar bill and handed it to me. "Here. Go buy yourself a soda and candy bar. On me."

I thanked him, realizing that sharing the wealth was part of the bingo culture. And after all the wine I'd drunk with the truck food, a coffee sounded just right.

I bought two lattes and set them down in between Brad's place and mine, just as the bingo caller announced the next game, this one called the Kite.

"Thanks," Brad said.

I turned to the old guy next to me. "What's the Kite?" I asked him. He shushed me again.

"Ignore him," Mary said. "That's what I do, after fifty-odd years of marriage. In the Kite, you have to get a block of four in any corner, with a diagonal line in three additional spaces, including the free space, to win. It looks like a kite with a tail."

Whatever happened to good, old-fashioned, five-in-a-row bingo? I wondered as I looked at the multiple possibilities on my sheet. About the time I thought I might have a winning card, someone yelled, "Bingo!"

This game sucked.

I stood up, tossed my sheet in the trash as if it were contaminated, and headed back to my seat. Brad was hunched over his bingo sheet like a prisoner guarding his food. This guy was getting bingo fever!

I sat down, but instead of filling in the free squares on my bingo sheet, I wrote down questions I had for Natalie so I'd be prepared when we chatted. When the last game finally ended, Brad and I waited outside for Mother and Larry.

Two smokers sat on a bench several feet away from the entrance to the hall. We kept our distance while scanning the people as they left the building. I spotted Allison exiting, accompanied by the elderly gentleman she'd been sitting next to during the games. He was using a walker and she had her hand on his shoulder.

"Allison!" I called. She turned around and saw me, looking startled. "Could I talk to you a second?"

Allison sighed, glanced at the man, then said, "I'll catch up with you, Delbert." He nodded and moseyed on to his car, a new white Cadillac parked in a handi-capped spot up front.

"What's up?" She pulled out a cigarette, lit it, and squinted as the smoke encircled her head. "Getting into bingo?"

I ignored her and asked, "Have you heard anything more . . . about the murder?"

She shook her head and blew smoke away from me. "You?"

"No," I said, then began weaving a lie as I contin-ued. "But I talked to Dennis Brien and he mentioned getting an urgent message from you earlier today. Something about wanting him to call you? I wondered if that was about JoAnne."

Allison blinked rapidly several times. I knew that blink. I'd taught "Blinking and Eye Movement" as part of my abnormal psychology curriculum, under the topic "micro-expressions." Allison had just micro-expressed a combination of surprise and concern.

She took another puff on her cigarette—a stalling technique often used when someone is about to lie. "Oh, that. I wanted to ask him about a special wine I'd ordered from his winery."

"That was urgent?" I asked.

"Yes, I wanted to give it to a friend for his birthday."

"You wanted to give your friend a wine from Den-nis's winery, not the Purple Grape?"

Allison gave me a harsh look. "Yes, if it's any of your business. It was a special occasion. Rob's wines are fine, but Dennis has some really great ones." She sucked an-other drag, dropped her cigarette onto the pavement, and stamped it out. "Any more questions? Otherwise, I need to get to the hospital. They say my sister tried to commit suicide, but she's denying it and so they're releasing her tonight."

"Yes, I heard." I wondered why Allison was here playing bingo instead of already at the hospital waiting for Marie. "I hope she's all right."

"She'll be fine. I'll take good care of her. So you'll be leaving us in the morning?" she stated more than asked.

"Uh, only if Marie doesn't need me for anything."

"Like I said, I'll take good care of her. Good night, Presley."

I watched as Allison headed for the white Cadillac still sitting in the parking lot. She leaned into the driver's window, said something, then gave Delbert a kiss on the cheek. He backed out, and she walked to her car, parked a few yards away, got in, and drove off.

Larry and Mother appeared in the doorway. "Oh, there you are, Presley," Mother said. "Did you have fun?"

"Yeah, it was great. Listen, Mom, I need to stop somewhere on the way back to the Christophers' place. Is that all right?"

"Sure, dear." She turned to Larry, leaned in and gave him a peck on the cheek, and said good night.

"I'll sit in the back," I said as we reached the MINI. I bent down and squeezed my five-foot-ten-inch frame into the tiny backseat, tucking my legs. I felt like a fetus, all curled up.

"Comfortable, dear?" Mother asked. "You could be driving my Cadillac, you know. It's just sitting there."

"I'm fine, Mother."

I gave Brad directions to the Napa Wine Train station, using my iPhone GPS. Along the way Mother related her evening, which was mostly gossip about who was having an affair with whom, which vintners were about to go under, and what to do about the food truck situation. By the time she was done tattling, it sounded as if everyone in Napa was having an affair. Must be the wine, I thought, wondering if JoAnne had had an affair with someone that had gone very wrong. She wasn't especially attractive, but that wouldn't keep her from finding a man.

Had someone broken her heart?

A few minutes later we arrived at the McKinstry Street station, where the gold, green, and maroon train was just pulling in. According to the details I'd found online, each car had a different name and theme, with its own kitchen, menu, and atmosphere. Train service began in 1864 when San Francisco millionaire Sam Brannan transported visitors to his spa resort. It soon became part of the Southern Pacific Railroad, bringing agricultural development to the Napa Valley. Train service was discontinued in the 1930s, but after preservationists got involved, the train was renovated and turned into a tourist attraction in 1989.

While we sat in the car waiting for the passengers to detrain, I read Brad and Mom some of the Wine Train details. "The three-hour trip goes from Napa to St. Helena and back, and guests enjoy lunch or dinner along with wine tasting. It stops along the way at several wineries too. Sounds wonderful!"

"Is that a hint?" Brad said, reading my mind.

Before I could answer, I spotted Natalie stepping

down from a train car. A young guy with long hair and a motorcycle jacket appeared to be waiting for her in the parking lot.

"Natalie?" I called, squeezing myself out of the car

"Yeah?" she said, looking up.

"Presley Parker," I said. "We met at the Douglas Family Winery earlier?"

"Oh yeah, sure. You were the one asking about JoAnne . . ." She lowered her voice. "So any luck finding out who killed JoAnne?"

"Not yet," I said. "But I wondered if I could talk to you for a minute. I have a couple more questions I think you might be able to answer."

Natalie glanced at the guy on the motorcycle, who stared at her blankly. His leather jacket read, "Devil's Playground." "Uh, yeah, sure. What's up?"

Natalie looked much different out of her winery uniform and now dressed as a retro train conductor, in a gray suit, short skirt, and wine-colored tie. Her long hair was loose and fell halfway down her back, and her nails were painted black.

"You said you've been working for JoAnne for the past year or so, right?"

"Yeah. Like I said, I heard she needed a pourer and I applied for the job when I couldn't get anything else in the business."

"Did you ever hear her talk about Rob Christopher?"

"Pretty much all the time."

"Really? What did she say?"

"Oh, you know. The Purple Grape was killing the environment. Rob didn't know what he was doing. Rob and Marie were out to get her. The Purple Grape was selling wine on the Internet at cut-rate prices. Things like that."

Hmmm. Wasn't that what JoAnne was supposedly doing—selling her wines on the Internet at lower prices?

"Did she say how Rob was out to get her?"

"Not really. Personally, I thought he was a nice guy. Kinda cute too, for an older guy." She giggled, then glanced at the parking lot. "Don't tell Will. Anyway, JoAnne really had it in for Rob, but I don't know why."

"Did you ever talk to Rob about her accusations?"

"No way," Natalie said. "That would have been consorting with the enemy. I'm sure I would have been fired for that."

"So you can't think of any reason why she had it in for him more than anyone else?"

"Nothing. No, wait—I do remember something. JoAnne said Rob was planning to switch to screw caps, instead of using corks."

I frowned. "Was that really an issue?"

A beep sounded from the parking lot. Natalie glanced over and waved to someone. I assumed it was her boyfriend, growing impatient. "Oh, you don't know the wine industry. The old-school vintners think wines should only be corked. But the new school wants to use screw tops. It's a quality-versus-style argument."

"What's the difference?"

"JoAnne said the screw caps affected the Mediterranean cork industry. That's where most of the cork is grown. She said losing the cork forests could threaten ecosystems."

"Interesting. I thought they were just considered tacky."

"I know, right? But vintners who switched to screw caps said they did it because they had problems with cork taint."

"Cork taint?"

"Yeah, it's a kind of mold that ruins the wine. You don't get it with screw caps. But then screw caps are made from nonrenewable material." She shook her head. "You can't win in this business."

"Wow. All these battles in the war of the wines," I said. It made sense that old-school JoAnne would be a corker while new-school Rob would be a screw capper. Was the corkscrew used to kill JoAnne some symbolic message? It had certainly screwed Rob.

The guy on the motorcycle raced his engine, signaling to Natalie that her time was up. She took a step toward him, indicating she was ready to go. I followed.

"Thanks, Natalie," I said. "Is there some way I can contact you if I have more questions?"

She lifted her skirt a little, hopped on the back of the bike, put on her helmet, and wrapped her arms around Will. "You can reach me at natloveswine at yahoo dot com."

"That's easy to remember," I said, and pulled out a Killer Parties business card. "Here's my card. Call me if you think of anything else. I appreciate your help."

"Sure," she said. She took my card and tucked it into her mini–shoulder bag, just before the two roared off into the night.

"What did she say?" Brad asked as I burrowed my way back into the rear seat.

"I'm not sure," I said. Before I could add anything, Mother gave a brief history of the Napa Wine Train. I don't know why I needed the Internet for background information when I had Mother.

We pulled up to the Purple Grape and followed the garden lighting to the front of the house. I used the key Rob had given me and I switched on the hall light as we entered the dark foyer. Obviously Allison and Marie weren't home from the hospital yet. I escorted Mother to her room, then joined Brad in our room next to hers.

I changed into my PJs, while Brad just dropped his clothes; then we snuggled into bed. He switched on the TV to catch the ten o'clock news. JoAnne's death and Rob's arrest were the lead stories, but thankfully there was no mention of Marie's so-called suicide attempt. The reporter, a young African American man, gave a brief history of JoAnne's life, mentioning the *"many controversies she'd been engaged in 'trying make a better tomorrow for the Napa Valley.'"*

The screen shot changed to a large, red-faced man standing in front of what looked like a rustic cabin, leaning on a cane. Next to him was a female reporter holding a microphone near his lips as he spoke.

"JoAnne's death is a great loss to our community," he said in a gruff voice, *"but our fine police department has arrested the heinous person responsible for her murder, and justice will be served. That's all I have to say."* The man pressed his lips together in a gesture of finality.

The name captioned at the bottom of the screen read, "Angus McLaughlin, President and CEO of Napology Corporation."

Why had they interviewed the head of Napology for the story? I wondered. What did he have to do with JoAnne Douglas?

I didn't have time to ponder that. Brad turned off the TV and temporarily helped me forget about JoAnne Douglas, Rob Christopher, and everything else associated with murder. And he did it better than any bottle of wine could ever do.

When I woke up the next morning, Brad was already up, dressed, and packed. He held two Fiestaware coffee mugs in his hands.

"What time is it?" I asked, rubbing my eyes.

"Seven thirty," he said, handing me a coffee.

"Too early," I muttered, setting the mug on the nightstand. "Need more sleep . . ."

"I got a cleanup call, so I'm heading back to the city now. I'll see you when you get back to the island. Drive safely." He leaned over and kissed me.

"Don't go!" I whined, then grabbed his arm. "Come back to bed . . ."

Brad laughed. *Could he be any cuter?* I thought.

"If I do, I might never get up again," he said. "Besides, I want to get out of here before I'm caught shacking up with the hired help."

"I think that ship has sailed," I murmured.

He rubbed my bed hair. "Come on. Marie's in the kitchen. I'm sure you want to see her."

That did it. I sat up, patted down my hair, retrieved my coffee, and took a sip.

"Okay. Call me when your job's done."

He bent down and kissed my coffee mouth, tousled

my hair again as if I were an impish child, and left the room with his overnight backpack. I took a few more sips of coffee—enough to make me human—then got in the shower, dressed in black jeans and a lavender Purple Grape T-shirt Rob had given me, and checked on Mother. Still asleep, she was softly snoring. Lucky girl.

I headed for the kitchen with my nearly empty coffee mug and found Marie sitting over a plate of untouched toast, staring out a window. Allison was nowhere in sight.

"Marie, I'm so glad you're back," I said. What do you say to a person who may have tried to commit suicide the night before? "Life is good"?

My presence seemed to bring her back from wherever her thoughts had wandered. "Morning, Presley. Did you sleep well?"

In spite of everything, the pleasantries continued.

"Great, thanks. How're *you* doing this morning?"

"Better, thanks, although my throat still hurts from that darn tube." She looked down at her cold toast.

"Can I get you something else? Yogurt, maybe? Some fruit?"

"No, I'm not hungry. I'm waiting for a call from Kyle about Rob. He said he'd let me know what's going on."

I nodded. "Well, Mother and I'll be out of your hair soon."

Marie reached across the table for my hand. "Presley, don't go," she said. "I meant what I said last night. You're no trouble at all. And I could use the company now that Rob's . . ." She left the sentence unfinished but implied.

"I'd love to, Marie, but I need to get my mother back to her facility," I said, feeling a twinge of guilt at the thought of abandoning Marie. "But listen. I'm going to do more background research and I promise to come back in a day or two."

She looked glum but forced a smile onto her sad face. "I understand. I just don't know what's going to happen with Rob. You're such a take-charge kind of woman—I was hoping you'd help me find out who really killed JoAnne. I know he's innocent." A tear rolled down her pale cheek.

I'm a sucker for tears. "I promise—I'll do what I can, Marie. I've already talked to quite a few people who were at the party. Now it's time to do some background research—and that I can do from my office. But I'll be back soon. Don't worry."

More tears. "Thank you, Presley."

She reached out to take my hand and suddenly froze, looking over my shoulder.

I turned to see what had caused her to tense up so abruptly.

Allison stood in the doorway holding a cup of coffee. She was wearing an oversized blue madras camp shirt, unbuttoned, over a too-small white tank top and too-tight jeans. The shirt looked vaguely familiar. "Good morning, ladies," she said.

Marie rose from the table, her face twisted in anger.

"Take that off!" she screamed at her sister. "That's Rob's shirt!"

Chapter 17

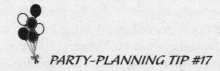

PARTY-PLANNING TIP #17

Another popular—and inexpensive—corkscrew is called "the Waiter," since so many waiters prefer it. Use the serrated knife blade to remove the foil cap, insert the screw (also called the "worm"), and pull out the cork. Sounds easy, but you may want to practice so you don't bend the worm inside the cork and end up with chunks of floating cork in the wine.

On the drive back to San Francisco, I thought about the significance of Allison wearing Rob's shirt—and Marie's angry reaction to seeing her in it. Why had a shirt provoked such a visceral response?

By the time we reached Mother's care facility, I still didn't have an answer. And while I'd had an "interesting" time in the wine country, I was eager to resume my real life back in the city. I missed my cats, my condo, and my co-workers. I dropped Mother off with a promise to take her to lunch soon, and drove home to Treasure Island.

After taking the exit off the Bay Bridge, I opened the

sunroof on the MINI Cooper and inhaled the familiar salt air. TI sits in the middle of the San Francisco Bay, completely surrounded by water, a floating relic of the city's past. The location was convenient, the rent cheap, and I loved the nearly three-hundred-and-sixty-degree view.

I drove by the huge rusty anchor left by the navy when it departed in 1997 and past the concave Building One that once housed exhibits during the 1939 Golden Gate Expo and now served as my office building.

I whizzed by the ginormous hangars once harboring the Pan Am Clipper Ships—now rented by movie studios—and on beyond the skeletal remains of naval housing that was soon to be demolished. High-rises were planned for the future of Treasure Island, something I could not imagine for this gem of the sea.

Turning into the small housing area, I pulled up to my condo, parked the MINI in the carport, got out of the car, and unlocked the front door of my home, hoping my neighbor had remembered to feed my three cats.

The moment the door opened I was attacked.

Thursby, my black watch-cat, leapt at my feet and tried to kill them. Fatman, my white longhair who could live on his fat for a month if no one fed him, tried to trip me while dodging between my ankles. And Cairo, my orange scaredy-cat, hightailed it for cover under the living room futon. He wasn't a cat; he was a chicken.

"My babies!" I said, hoisting Fatman and snuggling my face into his fur. I set him down, scratched Thursby's back, then called to Cairo, cajoling him into facing his fears. The sound of cat food rattling into bowls eventually brought him out from his hiding place.

"I missed you guys! Were you good boys while I was gone?"

What was it about cats that turned a grown, independent woman into a mushy, baby-talking idiot? While contemplating that, I refreshed the cats' water, made a mental note to thank my neighbor (a bottle of wine from Napa?), and threw my suitcase on the bed.

An hour and three cat massages later, I drove back to my office at Building One, a homemade latte in hand. I parked the MINI and walked up the steps to the glass entry doors, past the Rubenesque statues that had stood guard over the building for seven decades.

"Hey, Raj," I said to the TI security guard currently manning the front desk. "Have you recovered from the party the other night?"

He raised his animated dark eyebrows. "I am no longer surprised at what's happening at your parties, Ms. Presley. By the way, are you catching the killer?"

"Not yet," I said. "The police have Rob Christopher in custody, but his wife is certain he didn't do it. Frankly, I don't think he did either, but I have no idea who did."

"You are helping him, I suppose?"

"I'm doing what I can," I said, then moved on to my office a few steps beyond the desk.

The door stood open and I found Delicia, dressed in leggings, a denim skirt, and a long, gauzy top, working at her laptop.

"You're back!" she said with theatrical delight. As a

part-time actress, she couldn't help adding drama whenever she could.

"Finally," I said, plopping my purse down and picking up the "while you were out" forms piled on my desk.

"Those are just the ones I took for you while you were gone. You've got a dozen more messages on your machine."

I dropped into the seat at my desk, which faced hers. "Great. Getting back to callers should keep me busy for the next year. So what are you up to? Looking for an acting job?"

"I'm looking for wine. That merlot at the Purple Grape was awesome, but I can't afford it. Someone told me about this site called 'CheapbutGood.com,' where they have all kinds of name brands at way lower prices."

"Name brands . . . ," I said, remembering the rumor that JoAnne was selling wines online under a different name—and a lower price. I turned on my laptop. "I wonder . . ."

"Believe it or not," Dee said, "I found Two-Buck Chuck for a buck!"

I typed in "CheapbutGood.com" and the site appeared. The opening page showed a wine bottle with a dollar sign on the label, circled in red with a line through it. I did an on-site search for Douglas Family Wines, but nothing came up. Of course, she wouldn't use the name of the winery, not if she was trying to sell her wine cheaply on the Internet. So what was her "boutique" wine called?

No clue. But before I left the site, I typed in the name

"Purple Grape," just to see what might happen. Seconds later a link to "Purple Great" came up.

Purple Grape equals Purple Great? I wondered.

I tapped ENTER, which brought me to another Web site. This time a picture of a wine bottle with the label "Purple Great" appeared, along with a description: "Made from *great* grapes grown in the Napa Valley, this marvelous boutique merlot, comparable to the Purple Grape's signature wine, is available to you at a deep discount. Join our wine club and order a case or two today!" Below was a request to fill out information, such as name, address, credit card number, and so on.

A wine "comparable to the Purple Grape's signature wine"? Was someone at the winery selling the wines at lower prices too? Maybe in an effort to stay afloat in the winery business? If JoAnne did it, maybe Rob thought he could too. How hard would it be to create a new label, set up a Web site link, and undercut your prices, selling directly to the consumer?

Or was someone else trying to rip off the Purple Grape?

JoAnne?

"Dee, would you do me a favor?"

"Depends," she said. "Will you pay me in chocolate?"

"How about in wine?"

"Works for me!" she said, sitting up. "Who do I have to kill?"

"No one. At least, not yet. I'm going to send you a link to a site called ThePurpleGreat.com, and I want you to join their wine club and order a case. Use my credit card." I gave her the number.

"Sweet!" she said. "But why don't you order it yourself? Is there a catch? Will my name be sold to a penis-enlarging site?"

I laughed. "Because I don't want the seller to recognize my name. Use your home address, not this one, okay? And overnight it."

Moments later she was typing information into the site. "Must be good stuff if you want a case," she said. "I better start planning a party!"

"Good idea." I got up from my desk. "I'll be right back."

"Don't forget to write where you're going on the message board," she called, referring to the annoying whiteboard she'd hung on the wall. Too late. I was already out of the office. Besides, I was only going down the hall.

"Hey, Duncan," I said to our neighboring computer savant when I entered his office. Apparently it was casual Monday, because he'd come to work in SpongeBob pajama bottoms and a threadbare Star Trek T-shirt riddled with holes.

The part-time deejay and game player looked up from his computer, where he spent most of his time when he wasn't helping me with a party. I wondered whose secret site he was trolling at the moment. The FBI? CIA? TMZ?

"'S'up, Pres?" he said, typing at rapid-fire speed.

"Got a question for you." I sat down in Berkeley Wong's vacated chair at the desk opposite Duncan's and swiveled back and forth. Berkeley shared office space with Duncan and the two spent much of their time battling each other online. Apparently he was out videotaping something.

"Uh-oh," he said, still typing.

"I need some information."

"Like what?" Still typing.

"Like how to find out more about people using the Internet."

"Oh, you mean you want to find a needle in a haystack? Like who murdered that lady at your party?"

"Maybe," I said coyly, fully aware that he saw right through me.

"So you don't think that winery owner did it?"

"Rob? I'm not sure, but my gut says no."

Duncan finally stopped typing, sat back, and folded his hands in front of him. "Okay. Well, there are lots of ways to find out stuff about someone—as long as you're using the information for good instead of evil." He raised a devilish eyebrow.

"Like you?" I said, sarcastically.

He grinned. "Yeah, so if you want to check out, like, a potential employee, or a possible date, or find out if your new roommate is a serial killer, you can pay a professional investigation site to do the work for you. But if you want to save money and do it yourself, try Zaba Search.com—it's free if you want to track down names, addresses, phone numbers, e-mail addys, birth dates, stuff like that. If you want more info, you can pay them or go to another site like NetDetective.com and find out about criminal backgrounds, sex offenders, home values, court records, long-lost relatives. Then again, you could just Google them or use Facebook to find them. You'd be surprised how much you can learn that way."

"Okay, what do I need to know besides the person's name?"

"Their relatives' names. Friends. Their interests or hobbies. Any clubs they might belong to. Professional organizations. News clippings. What school they went to."

I jotted down his tips on a piece of scrap paper on Berk's desk.

"If you have a phone number, Google it or use a reverse-directory Web site. Try Craigslist and eBay using their names. And Classmates.com will tell you all kinds of things—if the person has signed up for it."

"Thanks, Duncan. This is great. A little overwhelming, but helpful."

Duncan spun back to his computer and resumed his bullet-speed typing. "Let me know if you find anything interesting—or you get stuck."

I spent the next two hours in my office trying to find out more information about anyone closely associated with JoAnne, including Rob—Allison, Javier, the Briens and Madeiras, even Kyle Bennett. When Brad peeked in the door two hours later and said, "Lunch?," I was surprised at the time: two o'clock. I'd forgotten all about eating.

"Hi!" I said, sitting up in my chair and stretching my weary back, hands, and fingers. Everything ached from all the typing I'd been doing.

"Welcome home," he said. "You hungry?"

"Starved, as usual. And I could use a break." I rolled my head to loosen my stiff neck. "How did your cleanup go?"

"Don't ask, or you won't want lunch. I need something to get the smell of cleaning fluids out of my nose."

I turned off the computer and stood up. "Can we keep it short and simple? A burger and garlic fries from the Treasure Island Grill would be perfect. After that dinner last night, I swore I'd never eat again. Besides, I've got so much event-planning work to catch up on."

I grabbed my purse and we walked the few hundred yards to the tiny café next to the yacht club, ordered the food, then sat out in the covered patio to enjoy ice-cold beers and a view of the windsurfers.

"Do you have a lot of party requests?" Brad asked after a sip of beer.

"Yeah, and I haven't gotten back to any of them."

He frowned. "What have you been doing?"

I nodded toward the windsurfers. "Surfing."

"Oh. So you're trying to find the killer online?" he asked smugly.

"Very funny. Duncan gave me some tips on how to search for people on the Internet." I opened my purse and pulled out several printed sheets of information.

"So whodunit?"

"Aren't you the comedian today," I said. "Well, for one thing, JoAnne Douglas's winery was about to go into bankruptcy, according to county records. She was hurting for money."

"A reason for her to be murdered?" Brad asked.

"Don't know." The hamburgers arrived and I ate a couple of French fries before continuing. "I also found out Rob Christopher and Marie Michaels attended Napa High School, according to the online yearbook. Rob played football, Marie was a cheerleader. Rob went on to study wine at UC Davis, while Marie majored in marketing there. All of this was on UCDAlumni.edu.

After they got married, they started their winery and seemed to be doing well, although last year they lost money, no doubt due to the economy. That was from the business section of the *Napa Times*."

"Wow. You found a lot. But I still don't see a strong reason for murder." Brad took a big bite of his burger.

"I'm not done yet," I said. "Listen to this: Allison was married for a short time to Angus McLaughlin—"

Brad stopped chewing, his eyes wide.

"That's the guy who runs Napology."

"Yep. The marriage only lasted a few months before he divorced her. Apparently she kept her maiden name and never married again. I also found a couple of police reports. Allison has been arrested several times over the years for buying and selling drugs. She was probably headed toward being homeless and on the streets if Rob and Marie hadn't taken her in."

"Hmmm," Brad said, taking a swig of beer. "Does she have a Facebook page?"

"Yes, but it's only open to people she accepts."

"Oh, you can get around that."

"How?" I took a mouthful of my burger before the rumblings in my stomach could scare off the seagulls flying overhead.

"Check out her friends list, friend them, then see what Allison has posted to their sites."

"Never thought of that."

Brad took another bite, letting the ketchup trickle down his fingers. There wasn't a juicier burger in the whole Bay Area.

"Brad," I said after a few more fries, "Allison was with a different old guy last time."

"Yeah?" Brad set down the burger and used three napkins to wipe the ketchup from his fingers. "Maybe that's why she plays bingo. Not because she's traded her drug addiction for a gambling addiction. Maybe it's because she has a sweet tooth . . ."

"A sweet tooth?"

"Yeah. All those lonely old men who come to play bingo. With all that money they've been saving over the years. Maybe she's playing a different game—like 'Who's Your Daddy?' . . ."

I looked at Brad. A light went on. "You think she's looking for a sugar daddy!"

Chapter 18

"It makes sense when you think about it!" I said. "Allison flirts with everyone. She even came on to you."

"Even?" Brad said, raising an eyebrow.

"I didn't mean it that way. You're hot. Of course she'd come on to you. But all those other old guys?"

"Old?"

"I didn't mean you!"

"Uh-huh."

"Listen. She probably thinks she'll find some elderly rich guy at the bingo hall and either marry him and take his money, or just scam him out of it. I mean, she is attractive. Maybe a little too thin . . ."

Brad grinned at my competitive comparison but said nothing. Smart move.

"Anyway, I need to get back to the office," I continued. "Parties don't plan themselves, you know."

We walked back to Building One, past a couple of windsurfers and an older couple with a dog, and parted at my office door with a promise from Brad to meet for dinner. I went into my office and found Delicia reading the want ads at her desk, a can of Diet Coke beside her.

"Looking for work?" I asked.

She closed the paper and rested her chin in her hand. "The job market sucks, and I need money!"

"I should have more party gigs coming up," I offered, sympathetic to her economic woes. I hovered precariously between staying solvent and going into debt. While the parties had certainly picked up for me after several recent headlining events—the mayor's would-be wedding, the de Young Museum fund-raiser, the séance at the Winchester house, and the zombie party in the cemetery—they were also expensive to produce. Renting tents, tables, chairs, and serving ware. Hiring caterers, entertainers, videographers, and deejays. Those were the tip of the sculpted iceberg. When a party ended, I was usually left with enough money to pay my office and condo rent, along with my mother's care-facility fees, cat food, and maybe a new pair of Mary Janes or some black jeans. Would I ever actually turn a decent profit? Not unless solving the occasional murder paid better. And speaking of pay, I hadn't collected anything from Rob and Marie yet, other than the advance.

"What kind of job are you looking for?" I asked Dee.

"Anything!" she said, throwing her arm in the air.

"As an actress, I've played every role from streetwalker to surgeon. That should qualify me for a few jobs."

I laughed at the thought of Dee playing a hooker.

"Seriously. I can fake just about anything. You want an administrative assistant? I can make coffee. You need a substitute teacher? I can write stuff on the blackboard. You looking for a medical technician? I can diagnose your disease using Wikipedia."

"God help us," I whispered under my breath. "Like I said, I've got a couple of big parties coming up and I'm sure I'll need your brilliant acting skills. One involves chocolate, so be thinking about your costume."

Dee folded the newspaper. "Thanks, Pres. Meanwhile, maybe I'll start my own bingo hall here on the Island and rake in the cash. That seems to be pretty lucrative. What do you think?"

I smiled. I knew her angst would pass and her enthusiasm for life would return with a vengeance. For now, I figured all I could do was keep her busy—and in the occasional paycheck.

"Here, I've got a job for you. Return some of these messages for me and find out what these people want in terms of an event." I handed her slips containing requests for a Historical Scavenger Hunt on Angel Island—the Ellis Island of the West—a Bay to Breakers 12K Run and Wacky Costume Party, a To Die for Chocoholic Extravaganza at the Ghirardelli Chocolate Festival, and a Día de Los Muertos—Day of the Dead—Celebration in the Mission. They all sounded like fun.

While Dee made phone calls, I returned to the Internet to look for more information. I did a search for ex-governor Dennis Brien and was overloaded with hits. When he was governor, his name had been in the papers on a daily basis. News had quieted down since he left office, with only a brief mention of his winery purchase and construction of his Napa mansion.

I thought about the message Allison had sent to Dennis. She'd wanted him to contact her and said it was urgent. What could have been so urgent? Had he called her after I left his winery? Was something going on between Allison and Dennis? Like an affair?

I had no evidence of anything like that. Not yet, anyway. Finding physical evidence would require another visit to the Purple Grape—and Allison's room.

Temporarily pushing aside thoughts of illegal search and seizure, I wondered if I could find anything on the other neighbors, Nick and Claudette Madeira. I typed in their names, but all that came up were accounts of various social events they had hosted or attended. I finally found one mention of their legal fight with JoAnne Douglas—she had sued them for "disturbing the peace, congestion, and littering, due to the heavy influx of tourists each weekend," but she had withdrawn the suit when they made a "donation" to her cause. Nick and Claudette were allowed to continue opening their "castle" and grounds to the public—and charging a hefty fee. Had the Madeiras held a grudge because of JoAnne's attempts to halt their business? Had JoAnne been planning something else to interfere with their moneymaking enterprise?

When I hit a dead end, I entered in Javier Montoya's name, remembering his last name had been written on the side of his pickup truck.

Nothing.

No Facebook, no Web site, no news articles, no property reports, no legal infractions.

How had the Internet not yet caught up with Javier Montoya? I wondered. I figured anyone with a birth certificate was Google-able.

Birth certificate.

Could that be it? Was Javier here illegally? He'd certainly kept a low profile. If he was illegal, had JoAnne found out and threatened to turn him in? Was she blackmailing him and he killed her for it?

I rubbed my forehead, trying to keep a grip on my imagination. The possibilities seemed limitless. My gray cells were turning into black holes. At this point I was convinced everyone had done it, just like the plot of *Murder on the Orient Express.* Where was Hercule Poirot when I needed him?

I made one last circuitous effort to find out more about JoAnne via Natalie Mattos, her hired pourer. I typed in Natalie's name and the word "Facebook" and watched her page come up. Unfortunately, it was blocked: "Natalie only shares *some* profile information with everyone. If you know Natalie, add her as a friend or send her a message."

I friended her but knew it would be a while before I got a response. Remembering what Brad had suggested, I checked her friends list. There were more than three hundred of them. I clicked "Friends in Common." Bingo! The Purple Grape Winery popped up. Interesting. I searched further and found she'd also friended the Briens' winery and the Madeiras' winery, as well as several others in the area.

I clicked on the Purple Grape link and read over the

latest entries from the winery. Nothing about the murder, of course. In fact, nothing posted at all since the party, which made sense. I scrolled down, searching for an entry from Natalie or anyone else I recognized. After going back several weeks, I had found nothing significant.

All I knew at this point was that Natalie knew the Christophers, along with several other vintners in the area. Probably because she had tried to get jobs at their wineries.

"Done!" Dee announced, hanging up the phone after completing several calls.

"Already?" I asked, her news jerking me out of my search.

"Yep. You'll be busier than Martha Stewart for the next few months if you take all these jobs. They're very high profile, which means big money and great for business. For the Angel Island one, I thought I'd dress up as one of the Chinese immigrants. I'm one-quarter Vietnamese, you know. Maybe I'll come as a skeleton for the Day of the Dead party. I'm thinking a Beach Blanket Babylon outfit for the Bay to Breakers gig. And I could do a sexy chocolate goddess for the Ghirardelli thing. What do you think?"

After only a few phone calls, Delicia had her spark and spirit back. I could see it in her dancing eyes. That's what parties do for people—lift their spirits even in the worst of times. It was part of the reason I enjoyed this event-planning business. I had a career I would never have chosen for myself if I hadn't been downsized from teaching at the university—and been encouraged by my socialite mother.

Brad stuck his head in the office. "Ready to quit for the day? Thought we'd have a quiet night at my place. I'll cook pasta. We can watch a video, play a board game, do some role-playing, you know . . ."

"Role-playing?" Dee repeated, giggling.

"Ignore her," I said to Brad, regarding Dee's nasty innuendo, and sent her a daggered look. "She's giddy from all the jobs she just snagged for Killer Parties.

"Sounds wonderful. Let me finish one more quick thing here and I'll be ready."

Brad pulled up a folding chair and sat down to wait. I guess he knew me well enough to know that "one more quick thing" meant "Have a seat 'cause we're not going anywhere for a while."

I typed in the name "Kyle Bennett," wondering if I could find any dirt on Rob's attorney. Again, I was besieged with links. The first was to his Web site, which featured a large photo of Kyle casually sitting on the corner of his desk holding a law book. Typical. His bio read, "The Kyle Bennett Law Firm, located in the Napa Valley, is a full-service office providing aggressive representation on all legal matters. Please call 1-800-555-5309 to arrange a free consultation."

"Listen to this," I said to Brad; then I read him the short paragraph.

"Pretty broad," he said. "And vague."

"I know. You'd think he'd be more specific. He doesn't include his office address, just says 'in Napa' and gives his phone number. Personally, I wouldn't hire him to bail my cats out of the pound. Even his picture looks fake."

I closed that site and pulled up another link—a

newspaper article mentioning him—and read it over. "Here's a story from the *Napa Times* about how he worked with JoAnne Douglas and her Green Grape group pro bono to help 'save the Napa Valley.' Nothing specific, just generalities. But he'd actually been paid for his work."

Brad didn't answer, busy checking his new Android phone for messages.

I opened another site, and another. All implied much the same thing—that Kyle Bennett was "doing all he could to prevent the Napa Valley from falling to environmental destruction."

I read the last line to Brad.

He looked up from his cell phone. "The guy's a saint," he said, tongue in cheek. "An altruistic savior of the valley."

I frowned. "And now he's supposedly defending Rob Christopher, who's charged with murdering one of his former clients, JoAnne Douglas. Isn't that interesting?" I chewed my lip, pondering what I felt was a conflict of interest for the lawyer.

I shut down the computer. Brad stood up.

"Just one more thing," I said, holding up a finger.

Brad slumped back in the chair.

I picked up my cell phone and dialed a number I had jotted down. A machine answered. I left a message: "Kyle, this is Presley Parker, from the party the other night. I understand you're representing Rob. I need to talk to you—I may have something that will help his case. Could you call me back as soon as possible so we could set up a time to meet?" I left my number and hung up.

"You found out something to help Rob?" Brad asked, surprised. "What is it?"

I laughed. "I've got nothing. I just want Kyle to think I do so he'll make time to meet with me."

Brad shook his head at my logic. "So what are you going to tell him when you meet? That you forgot?"

"Very funny. I'm not sure yet, but I hope it'll come to me on the drive back to Napa."

"You're going back tonight if he calls?"

"No, tomorrow. I don't want to miss your home-cooked meal and the after-dinner entertainment you promised." I winked at him.

"Oh, get a room," Dee said as we headed out the door.

After I checked on my cats, I headed over to Yerba Buena Island to see Brad. The drive between the connected islands was always disconcerting. Where Treasure Island is flat and fairly barren, Yerba Buena is hilly and lush with vegetation. The contrast emphasizes not only the differences in past living quarters between the enlisted men and the officers, but also the esthetics of both environments. While the navy men were bunched together in multistoried or cramped housing, their superiors were provided with individual homes, some of which were palatial.

Brad currently lived in Admiral Bryson's grand three-story home near several other high-ranking officers' houses, including that of Admiral Nimitz. As a part-time security guard for the island, he lived in the place rent-free in exchange for keeping an eye on the historic properties, now abandoned by the navy. To discourage curious tourists from peering into his windows, he'd strung a "Crime Scene—Do Not Cross" ribbon across the front entrance.

I parked at the side of the house, maneuvered myself between the lower and upper ribbons, and headed up the gray painted steps. Brad opened the door and let me inside. I was immediately greeted by Bruiser, the Paris Hilton–type dog Brad had sort of inherited from one of my former clients. He'd renamed the pooch, unable to utter the former name, Chou-Chou, and had planned to find a home for him as soon as possible. Naturally, he fell in love with the ADHD poodle-something cross and didn't have the heart to give him away. When he had to work cleaning up after dead people, he'd hired the neighbors—a single mom and her young son, Spencer—to dog-sit. Needless to say, the one time we tried hosting a play date with his dog and my cats, we were lucky to get out alive. And so was Bruiser.

I followed Brad into the kitchen, the heart of the home, mainly because most of the other rooms lacked furniture. He'd outfitted only the dining room area, next to the kitchen, turning it into a classic man cave, with more electronic entertainment equipment than a Hollywood studio.

I preferred the cozy nook between the kitchen and the dining room and sat at the small table, which was currently covered with Legos, Star Wars action figures, and a plastic Spider-Man cup.

"Been entertaining?" I asked, sliding the toys and cup aside to make room for dinner plates and wine-glasses.

Brad pulled out some red peppers, tomato, bacon, and half-and-half from the refrigerator. From the cupboard he retrieved an onion, some garlic, and a bottle of Charles Shaw—aka Two-Buck Chuck. That wine was seemingly everywhere, thanks to its cheap price.

"Yeah, Spencer was over earlier. He brought Bruiser back. His mother had to do an errand and he didn't want to go, so I let him hang out here."

"You bought him these toys?"

He nodded. "I figured that way he wouldn't touch any of mine," he said, nodding toward the HDTV flat screen, Xbox, and other guy toys in the dining room.

"You're so sweet!"

"Knock it off. I'm not sweet. I'm a tough macho man who just happens to have a girly dog and a five-year-old best friend. Wine?"

"Two-Buck Chuck? Sure you can afford it?" I teased.

"Hey, it's not half-bad. You know the story behind this wine?" He filled two glasses with the deep purple cabernet.

"I heard it had something to do with a divorce. The husband wanted to screw over his ex-wife so he slashed the price of the wine and that way she wouldn't get as much money." I took a sip. It passed my "drinkability" test.

Brad grinned. "Nope. Urban legend, although it makes a great story. I've also heard that an airline went out of business because it bought too much wine and had to unload it. And that Charles Shaw—who doesn't exist, by the way—is a billionaire who wanted to share the nectar of the gods with the common people."

"Funny! So what's the real story?" I took another sip.

"The company is owned by Fred Franzia, a relative of Ernest Gallo. He runs Bronco Wines, the fourth-largest wine producer in the country."

"You're kidding!" I took another swallow under the guise of "tasting" it.

Brad took a sip and licked his lips. "Truth is, Franzia had a lot of grapes, which made Two-Buck Chuck cheap to produce. Now the wine has this whole cult following."

"I'll bet the people in Napa don't like him undercutting the price so drastically."

"No doubt. He owns something like thirty square miles of vineyards and produces a bunch of other cheap brands, like Napa Ridge, Red Truck, Fat Cat."

"I love Red Truck! The label is so cute!"

"You buy wines because of the labels?" He looked at me as if I'd lost my mind.

"Sometimes," I said defensively. "I got a great one from Target called Mommy Juice that I gave to a friend with a new baby, figuring she'd need it. And one I found online called Bored Housewife. Gave that one to another friend who'd just gotten married. They make great gifts. And they cost more than two dollars, I can tell you that."

Brad shook his head and returned to the kitchen to magically change ordinary ingredients into a tasty pasta ragout. "By the way, I heard from Luke," he said, as the smell of simmering garlic overcame the bouquet of the wine.

I sat up, eager to hear the news. "What did our detective friend say?"

"Not much, I'm afraid. The Napa cops claim to have solid evidence that Rob killed JoAnne, but they're keeping it close to the vest. Sounds like they have an airtight case. They're probably going to proceed with murder one, Luke said."

"Oh God." I sank down, disappointed, and worried about how this would affect Marie.

My cell phone rang.

"Hello?"

"Presley? This is Kyle. So glad you called. I'd love to meet with you. Are you free tonight? I know a nice little bar downtown where we could get a drink."

Kyle. I'd nearly forgotten about him.

"Oh, hi, Kyle. Thanks for returning my call. I can't make it tonight, but how about first thing tomorrow morning?"

"Sounds good. We can have coffee. So what's this promising news you have regarding Rob's case?"

"I don't want to discuss it over the phone, Kyle. I'll talk to you tomorrow. Where's your office located?"

"Why don't we meet at From the Ground Up, near the police station? My treat." This guy was awfully eager to hook up.

"Actually, I'd prefer somewhere more private, like your office. This is pretty sensitive information."

He paused a moment, then said, "Sure, I understand. All right. Come to my office. I'm at 1984 Main Street in downtown Napa. See you tomorrow. Around nine?"

"Perfect," I said. "By the way, how's Rob doing?"

"He's hanging in there. We'll chat more tomorrow."

"Okay," I said, and hung up.

I turned to Brad, who'd been watching me from the kitchen.

"You have a date?"

"Not a date. A meeting. That guy is a sleazeball."

"So what are you going to tell him?"

"Like I said, I'll think of something."

Brad hoisted cooked pasta onto two plates, covered it with chunky red sauce, added a slice of fresh sourdough bread on the side, and set the plates on the table.

"Seriously, Presley. You need to be careful. Someone murdered JoAnne. And if it wasn't Rob, the killer is probably still running around the Napa Valley. That includes Kyle Bennett."

"I know. I've learned from experience not to be too trusting. Believe me, I'll be careful." I stabbed my fork into the steaming pasta, twirled it around, and brought it to my mouth, savoring the garlicky flavor. Yum. I washed it down with a gulp of Chuck. "Delicious!"

"Thanks. Got the recipe from one of those cooking shows. Just wait until dessert . . ." His eyes sparkled and he took a sip of wine.

"Something chocolate, I hope?"

"Yes, but you'll have to win it in a game I have planned. I'll give you a *clue*," he said, emphasizing the last word. "You're going to be Miss Scarlet. I'll be Professor Plum. And there's an edible rope involved . . ."

Chapter 19

PARTY-PLANNING TIP #19

If you want to offer your guests the total wine experience—and you don't own your own large winery—consider purchasing a WinePod. Grow a few grapes in your yard (or buy some); then use your home-winery gizmo to crush, ferment, and serve your wine. The price, however—two thousand dollars—could go a long way toward buying nearly a hundred cases of Two-Buck Chuck instead.

By the time I reached Napa early the next morning, I still had no real plan for my meeting with Kyle Bennett. My ADHD kept me from focusing on the task, and instead my mind wandered back to the short list of suspects I'd developed. But by the time I pulled up to his street, I knew one thing—Kyle would be a great source of information, perhaps more so than the bingo players, given his job. I just hoped I didn't have to Mace him if he tried anything. Mainly because I didn't have any Mace.

But I did have one of the souvenir corkscrews in my purse that I'd passed out as party favors, just in case.

I parked, then double-checked the address he'd given me to make sure I was in the right place. I didn't know what I'd been expecting, but certainly not the rundown two-story Victorian mansion squeezed between two modern three-story buildings. This shabby place was Kyle's law office?

I stepped over a crack in the crooked stone path, which was outlined with weeds that had been mowed down but not removed. The white house paint on the exterior walls was peeling and the door had black scuff marks at the bottom, as if it had been kicked. To my surprise, the door was wide open.

I stepped inside and realized that the mansion had been divided into small offices. I found Kyle's door with a brass plate that read "Law Offices" and rang the bell. After several seconds, his door opened.

"Presley!" Kyle greeted me as if I were his long-lost love. "Come in, come in. Excuse the place. I don't spend much time here—it's just temporary. I'm waiting for my new office building to be finished. But you wanted privacy and that's what you'll get here."

He ushered me inside to a small room. A cluttered desk took up much of the space, stacked with what looked like mail, notepads, and legal forms. Apparently Kyle didn't have a secretary, at least not from what I gathered. The walls were cheap paneling, bare of pictures or posters, and the hardwood floors were nicked and scratched and hadn't seen wax or a cleaning in months, if not years.

Overall, not much of a law office. But like he'd said, it was temporary.

Kyle gestured toward a garage-sale chair, then unbuttoned his suit jacket, hiked up a pant leg, and sat on the corner of his desk, just like in his Web site picture. I looked up at him as he grinned down at me. The power seating was obvious.

"Now, what have you got that's so important to Rob's case?" he asked. "I could sure use something solid, I'll tell you that."

"Well, I just don't think Rob did it," I said simply.

He blinked a few times, shaking his head as if he didn't understand me. "That's it? You don't think he did it?"

"No, of course not," I said, brushing invisible lint off my black jeans. "I have my reasons."

"Like what? Because I'm going to need some heavy-duty evidence, not just your opinion."

I held up a finger, beginning my countdown. "First of all, motive. There's no logical reason for Rob to kill JoAnne."

"What about their constant arguments and her threats against him?"

"Circumstantial." I'd learned that word from watching *Perry Mason* reruns. I held up another finger. "Second, opportunity. It seems like nearly everyone had the chance to kill JoAnne at that party, not just Rob."

Kyle's shoulders sank. "I suppose, but he manned the table off and on where they found JoAnne. He could have spotted her, hit her over the head with a wine bottle, stabbed her with the cheese knife, then stuck in the corkscrew and gone on with the party."

"So could Allison, or Javier, or anyone else who happened to stand behind that table anytime during the evening."

Kyle ran his hands through his moussed hair, obviously beginning to realize I was full of crap. I noticed he was wearing an expensive diamond ring.

"Finally," I pressed on, "method. The weapon came from his own antique corkscrew collection. If Rob wanted to get away with murder, he isn't going to incriminate himself by using something that points to him. Especially when there were all those cheese knives and Killer Parties corkscrews lying on the tables for anyone to grab."

Kyle sighed. "Presley, the cops think he was trying to make a point."

"What, that he's guilty?"

Kyle jumped up from the corner of the desk, essentially dismissing me. "No, that she tried to screw him, so he screwed her." He sighed. "Is that all you've got, Presley? I was hoping—"

I was losing him—and I couldn't leave without accomplishing what I came for—information. In a panic, I blurted, "I know who did it."

He raised a suspicious eyebrow. "You know who did it?" he repeated.

"Yes," I said, looking up at him standing over me. "I can't prove it yet, of course. But I'm close."

"Uh-huh," he said. He crossed his arms, clearly tired of my antics.

I quickly redirected the conversation. "You worked for JoAnne for a while, right?"

"Yes?" he said, his knuckles tightening and turning white.

"Why did you stop?"

"Because she was going off the deep end with her

fanatical ideas. I want to save the Napa Valley as much as anyone, but she was becoming deranged."

"That's what I keep hearing from people in town. That's why I think someone else at the party that night killed her. Someone who, for some reason, wanted to make it look like Rob did it."

"You're saying you think someone framed him?" Kyle said, frowning.

I heard a sound at his office door. Distracted, I turned around and watched the mail slot open. Several envelopes cascaded onto the floor.

Kyle swooped down and scooped up the pile. He riffled through the envelopes, then paused at one. His eyes narrowed as he slit open a plain white legal-sized envelope. Instead of removing the contents, he peered inside, pressed his lips together, turned the envelope facedown on the mail pile, and set it on his desk.

Hmmm.

"Uh . . . where were we?" he asked, sitting back down on the desk corner. "Oh yes, you were saying something about Rob being framed."

I started coughing.

He leaned over. "Are you all right, Presley?"

I coughed again. "Could you"—*cough*—"get me"— *cough*—"some water?" The trick had worked for my mother—why not me?

"Certainly." He hopped off the desk and went into a back room. When I heard water running, I snatched the opened envelope. No return address other than the stamped words "Napatite Company."

I thought about stuffing the thing in my purse but didn't want to be arrested for mail theft.

I didn't have much time. Kyle would be back in an instant with a glass of water.

To stall, I called out, "Could I have ice please?" hoping that would take him longer. Still fake coughing, I looked inside the envelope to see what had caused a reaction in Kyle.

Oh my God.

"Here you go," Kyle said, appearing from behind the corner. My back was to him.

Startled, I dropped the envelope. It fell to the floor and floated under the desk.

Uh-oh.

"Thank you," I said, taking the water with trembling hands. I sipped it, miraculously curing my cough, and handed the glass back to Kyle. "Sorry about that. Allergies."

Kyla nodded, eyeing me strangely. Had he seen me reading the contents of the envelope?

"Well, I have to be going," I said, and abruptly rose. Reaching down for my purse, I caught a glimpse of one corner of the envelope. There was no way I could retrieve it now.

"All right. Uh, let me know if you find the killer—and the evidence to support that."

I laughed nervously. "Yeah, I guess I think I'm Nancy Drew, huh?" I laughed again, louder this time, in an effort to show him how silly I was being. "Oh, by the way, do you happen to know Natalie Mattos?" Of course, he had to know her, if he'd worked for JoAnne.

His eyes widened in a flash of recognition before he shook his head. "I . . . don't think so. Is she a suspect?"

Odd response, I thought. "No. She works—worked—

for JoAnne. I thought you might know her, since you used to represent JoAnne."

Kyle clapped his hand on his forehead. "Oh yes, now I know who you're talking about. Nice young girl. Pretty. All that dark hair. Cute figure. Smart too. She knows a lot about wine. Do you think she did it?"

The guy needed acting lessons if he wanted to be a good liar. I wondered how he came across in a court of law. "No, no. I just wondered if you could tell me anything about her."

"Why?"

"I met her the other night . . . at bingo." I decided not to mention visiting JoAnne's winery.

Kyle looked away when he said, "Not really. Only saw her a couple of times."

From the way he'd described her, I got the feeling she'd made a big impression on him. Was he hiding something?

I headed for the door, then had a second thought about the envelope I'd accidentally dropped under the desk. Napatite Company—was that another of Angus McLaughlin's properties, under the umbrella of Napology?

"Sorry, one last question," I said again, feeling like Columbo with his endless "last questions." All I needed was a trench coat and a cigar.

"Yes?" He looked truly impatient now. Time to leave.

"Do you know Angus McLaughlin very well? His name keeps coming up."

"No. I mean, everyone knows who he is. He's been buying up all the wineries that are in default. But I don't know him personally."

"Did JoAnne know him?"

"I doubt it," he said. "Why, you think he might have had something to do with JoAnne's death?"

I shrugged.

"What reason would he have? Sure, they were at odds over the environmental issues, but if Angus McLaughlin wants something, he just buys it."

"Did he ever try to buy Rob's winery?"

Kyle looked at the door, as if visualizing me on the other side. "I don't know. They've always been competitors. I think they went to school together. Angus has done better than Rob in terms of business success, but physically, the years have been a little kinder to Rob than Angus. He's not in great shape."

"I heard a rumor that Marie's sister, Allison, was married to Angus for a short time. Is that true?"

"That's the rumor, although she doesn't talk about it, and it was years ago. I heard she married him right after Marie married Rob—I think she had a crush on Rob. But then she got into drugs and Angus divorced her. Unfortunately for Allison, that was before he made all his money."

"Ouch. That must have hurt," I said, intrigued at this juicy information.

"No doubt," Kyle said. "The Christophers were saints to take her in, after she got out of jail and rehab. But now I don't know what's going to happen to her."

My question was: What was going to happen to Rob with Kyle as his lawyer?

I started the car, stunned by something I had learned at Kyle's office that he hadn't told me. Inside the envelope

that Kyle had opened was a personal check from Angus McLaughlin.

For ten thousand dollars.

No wonder peeking inside had caused my hands to
shake and the envelope to drop. I'm sure it was something I wasn't supposed to see.

I drove off, certain that Kyle would come chasing me
down the street when he noticed the envelope was
missing. I hoped he'd spot it on the floor and just figure
a gust of wind blew it off the desk. Otherwise, he'd
know I'd been snooping—and think I'd stolen it.

And maybe kill me? Maybe—if he was hiding some
kind of shady business relationship with McLaughlin.
After all, he denied knowing the guy when obviously
he did.

I had to find a safe place to think until I figured a few
things out. The Christophers' winery was only a few
miles away. I wanted to check on Marie anyway, and
ask Allison a few questions. I sped away, reaching the
Purple Grape in record time.

The crime scene tape still encircled the party area
when I arrived. Grabbing my purse, I hopped out of
the MINI, followed the path to the front door, and
knocked. No answer. I knocked again and rang the bell.
Still no answer. Granted, it was a large home, but surely
if someone was inside, they'd have heard me ringing
and pounding.

A chill suddenly ran down my back.

Oh God. What if Marie had tried to commit suicide
again?

I pounded on the door, rang the bell until my thumb

hurt, then remembered—I still had the key! I jammed it into the lock, turned the handle, and let myself in.

"Marie? Allison?" I shouted their names several more times.

The house was deadly silent.

I raced down the hall to Marie's room. Empty.

Growing more frantic, I searched the other rooms, then knocked on the door of Allison's "suite" at the back of the house.

No answer.

I tried the handle. It was locked.

I peered through the window. All I could see were strewn clothes, entertainment magazines, and food cartons, but no sign of Allison.

I wasn't particularly surprised that Allison wasn't around, but where had Marie disappeared to?

I returned to the kitchen and saw no signs of a struggle or anything unusual. Aside from Allison's messy place, the rest of the house was perfect. I checked for a note or some sign Marie had gone out—missing car keys, missing purse—but I found her handbag where she kept it on a small stand in the hallway, her keys inside.

Maybe she'd taken a walk in the vineyard.

With a killer on the loose?

Chapter 20

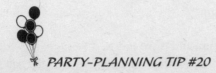

PARTY-PLANNING TIP #20

Add to your wine-tasting experience by having guests stomp harvested grapes! Sure, machines can get the juice out of grapes faster (and more hygienically), but where's the fun in that? In fact, grape stomping is quickly becoming a championship sport, so help your guests start training for the Wine Olympics!

I was about to head out for a vineyard hike in search of Marie when my cell phone rang.

I checked the ID.

Uh-oh. Kyle Bennett. I had a feeling he was wondering where his check had gone to.

"Hello?" I said, bracing myself.

"I think you have something of mine," Kyle said. His voice, low and even, scared the crap out of me.

"What do you mean?" I asked, playing dumb.

"You know exactly what I mean," he said. "Where's the check?"

I immediately went on the defensive. "You mean the

one for ten thousand dollars from Angus McLaughlin?"

No response.

"I'm curious why you received a check from the CEO of Napology," I continued. "I thought you represented the underdog wineries in their fight against corporate takeovers. It looks like a conflict of interest, to say the least."

More silence, then, "We have to talk. Where are you?"

I thought about telling him I didn't have the check, that it had fallen under his desk, but decided I might be able to use this to gain information. Still, no way was I going to meet this guy alone again. For all I knew, he could be the killer.

"Okay, where do you want to meet?"

"Where are you?"

"In my car," I lied.

"Come to my office."

"How about somewhere public, like that café you mentioned?"

"From the Ground Up. It's just down the street from my office. I'll see you there in twenty minutes—or I'll call the police and have you arrested for theft. And that will just be the beginning of your problems."

He hung up the phone before I could say, "Are you threatening me?"

Twenty minutes. I checked my watch. My search for Marie would have to wait. I just hoped she wasn't in any kind of trouble. I headed out the door, planning to call Brad and let him know where I was going—just in case.

And I'd keep the corkscrew party favor in my purse handy too.

I was about to get in my car when I heard a noise coming from the wine-storage building, adjacent to the Christophers' three-car garage. Thinking it might be Marie—and still anxious to make sure she was safe—I stepped over and peered in the open sliding door. The large, cavernous room was dim, but shards of morning sunlight pierced the semidarkness, allowing me to see the rows of giant wine barrels lining both sides of the walls.

The noise came again, from deeper inside.

It sounded like the clink of a bottle.

"Hello?" I called out, hoping to hear Marie's voice.

The sound stopped.

Someone was in here. And I sensed whoever it was didn't want me to know.

Javier?

I reached into my purse, pulled out the corkscrew, and gripped it in my hand like a knife.

I took a step forward, straining to see into the semidarkness ahead. Off to the right, I spotted a dim light emanating from another room. I recalled from the tour Rob had given Mother and me that this was a storage room for the bottled wine.

I broke out into a sweat. The corkscrew in my hand felt slippery in my moist palm. My heart pounded like something out of a horror movie. "The Tell-Tale Heart."

I thought about backing out and calling the police. My mama didn't raise no dummy, like that scantily clad teenage girl who hears a noise and goes into the dark basement, only to be murdered by a demented killer. Unless it's just a cat. But what would I tell the cops? Someone is making noises in the Christophers' winery? And then they'd ask me what I was doing there, and then I might be arrested for trespassing, and then I'd go to prison . . .

Forget that.

If it was Marie, maybe she was in trouble. Tied up, bound and gagged, stabbed with a corkscrew, and left for dead . . .

I really needed to stop watching old horror movies.

I took a few more steps, as quietly as I could manage on the cement floor. Luckily Mary Janes don't make noise like spike heels. Another good reason to wear them, besides comfort.

Yeah, Presley. Good time to stop and think about shoes.

I paused and listened.

Silence.

I stepped closer to the lighted room. Just as I was about to reach the doorway, the lights inside went out.

Uh-oh.

"Who's there?" I said. "I've got a weapon." The "weapon" nearly slipped out of my hand from the sweat and shaking.

The light went back on.

"God, Presley, you scared the crap out of me!"

Allison stood in the doorway, a bottle of wine raised above her head. She lowered the bottle. "Don't come sneaking up on people like that!"

"Why didn't you say something when I called out?" I asked, eyeing the bottle.

She flicked one of the earplugs that hung around her

neck. "I didn't hear you." She'd been listening to her iPod. "I saw your shadow."

We both let out breaths of air. To my relief, Allison set the bottle on a nearby table just inside the door, which held about a dozen other bottles.

I followed her inside, relaxing my grip on my corkscrew. Allison spotted the weapon in my hand and her eyes widened. "You . . . ?"

I realized she thought I might be the corkscrew killer. "What? Me? No! I was just holding this to protect myself."

"You always carry around a corkscrew for protection?"

"No. I had it in my purse from the party the other night," I said, defending myself. I tried to turn the tables of the inquisition. "So what are you doing in here, anyway?"

"I was . . . just getting some wine. For personal use." Her eyes shot to a large envelope lying on the table next to the bottles. On top was a stack of wine labels that read "Purple *Great* Merlot."

I looked at her. "Oh my God. You've been selling the Christophers' wine on the Internet, haven't you? Under your own homemade label. Just like JoAnne was supposedly doing."

"So?" she said, stuffing the labels back into the envelope to hide them. "I'm part of the family business now."

"Yeah, but I don't think Rob and Marie meant for you to undersell them. On the sly."

"Listen, Presley, you know nothing about me or my sister. We're very close. No one, not even you, can come between us. So just butt out and mind your own damn business."

"Allison, I'm trying to help Rob," I said. "From the way you've been behaving, it doesn't seem as if you're doing much to clear his name."

She gave a cold smile that made me shudder. "Don't worry. Kyle is taking care of Rob. And I'm taking good care of my sister."

"How? By stealing bottles of wine and selling them at a discounted price? If he finds out you're undermining his business—"

"His business? This is *Marie's* business. She's the one who built this company up from nothing. Rob is a dreamer. Sure, he knows a lot about wine, especially about drinking it, but he has no idea how to run a company. If it weren't for Marie, there would be no Purple Grape."

"Selling behind their backs isn't helping things," I argued. "Obviously Marie doesn't know you're doing this or she wouldn't put up with it."

Allison sighed. "Listen, Presley. I had no choice."

"What?"

She took a deep breath, then said, "JoAnne was blackmailing me. She . . . found out about my affair with Rob and threatened to tell Marie unless I helped her with her online business."

"Wow," I said, stunned at these revelations. "So you two were doing it together?"

"Like I said, I had no choice."

A look of panic crossed Allison's face, then faded just as quickly. Maybe it suddenly dawned on her that I might rat her out.

It suddenly dawned on *me* that she might try to stop me.

Where was Javier?

Where was Marie?

Would anyone hear me if I screamed?

Allison took a step toward me.

I took a step back and gripped the corkscrew I still held in my hand.

"I don't think you're going to do that, Presley." Her eyes almost glowed under the fluorescent lights.

I took another step back, ready for fight or flight.

"Why not?" I asked, stalling, hoping to keep her talking.

She smiled. "Because I got a call from Kyle before you came in here."

Kyle! I'd forgotten all about meeting him at the café to get his check back. Maybe he had news about Rob.

"Why did he call you? Was it something about Rob?"

"No, actually. It was something about you." Allison picked up one of her newly labeled bottles by the neck, supporting it with the other hand while she continued talking. "Kyle and I are, well, you could say we're close. He told me you took something that belonged to him this morning. A check?"

I felt the blood leave my head. "But I didn't—"

She cut me off. "You wouldn't want the police to hear about your theft, would you?"

My legs felt wobbly. Pretending to steal that check was quickly becoming one of the stupidest things I'd ever done. Now both Kyle and Allison were threatening me.

I decided to go along with it. "Listen, Allison. I'll go to jail if I have to, to protect Rob and Marie, so go ahead and call the cops. I've got a bigger issue on my mind—unlike you—and that's trying to save your brother-in-law's neck."

Allison snickered. "Yeah? How's that going for you?"

I shook my head in disbelief at her callous attitude toward Rob. "You really are a piece of work, Allison. What do you think this is going to get you? The winery?"

Allison set her jaw. I was onto something.

Allison took another step toward me, bottle in hand. "It's time for you to leave, Presley. The party's over for you. Your services are no longer required. And from this point on, you're trespassing here. So stop sticking your nose into my family's business. Got it?"

"I'll stop if and when Marie tells me to. She's the one who asked me to help clear Rob, and I'm not leaving the Purple Grape until I see her—alive and well."

Allison's face hardened. She looked as if she wanted to stomp me like a plump grape.

A bloodcurdling scream pierced the tense air, startling us both.

Allison froze.

My heart stopped.

"That sounded like Marie," Allison said. Bottle still in hand, she dashed past me and fled the storage room.

I was right behind her.

Chapter 21

PARTY-PLANNING TIP #21

Dress up your wine bottles by making your own personalized labels! Find some clip art, such as a picture of grapes, or scan in a snapshot of yourself
dressed like Lucy in her wine-stomping episode.
Make up a name for your wine, such as "Presley's
Pinot" or "Blood Red"; then print the labels out on
adhesive paper. Cut out your labels and adhere
them to your wine bottles.

"Marie!" Allison yelled as soon as she reached the outside of the building.

Another scream.

Allison ran in the direction of the sound, which led
her—and me—to another storage building behind the
garage, where the Christophers kept their winemaking
equipment. I followed her as she darted past giant
metal tanks, large glass jugs, wine bottles, siphons, fun-
nels, oversized rubber stoppers, and what looked like
a complicated printing press.

Marie stood in the center of the room, her back to us. She appeared to be staring into a large metal vat, about the size of a hot tub.

Allison slowed her pace as she neared her sister.

"Marie! What is it? What's—"

Allison choked on her words as she looked down into the vat.

I caught up with them and peered inside.

My stomach lurched.

A body was floating facedown in a pool of red wine.

It wore a flannel plaid shirt. A straw hat lay at Marie's feet.

"Oh my God!" I croaked, unable to find my voice.

"Javier," Allison said, recognizing her co-worker. The back of her hand covered her mouth.

Marie grabbed her sister's arm. "I just found him here . . . floating . . . ," Marie said through tears. "I came in looking for him, and saw his hat . . . then, there he was . . . Javier . . ." More tears flowed down her cheeks. Her shoulders shook.

I stepped back, not wanting to see the horrible scene anymore, and pulled out my cell phone with shaking hands. I punched 911, waited for the operator, and said, "We have an emergency. A man has drowned." I gave her the particulars and hung up, my hands still trembling.

I was about to call Brad when I noticed there were two phone messages I'd apparently missed. No wonder, considering the day I'd had. Both had come from the same caller—a number I didn't recognize. While Allison guided Marie outside to wait for the police, I pressed the button on my phone and listened to the first message, in case it was Brad calling from someone else's phone.

"Ms. Parker," the Spanish-accented male voice said. "This is Javier Montoya, Mr. Christopher's winery manager. I know you have been working to free him from jail. I have some information that could help. Can you come to the winery today so I can talk with you? You can call my cell phone when you get here and I will meet you. Please do not tell anyone of this. Is very dangerous."

He left his number and hung up.

I shuddered, remembering the disturbing scene I'd just witnessed.

Javier had called me sometime before he died!

I checked the time: nine ten a.m. He must have called during my drive to Napa. I'd had the radio on and hadn't heard the phone ring.

I listened to the second call from the same number. Nine fifteen. A hang-up.

He'd phoned back only minutes later. Why?

Javier had wanted to tell me something. Something urgent, if he'd called twice. Was it about the murder? What had he known?

And how had he gotten my number?

"Presley!" Allison called from outside the storage building. "Would you mind waiting for the police? I'm taking my sister inside." She wrapped her arm around Marie's waist as she walked to the house.

I dialed Brad. No answer. He often couldn't answer the phone while he was on a cleanup job, with his gloved hands full of chemicals. I left an urgent message asking him to call me back ASAP but decided not to offer the details until I could talk to him in person.

After hanging up the phone, I stepped back to the entrance of the building and looked around for anything that might explain what had happened. Obviously this was no accident—a person didn't just fall into an open vat of wine and drown.

So how had Javier ended up there?

The barrel was at least six feet across, four feet deep. There were no steps to climb on, if a person suddenly wanted to take a wine bath, but one could lean over and perhaps try to take a sip. But who would?

I moved in closer, avoiding the sight of the body, and instead focused on the floor around the vat. I saw the hat and some wine stains, but there were no weapons lying about. I glanced at the shelves nearby and spotted plenty of solid, heavy objects the killer could have used to clobber the victim—a steel bar, a metal tool, a heavy piece of equipment. But none of those lay near the vat. Did the killer grab one of the objects and hit Javier over the head, then carefully replace it, making it a needle in a haystack for the cops to find? A careful killer would probably have wiped off any fingerprints as well.

But if the killer beaned Javier first, wouldn't he have to drag the body over to the vat, lift it up, and dump it in? That took muscle. And would surely cause a splash. There would be wine stains on the killer's clothes, as well as on the floor around the barrel. There were plenty of stains around the vat, but all appeared to be dry.

I'd have to see what the police found before spinning my wheels any further. All I knew at this point was that Javier had had something urgent to tell me and had wanted to meet.

And now he was dead.

A light went on in the fog of my brain. Rob couldn't have killed Javier—he was in jail. That meant Rob could be released—right? It didn't clear him of JoAnne's murder, but it had to be the same person—didn't it?

Or would the police think there were two killers running around Napa Valley?

I heard sirens and stepped out of the storage area into the daylight. Two police cars pulled up, followed by an ambulance and a crime scene van. Detective Kelly stepped out of the car.

"You again?" he said by way of hello, and signaled his men to go inside. "What happened this time?"

"I don't know," I said, then nodded toward the storage building. "Allison and I were in the building next door and we heard a scream. We came running and found Marie hysterical, staring into that vat of wine. She'd discovered her manager, Javier, floating inside."

The detective entered the crime scene building while I waited in the doorway, not wanting to see the body again, yet hoping to overhear any discoveries the police made. After a preliminary search by the detective and crime scene techs, the EMTs began removing the body from the vat. I turned my head, not eager to view Javier's wine-soaked corpse. Again I wondered what he had been planning to tell me. Was it something that could have saved his life?

After the body was placed on a stretcher and taken to the ambulance, one of the officers searched the shelves. I thought he might be looking for the murder weapon, but instead he picked up a long-handled sieve the size of a butterfly net. He rolled up his shirtsleeve and dipped the sieve into the barrel, dredging the wine. After a few moments, he raised the sieve. Inside was a small round object.

Shaking off the wine residue, the officer retrieved the object from the net and handed it to Detective Kelly.

"What is it?" I asked, stepping in closer as the detective examined it.

"It looks like a class ring," he said, squinting as he turned the object around in his hand. He pulled a pair of glasses from his pocket, put them on, and read the details aloud: "UCD, Class of '89." Peering inside the ring, he continued. "To Marie, Love Robert."

Huh. What was Javier doing with the ring Rob had apparently given to Marie?

My cell phone rang. I answered it, hoping to hear Brad's voice.

"Hello?"

"Where the hell are you?" I recognized Kyle's voice. Crap. I'd forgotten all about meeting him.

"I've . . . been detained," I said softly, and stepped away so the detective wouldn't hear me.

"I want my check, Presley!" he demanded. "If you don't bring it over now, I'm going to the police."

I thought about telling him the truth, then changed my mind. I took a deep breath and said, "You know, Kyle, I don't think you're going to do that. I have a hunch that check—written against Angus McLaughlin's personal account—isn't something you want anyone, including the police, to know about."

Dead silence on the other end.

I continued. "I'll meet you, but meanwhile, something's come up that might help your client get out of jail free. I suggest you talk to the police. I'll see you at the station in half an hour and we can have a little chat."

I hung up. That felt good. I should pretend to have blackmail materials more often.

But I still had questions I wanted Kyle to answer—like why he had a check from the CEO of Napology. For now, Javier's body trumped that. Either we had a new killer on our hands, or the person who'd murdered JoAnne was still on the loose and had just doubled his count.

Detective Kelly came out of the house, where I assumed he'd been taking statements from Marie and Allison.

"Ms. Parker," he said, holding his notebook at the ready as he reached me.

Before he could pounce, I blocked him with my own question: "How's Marie?"

"Upset, as you can imagine. Two murders on her property in less than a week. Her sister gave her a sedative, which cut my questioning short. She's lying down."

I thought about Allison giving Marie more drugs. Was that a good idea? Marie was already fragile, and I didn't trust Allison to medicate her, since there seemed to be some animosity between them.

"Did Marie say anything about seeing Javier before he was . . . murdered?" I asked.

Detective Kelly looked at me. "Detective Melvin warned me about you. You like to moonlight as Agatha Christie, don't you?"

"More like Nancy Drew," I said. "Listen, Marie asked me to help out. I may know something that will help you. Quid pro quo?"

He eyed me suspiciously. "If you're withholding evidence—"

"I'm not!" I said. "But I've learned a few things that maybe will help you with your investigation."

"Like what?"

"Like JoAnne had threatened quite a few people in this town. Like Allison had been selling the Christophers' wines under a false label. Like Kyle Bennett is involved in unethical lawyering, or whatever you call it."

The detective cocked his jaw.

"So what did Marie say?" I asked.

He sighed and glanced at his notes. "She said she was taking a walk around the vineyard, looking for Montoya. She wanted to ask him about something. That's when she found him floating in the wine barrel."

"It must have given her quite a shock," I said, remembering her screams. It had certainly given me a shock. "Did you ask her about the ring you found?"

He nodded. "She said it had gone missing a few days ago."

"During the party?"

"Before that."

"Did she say she lost it, or it 'went missing'?"

The detective looked at his notebook again. "She claims she kept it in her jewelry box, along with some other valuable pieces. When she went to retrieve a necklace a few days before the party, she noticed it was gone."

"Did she say anything else was missing?"

"As a matter of fact, she mentioned diamond earrings and a diamond tennis bracelet."

I sucked in a breath. "Did she suspect Javier of stealing her jewelry?"

"She was pretty surprised when I told her what we found in the vat of wine. She said she didn't think Javier would do anything like that, but she couldn't explain why we found it with his body."

I thought a moment. "Okay, I could understand Javier stealing the diamond jewelry in these hard times, especially since he'd been losing work. But why a class ring, since it was engraved—and probably not worth enough to make it worth his while?"

"Diamond studded," the detective said.

It still didn't make sense. "Then why did he end up floating in the wine barrel?"

The detective shrugged. It was becoming his favorite mode of communication. "Maybe he was a fence and planned to keep the money himself.

"Any marks on him?"

"Yeah, the EMT noticed a contusion at the back of his head. Looks like someone hit him first, good and hard, just like JoAnne. Then somehow the perp got him into that barrel and let him drown—or held his head under until he drowned."

I shuddered at the details of his death, as if a wind had swept through me. What had the killer used to bean him?

"Well, if anything," I said, "this lets Rob off the hook, doesn't it? Obviously he didn't do it since he was in jail."

Detective Kelly flipped his notebook closed. "Not so fast. True, he didn't kill Montoya, but that doesn't mean he didn't kill Douglas. We'll hold him until we hear back from the ME and the crime scene techs. We may have a second killer who could have been working with Rob on the outside."

"That's ridiculous!" I said. "Rob's not some mastermind gang leader. He's a winemaker who happened to be at the wrong place at the wrong time. You can't possibly still think he's guilty."

"I don't know what to think yet, Ms. Parker. But if you'll let me do my job, maybe I'll figure it out. And by the way, what I've told you is in confidence. Melvin said I could trust you to be discreet. Annoying, but discreet."

With that, the detective got in his car and drove away, leaving the techs behind to pick over the scene, and me to wonder what the hell was going on in the wine country.

I decided to check on Marie and Allison and make sure there were no suspicious cups of tea or empty pill bottles lying around. Allison was on her cell phone in the kitchen, talking mushy baby talk to someone on the other end. I couldn't make out the words, but her flirtatious tone was clear. I wondered who was on the receiving end of the call. One of her sugar daddies? It seemed awfully inappropriate, considering the recent circumstances. But I expected nothing less of Allison.

I tiptoed past the kitchen entry and walked to Marie's room, hoping to talk to her before she was completely zonked out. I opened the door and peered inside the dark room. The shades had been drawn. Marie lay on her back under a thick comforter that was patterned with grapes and leaves. When I heard her rhythmic breathing, I took a step back, prepared to leave.

"Allison?" Marie's scratchy voice whispered. Her eyes blinked open and she looked at me as if trying to place me.

"It's me, Presley, Marie. I just came to check on you and see if you need anything. I didn't mean to disturb you."

"Allison?" she repeated.

I stepped inside and neared her bed. "No, it's Presley Parker. Allison's in the kitchen. Can I get you anything?"

"Allison . . . ," she said again, her eyes fluttering under the influence of the sedative she'd been given. I hoped it was only a sedative.

"Do you want me to get her?" I asked.

"Allison . . . please . . . leave Rob alone . . ."

I tensed. Marie still thought I was Allison. What was she saying about Rob? I stood still and listened.

"Allison . . . you're young and beautiful . . . you have others . . . please . . ."

Her voice faded off. The heavy breathing resumed. She was out like a light.

I tiptoed out, closing the door behind me. But instead of returning to the kitchen to question Allison, I went to the back of the house, where her in-law unit was located. Listening for Allison's voice, I could hear her still talking on the phone in the kitchen. I tried the door. Unlocked.

I didn't have much time.

Chapter 22

Before your party begins, send the guests tips on wine-tasting etiquette, such as (1) no second tastes; (2) dump unwanted wine into the provided bucket; (3) eat a neutral food such as a cracker between tastes; (4) do not overdrink and become intoxicated; and (5) avoid hitting on the server.

Praying the door to Allison's room didn't squeak, I eased it open, holding my breath. So far, so good. Before I entered, I thought up something to say if I got caught: "Marie asked me to retrieve something-to-be-named-as-soon-as-I-find-it in your room, Allison." Weak, but plausible, I figured. What could she do—hit me over the head and drown me in a pool of wine?

Maybe.

Adrenaline pumping, I scanned the one-room-plus-bath suite to see if anything suspicious jumped out. Of course, nothing did. That would have been too easy. I opened drawers, hoping to spot a hidden will or a wad of cash or a pile of incriminating love letters she'd been using for blackmailing purposes. Nothing.

Hands on my hips, I twisted back and forth, searching for other hiding places. I knelt down and looked under the bed. Nothing but dust bunnies, a single bedroom slipper, and some discarded underwear. Yuck.

Standing and wiping my hands on my jeans, I glanced at the pictures on the walls and easily recognized more scenes from the Mustard Festival painted by Guy Buffet. Unfortunately, there were no safes hidden behind any of them. And I was running out of ideas—and time.

Where would I hide something in a room like this? I wondered. When I was a teenager and didn't want my mom to find my journal, I'd hidden it in my bathroom in my tampon box, figuring she'd never look there.

I entered the opened door that led to the bathroom and checked the medicine cabinet. Inside I found an array of over-the-counter and prescription meds, everything from pain relievers to stomach soothers to fat melters to gas eaters. Even though Allison was supposedly off drugs, she still had a whole pharmacy of common medications at her disposal. Just in case, I checked to see if Marie's name was on any of the labels—it wasn't—but that didn't mean Allison couldn't overdose her sister with some of the meds she had on hand.

I closed the medicine cabinet door and started to back out of the bathroom when I heard footsteps in the hall.

Allison!

While I'd come up with a flimsy excuse to be in her

room, I still didn't want to get caught. If I did, then she might suspect I was investigating her—and that could put me in jeopardy. Frantic, I slipped out of the bathroom and opened another door that I assumed led outside to make my escape.

To my surprise, I found myself not outside, but inside Allison's closet.

Ha! I should have known. No one, especially a woman, can live without a closet.

I pulled the door shut behind me as quietly as I could, ducked under a long raincoat, and prayed it didn't rain. Holding my breath, I listened as she entered the room.

For what felt like an eternity, Allison seemed to putter around, opening drawers, using the toilet, checking the medicine cabinet. Those were the actions I could hear. During the periods of silence, I could only imagine what she might be doing.

Plotting a murder?

Mine, perhaps?

Finally I heard her leave the room, closing the door behind her. Thank God she hadn't wanted anything from the closet. It would have been harder to explain why I was hiding behind her coat than just being in her room.

I exhaled, waited a few more minutes, then opened the closet door and peeked out. The coast was clear. But before I rushed to safety, I decided to tempt fate and take a few more minutes to scour the closet I hadn't known was there.

I checked the shoe boxes—and found shoes. Chanel, Louboutin, Manolo, Choo, Dolce & Gabbana. I checked the pockets of coats and pants—and found some bingo sheets with phone numbers written on them. Finally I reached for the boxes on the overheard shelf and pulled one down. This one held shoes—Stuart Weitzman pumps—but underneath lay a manila envelope, unmarked. I set the shoe box down on the floor and pulled out the envelope. Inside were a bunch of papers.

I switched on the closet light and looked them over. Invoices. Most of them appeared to be from local restaurants.

I read the details and discovered that Allison had been selling the Purple Grape wines to restaurants— and no doubt keeping the payments. She'd probably been costing Rob and Marie hundreds if not thousands of dollars.

Excited about my find, I pulled down another shoe box. Under a pair of expensive Christian Louboutin heels was another manila envelope. I reached inside the envelope and withdrew a handful of letters addressed to Allison.

Curious, I read the letter that was on top.

Allison, please stop sending me letters, e-mails, texts, and stop calling. I love my wife and have no interest in having a relationship with you. That day in the storage room was a mistake I will regret for the rest of my life. I've done what you asked. Now please live up to your promise and leave me alone or I'll tell Marie myself, as much as it would break her heart.

It was unsigned but obviously written by Rob.
So it was true. Rob and Allison had had an affair. If

JoAnne was blackmailing her, could she have been blackmailing Rob about it? If so, what had Rob promised her? Was she somehow responsible for putting Rob in jail? And for Marie's suicide attempt?

I stuck the letter and one of the invoices in my purse, figuring if I got caught now, I wouldn't live to drink another glass of wine anyway, so why not try to take some evidence with me. I checked one more box, and this time found a copy of Rob and Marie's will. Figuring I couldn't steal the whole thing, I left it there, planning to return when I had more time and read it over.

Arranging the shoes boxes the way I'd found them, I closed the closet door, listened for any sound from Allison, and quietly left her room.

My phone rang the second I stepped out into the hall.

If it had rung two minutes earlier . . .

"Presley?"

Allison stood at the end of the hall, eyeing me suspiciously. She'd heard the ring. Crossing her arms in front of her, she said, "What are you doing here? I didn't see you come in."

"Oh, just checking on Marie. She's sound asleep." The phone continued to ring.

"Marie's room is over there," she said, pointing in the opposite direction.

"I know. I needed to make a phone call and didn't want to disturb her, so I stepped down the hall."

"But your phone is ringing."

"Yes, uh, when I called, he didn't answer, so I left a message and I guess he's calling back." The tune—the theme from *The Sopranos*—continued.

"Don't you want to answer it?"

I looked at the phone in my hand. "Yes, of course. Will you excuse me for a minute?" I turned away and softly said hello. It was Brad. I'd recognized his ringtone.

"You okay?" he asked. "You called—it sounded urgent."

"Yes, I mean, no. Uh . . . could I call you back? I'm right in the middle of something."

"Presley . . . ?"

I hung up.

Allison still stood at the end of the hall. "Everything all right?" she asked.

"Oh yes," I said, moving toward her. "It was just my mother. She worries about me. You know how it is."

Allison gave no sign that she did.

"Well, I should be going. I'm hoping Rob will be released from jail soon, since he couldn't have killed Javier. I'm heading to the station to meet his lawyer."

"You're going to see Kyle?" she asked, her jaw working.

"Yes, and I'm late," I said, checking my watch. I gave her a wide berth as I went to the front door.

"You'll keep an eye on Marie?" I said, turning back to her.

"Of course. I'll take good care of her. She just needs to sleep. This has all been very traumatic for her."

"Well, when Rob gets back home, I'm sure she'll feel better," I said.

"*If* he's released, you mean," she said.

"*When*," I returned, and closed the front door behind me.

*   *   *

Bee-otch, I said to myself, a word I'd often heard Delicia use. That's what I thought of Allison. But she was one dangerous bee-otch . . .

I called Brad and told him I was headed back to the police station and would call him soon with an update. I arrived at the station, which was fast becoming my old stomping grounds, and saw Kyle sitting on a railing outside, checking his watch. As soon as he spotted me, he jumped off his perch—the man was quite the percher—and met me as I approached.

"We need to talk," he said, grabbing my arm. He spun me in the opposite direction from the police department. "But not here."

"Let go of me!" I snapped, jerking my arm out of his grip. "First I want to see what's going on with Rob's release."

"I'm handling it. There's no word from the detective yet. You can't do anything at the moment. And you have something of mine I want."

"Fine," I huffed.

"The café is just down the street. Come on."

"God, you're bossy," I said as he led me along. "I'm glad you're not *my* lawyer."

"Don't worry. There's no chance of that happening. If they arrest you for the murders, you're on your own."

I stomped in silence next to him until we reached From the Ground Up café, two blocks from the station. "What kind of coffee do you want?" Kyle asked bluntly, pulling a wad of bills from his wallet when we reached the counter.

"A latte, please. Nonfat. Decaf. Grande. One shot. With a little caramel on top. Hold the whipped cream." I smiled at him, enjoying the irritation I was probably causing.

"Sorry, they don't call it 'grande' here," he said sarcastically. "They call it medium, like they should." He turned his attention to the barista, a girl with piercings in her eyebrow, lip, and nose, and a tattoo around her neck. I shivered from the perceived pain.

Spotting a couple of free stools at the front window, I headed over and sat on one and saved the other for Kyle, knowing he liked to perch. At least if he tried to kill me, anyone walking by would be a witness. Although I didn't have any hard evidence—unless getting a payment from Napology for a hit worked—I certainly hadn't ruled him out.

He returned with what looked like two espressos and set them down on the narrow counter in front of us.

"Perfect," I said, not giving him the satisfaction of getting annoyed that he'd deliberately screwed up my order. "This should keep me going for a few minutes." I added sugar and cream to the tiny cup and took a sip.

Ignoring his coffee, he faced me. "Hand it over," he said. Where was the flirtatious nice guy who'd come on to me at the party?

"I don't have it," I said, and took another sip of the hot drink, knowing I'd just jumped into hot water.

His face grew bright red and I thought he might be experiencing sunstroke. "What do you mean, you don't have it?"

"I don't have it. It fell under your desk. I assume it's still there."

He ground his jaw, then said, "I don't believe you."

"Go see for yourself. I'm not into stealing U.S. mail, but I do want to know why you have a check from Napology. Are you working for Angus McLaughlin? Or is he sending you checks for ten thousand dollars because you're such an honest lawyer?"

"That's none of your damn business," he said, not finding my sarcasm amusing.

"It is if there's a conflict of interest. You could be disbarred for representing people with opposing agendas. And if your clients include JoAnne Douglas and Rob Christopher and Angus McLaughlin, I'm sure there's a conflict."

Kyle's eyes darted around the café. "Shhh! Keep your voice down. People know me in this town."

Only because your mug is on every bench, I thought. "Then I want answers, Kyle. The truth. Are you working for Napology?"

"No." He shifted on the stool. "Well, not exactly, that is. I've been doing a little work for Angus. But nothing that directly conflicts with anything else."

"Really? Isn't McLaughlin trying to buy out wineries that are suffering in this economy? Like the Purple Grape?"

"That's not a *direct* conflict."

To the letter of the law, spoken like a lawyer.

"And what about JoAnne? You were working for her too, at least until recently."

"I admit I was helping her protect the environment. Pro bono, I might add. But that had nothing to do with my other clients."

"No you weren't. She was paying. When she

couldn't afford you anymore, you stopped working for her."

"That's not true. I told you. It was because she'd become a nutcase."

I sipped my espresso and thought for a moment. "So what exactly do you do for Napology?"

He glanced away, his espresso still untouched. "That's attorney-client privilege. Even you should understand that."

Since I was already out on a limb, I decided to shake the tree a little with another wild question.

"What about the will . . . ?" I took another dramatic, lingering sip of my espresso. It needed more sugar and cream and caramel, but I refused to make a face. Instead, I watched his face closely.

He winced. Not much of a bingo player . . . er, poker player.

"The Christophers' will is confidential. I can't discuss it."

Ah-ha! "That's okay. I know all about it," I bluffed. "Marie told me everything. I wonder what the cops will think."

"Look, Presley, I only did what I was told. Rob and Marie asked me to change their will a couple of weeks ago. Originally it was their idea to leave everything to Allison if anything happened to them. But they wrote her out."

"Does Allison know?"

"Of course not. I would never reveal that kind of information. But apparently they told you."

"Are you sure you wouldn't tell Allison?" I asked again.

"I said no."

It was time to turn the corkscrew and dig a little deeper. "Were you having an affair with Allison?"

He pulled back. "Good God, no! That woman is a . . . ," he sputtered, unable to find the right word.

I snorted. "Well, you might be the only one who wasn't fooling around with her."

"Tell me about it. That woman is a geezer freak."

Geezer freak?

"Did you know Allison was selling Purple Grape wines to local restaurants at a discount, using fake labels? And doing it right under Rob and Marie's noses?"

"No, although I wouldn't put it past her."

Speaking of making money on the sly, I still didn't know why Kyle had a check for ten thousand dollars. The rumor around the bingo hall was that Angus McLaughlin was buying up wineries that were losing money and going into foreclosure. Was Kyle in on that in some way?

Another light went on. "You said you've been helping the smaller wineries go green while staying solvent," I said. "Yet several of the wineries you've represented have gone under. Have you been working with Angus McLaughlin in some way, with your insider information? Is that why he's paying you?"

Kyle worked his tight lips.

"Oh my God, that's it, isn't it? You're not only spying; you're double-dipping."

Kyle reared up and grabbed my arm forcefully. "Shut up!" he said, then remembered where he was, looked around, and relaxed his grip.

"Is everything all right?" said a college kid with a brown apron. He had a rag in his hand for cleaning tables.

I looked at Kyle pointedly.

He sat back down on his stool. "Yes, we're fine."

"Ma'am?" the young guy asked me to make sure.

"I think so," I said, still looking at Kyle. "Although I think his espresso is cold. Could you heat it up for him?"

"Sure," the guy said, and took the full cup.

"He'll be back," I said to Kyle, a reminder to keep his paws off me.

He stood up again. "I think we're done here."

"What are you going to do about getting the charges dropped against Rob?"

He ignored my question and stormed out, just as the bewildered café guy brought a fresh hot espresso.

"Can I get that to go?" I asked, sweetly. "And could you put some whipped cream and sugar and caramel in it?"

As the barista returned to the coffee counter to re-make the drink and retrieve a to-go cup, I watched Kyle walk down the street toward the police station.

I was fairly certain Kyle had been reporting information about troubled wineries to Angus McLaughlin, while collecting money from those wineries at the same time. No wonder he had the cash for all those billboards and TV spots, and those expensive suits and shoes, not to mention the car. That dump of an office he supposedly rented had to be a front. I wondered where his real office was—at Napology?

But what reason did he have to kill JoAnne? Had she

found out about his illegal activities and fired him? Or was she blackmailing him?

And what about Javier Montoya? What reason would Kyle have to kill the manager of the Purple Grape? Because Javier found out the truth about him and threatened to expose him?

Blackmail was a pretty common reason for murder. Especially if you were a lawyer trying to build up your reputation and your bank account.

If only I'd heard the ring of my cell phone when Javier had called—I might have all the answers.

What was he going to tell me before he was murdered?

Chapter 23

PARTY-PLANNING TIP #23

Be wary of serving counterfeit wines at your tasting party. To spot a fake, check the cork to see if the vintage is printed on it, look for a label that is "too perfect," and make sure there is a USA strip label on the bottle if it's imported. You can have your wine authenticated by a service if you suspect "foul pour."

Distracted by the recent events, I'd forgotten to call Brad back again. On my walk to the police station, I tried his number; no answer. I left a message asking him to call again when he was free.

There was no sign of Kyle when I arrived at the station. I wondered if he'd gone to the jail to see about getting Rob released. I asked for Detective Kelly, but the sergeant manning the front office said he was out. I hoped he was also at the jail freeing Rob.

I sat in my car for a moment, thinking about Allison and Kyle, who were now my two primary suspects, since their names kept bubbling up like fizzy champagne. If JoAnne had been blackmailing them—Allison for having an affair with Rob and undercutting Rob and Marie's sales, Kyle for conflict of interest and double-dipping—either of them might have wanted to stop her permanently.

Since both were at the party, either one could have set up Rob to take the fall. Why? I wasn't sure. Maybe Rob had discovered their secrets too. As for Allison, that would bring her one step closer to taking over the winery. All she had to do was get rid of Marie and she'd have bingo. And she could easily have put something in her drink.

As for Kyle, framing Rob would take the heat off him and make him look like a saintly lawyer when representing Rob. Kyle could also control the way the case was presented, ultimately screwing over his helpless client.

It was a win-win for both Allison and Kyle.

Maybe they had done it together.

But I was leaning toward Allison. By killing JoAnne and framing Rob, then helping Marie "commit suicide," everything would be hers. She could stop selling wine on the side and, at the same time, not have to worry about JoAnne and her Green Grape group hassling her. Nor would she have to find herself an aging sugar daddy to keep herself in designer shoes and handbags.

Something told me Allison was the favored suspect, but I had no physical evidence, only circumstantial—a letter from Rob regretting their brief affair, invoices proving she was selling wine on the side. What was in that will?

I thought back to the crime scene.

- JoAnne's body was found under one of the pouring tables with a can of green paint nearby. Why? Was she going to lunge out at an opportune moment and douse the party guests with green slime?
- The cheese knife—with Rob's fingerprints—had been inserted into the ground to look like a sprinkler head. Seriously? It wouldn't go undiscovered for long. Why not hide it better?
- The antique corkscrew was used to finish the job. But why? The knife was enough to kill her. Why use one of Rob's corkscrews and not use one of the Killer Parties corkscrews that lay on the table?
- How had the shoe come off, and why had Rob hidden it under his and Marie's bed? If he didn't kill her, how had his fingerprints gotten on the shoe?

I needed to know more about JoAnne, Kyle, and Allison. And I knew just the person who could tell me how to uncover more information.

I punched a number on my phone. "Duncan?" I said, after he answered my call.

"Pres, wassup?"

"I need your help again."

"What is it this time? Need someone's phone located? Some GPS coordinates? The file they keep on you at the CIA?"

"Jeez, I hope they don't have a file on me," I said. "No, I need to find information about a couple of people on the Internet. I've already Googled and Facebooked them and tried everything else. Is there anything else I can do?"

"You tried ZabaSearch? You could try Pipl—they search for stuff that's not so easy to find through Google. If that doesn't do it, you can try Wink, Spock, ZoomInfo, PeekYou, YoName. And the obits are always a good source for dead people."

"Goodness. This will take me all day. Thanks, Duncan." I hung up and tried the various sites he'd mentioned using my laptop. Nothing came up for JoAnne, except her obituary, which had been published in the local paper this morning.

JoAnne Douglas, 39, died unexpectedly on Saturday. Owner of the Douglas Family Winery, JoAnne was an advocate for no growth in the Napa Valley and belonged to the Green Grape Association, a grassroots organization that helps businesses become more environmentally sound. Preceded in death by her mother, Josephine, and her father, Albert, she leaves behind her seven cats: Azrael, Figaro, Fritz, Krazy Kat, Macavity, Mehitabel, and Pyewacket. No services pending. Please send donations to the Green Grape Association of Napa Valley and the ASPCA.

Seven cats? Maybe she wasn't all bad. Just a little off center.

I did a search for the Green Grape Association. A Web site came up, espousing the importance of "going green," and a link to "ten simple ways you can eliminate your carbon footprint." At the bottom, in a very tiny font, was the name of the Web master: "Napatite Company."

Where had I seen that before?

Oh my God. On the envelope containing that check for ten thousand dollars. And Angus McLaughlin.

I did a search for Napatite Company. Several businesses appeared, including Kyle Bennett, Attorney at Law, the Napa County Bingo Hall . . . and Napology.

Was Angus McLaughlin behind *all* of those businesses? It sounded as if he owned not only half the wineries in the valley, but several other companies as well.

It was time to pay the reclusive man a visit.

Napology Corporation looms large in the Napa Valley. The headquarters are situated on a hillside halfway between Napa and St. Helena. I remembered passing the sprawling, ultramodern plantation when Mother and I had gone for our mud baths but had thought nothing of it at the time. The estate posted signs announcing weekend tastings, accompanied by "live music, cheese on the patio, and a spectacular view of the valley."

I drove up the long driveway lined with rosebushes and parked in the mostly deserted lot. Apparently the place wasn't open for wine tasting during the week. I wondered if Angus McLaughlin would be around— and what ruse I'd use to question him.

Locating what appeared to be the front door to the winery, I knocked and waited. No answer. Standing back, I searched for another entry but saw nothing that would give me access to the winery.

I stepped around the side of the curved building,

which seemed more like a modern art museum than a home or winery. A garden path lined with topiaries in the shape of zoo animals led to the back, where a wrought-iron gate kept curious tourists and nosy party planners from trespassing onto private property.

Oddly, a small cabin-like dwelling sat at the back beyond the swimming pool, looking completely out of place in this futuristic setting. I spotted a gardener tending to more rosebushes nearby and walked over. He was short and dark skinned, wearing a straw hat, short-sleeved plaid shirt, jeans, and gloves, and snipping at the bushes.

"Excuse me," I said, "I'm here to see Angus McLaughlin and I'm not sure where to go."

"You the temp he's expecting? He's in his office." The man pointed with the cutting shears to the rustic-looking cabin inside the gate.

The temp? Perfect.

I looked in the direction he pointed. "That's his office?" I asked, surprised.

"Yes." The gardener smiled, revealing a gold-capped tooth. "Mrs. McLaughlin designed the winery, but Mr. McLaughlin built his office like a cabin. It's a replica of the one he owns in Montana."

"Ah, so they compromised," I said. "How do I get in the gate?"

The gardener pulled out a key card from his pocket and swiped it through a metal lock.

"Thank you!" I said, hoping I wouldn't be responsible for the man getting fired for letting me in under false pretenses.

When I reached the door of the log-style cabin, I

knocked and heard a booming "Come in!" from inside. Hesitating for a second, I opened the door.

"Come on, come on!" the voice came again. "You're late."

What a pompous ass, I thought. How long could I play along with this ruse without smacking him? I'd find out soon enough.

"Yes, sir," I said, slowly approaching his massive oak desk, which was roughly carved and notched and stretched nearly six feet across. Two large green leather chairs faced the desk, both resting on top of a white fur pelt. The heads of several animals—deer, boar, and coyote—appeared to lunge from oval plaques on the surrounding walls. Another wall held the hunter's rifle and gun collection in a locked case.

Uh-oh. Who was I about to confront?

"Your desk is over there." The big man pointed with a diamond-ring-studded pinky finger to a smaller desk in the corner. The desk, topped with a computer, faced out, toward McLaughlin.

I glanced at the desk, then back at the man. He was round faced, with a red and splotchy complexion, a bulbous boxer-type nose, and thinning gray hair greased back. Gold rings covered his fingers, matching a gold bracelet and gold chain around his neck. The gray silk shirt he wore was open enough to allow curly gray chest hairs to peek out. Sitting behind his desk, he could have been stark naked from the waist down, for all I knew. Where had that thought come from?

"Uh, yes, sir," I said again, not quite sure what he expected me to do. Go sit down and start typing?

"The temp agency said you type eighty words a

minute. That true? 'Cause I need someone who's competent this time."

"I'll do my best, sir," I said, standing at attention like a good little employee. I hoped the real temp didn't show up anytime soon. This opportunity was golden.

"Well, get to work, then. I need you to retype those forms on the desk and make the corrections I indicated."

I sat down at the desk and moved the pile to my right, as if preparing to do his bidding. Instead, I opened up Word and searched the files for anything that might look interesting.

Like "Payroll."

I opened the file, scanned the list of employees, and found Kyle Bennett's name, with the amount ten thousand dollars next to it.

Wow. Another ten grand? What was the lawyer doing for this man that was worth so much money?

I scrolled down farther, checking for other familiar names. There were several restaurants listed I recognized, some shops, and the Napa County Bingo Hall. I stopped when I discovered Allison's name. Next to it was the number five thousand.

Why was Angus McLaughlin paying Allison five thousand dollars?

"What's the hold-up?" Angus called out, his curly white eyebrows meeting at the center of his deeply lined forehead.

"I was just getting organized," I said lamely. "I think I opened the payroll file by accident."

"Well, close it and get to work!" he huffed.

"Okay, but I was just wondering why Allison's name

is on your payroll list. Doesn't she work for the Purple Grape Winery?"

Angus put down the papers he'd been holding in his hands and looked at me oddly. "Excuse me?"

The jig was up. I stood, ready for fight or flight.

Angus's blotchy face grew redder. He stood too, sending a stack of papers flying. "Who the hell are you?"

I grabbed my purse and dashed halfway to the door in order to make a quick getaway in case he went for the gun cabinet.

"I just think it's odd that you have so many businesses on your payroll—restaurants, shops, even the bingo hall. Are you paying kickbacks to all these places, Mr. McLaughlin? In exchange for what—information? Influence?"

Oh boy, I was asking for it now. I took another step closer to the door.

"Get the hell out of here!" the man sputtered. "How dare you . . ."

McLaughlin came around the desk on wobbly, bowed legs, using the desk as support—and wearing pants, luckily. I guessed he had some sort of hip or leg problems that slowed him down physically. Reaching over, he picked up a cane I hadn't noticed lying on the edge of the desk—I'd thought it was some kind of rustic decoration—and waved it threateningly at me.

"I know who you are! You're that snoop from the party that can't keep her nose out of other people's business. Kyle told me about you." He whacked the cane on the desk, and it made a loud, threatening crack.

I reached the front door and took hold of the knob.

"And you're the man who's trying to buy up all of Napa, including the Purple Grape. Are you also the one who murdered JoAnne Douglas because she got in your way? And Javier Montoya because he found out about JoAnne?"

I was taunting him, randomly making up stuff, but what the hell. I figured I could make a run for it and he wouldn't get far in his condition. And maybe, in his anger, he'd spill something important by accident.

To my surprise, he came at me, swinging his cane.

I yanked open the door and came face-to-face with a pretty young blond woman.

"He's all yours!" I said, and fled outside and out of McLaughlin's reach. When I got to the other side of the gate, I looked back.

The door to the cabin slammed shut. The girl still stood at the doorway, looking completely bewildered.

Thank God, I thought, panting from the adrenaline rush.

The gardener, working near the gate, stopped trimming a rosebush and stared at me quizzically.

"Mr. McLaughlin didn't like my résumé," I explained, forcing a casual smile at him.

The gardener nodded as if he understood and resumed his snipping. A perfect, long-stemmed red rose came off in his gloved hand.

Stepping through the gate, I said, "The roses are beautiful."

The gardener offered me the bloodred rose in his hand. "For you, señorita," he said, and gave a small bow.

I took the flower and inhaled its fragrance. "Thank you!"

"*De nada.* Have a nice day."

I smelled the flower again on the way back to my car, then unlocked the door and ducked inside. As I lay the long-stemmed rose on the passenger seat, my thumb caught on one of the thorns.

"Ouch!" I said aloud, and pulled the wound to my mouth.

After the bleeding subsided, I looked at my throbbing thumb. It was the second time I'd drawn blood during this investigation. This time, it was just a painful nuisance.

But that's when I realized the first time had been a significant clue.

Chapter 24

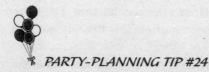

I had cut myself on a piece of glass from the broken
pane in the hallway. Whoever had broken the glass to
take the corkscrew had cleaned it up but overlooked a
shard or two. That had to be the killer—someone
who'd made it look like Rob killed JoAnne by placing
Rob's antique weapon at the scene.

All I had to do was find the physical evidence.

And I now knew how to do just that—pay a visit to
everyone at the party who had a reason to either kill
JoAnne or frame Rob. That let out Angus McLaughlin.
He wasn't at the party, unless he was hiding somewhere—and with those bum hips, I doubted he did
much on-site dirty work. Then again, he could have
paid someone to do it—like Kyle, who was apparently

getting checks from the old recluse, not to mention Allison. I put McLaughlin back on my list.

As for the rest of my suspects, I had to revisit a few people on my list. Figuring Kyle and Allison were the two most likely prospects, I decided to start with them. I knew they wouldn't be very cooperative, but I'd just have to get around that.

Somehow.

I called Kyle, wishing I could use the standard "I have some important new information for you" trick, but I'd done that last time. I needed to come up with some other ruse. My throbbing thumb gave me an answer.

"Hello," Kyle answered.

"Kyle, this is Presley."

"What do you want? I'm busy." He sounded agitated.

"I just came from Angus McLaughlin's cabin." I waited, letting that bulletin worm its way into his heart.

Silence on the other end, then, "Yeah? So what did he say?"

"Enough to get you disbarred," I said, bluffing. "I think I can save your butt, but you'll have to meet me as soon as you can."

I expected Kyle to argue, but instead he said, "Where?"

"Not your office. That place is obviously a front. And certainly not at Napology—if that's where you keep your real office. How about your home?"

"Why not the café?"

"It has to be private. Where do you live?"

He gave me an address in an apartment building in the newer part of town. "I'll see you there in about twenty minutes."

"You better not be playing more games, Presley. I'm tired of your accusations and amateur sleuthing. If this is another wild-goose chase, I swear, I'll—"

"You'll what?" I interrupted him. "Kill me?"

The line went dead.

That went well. I knew I was taking a risk meeting Kyle at his home, but I had a protection plan. For backup, I called Brad, left a message on his phone where I'd be, then called Delicia, who answered on the first ring.

"Pres! Where are you? Ever since your Killer Wine-Tasting Party made the news, the phone's been ringing off the hook. You're going to have to pay me overtime for all the messages I've taken!"

"Dee, I need you to listen," I said, trying to calm her down.

I told her my plan, then hung up and drove to the address that Kyle had given me. He lived in a gated two-story apartment complex, lavishly landscaped and obviously exclusive. It fit his expensive taste and showy personality. His unit was on the second floor, overlooking a large swimming pool and tennis courts. It obviously hadn't come cheap.

I knocked. While I waited for Kyle to answer the door, I redialed Dee.

"You there?" I said softly into the phone.

"Yep. You're coming in loud and clear."

"Okay, don't hang up or I'm screwed."

"Got it! This is so exiting!"

"Shh!" I said, just as the door opened. I lowered the phone as if I were done talking and put it in my purse, making sure the speaker was unobstructed. I hoped he'd figure I'd told someone where I was, but I still had my backup plan.

"Come in," Kyle said, sighing and frowning at my intrusion. Dressed in the same expensive suit he'd been wearing earlier, he gestured for me to enter. I took a quick look around at the expansive living area, staged with model-home furniture and matching art-work. It looked as if Kyle didn't spend a lot of time here—at least not in the living room. There were no magazines on the coffee table, no jackets on the back of the chairs, nothing personal to indicate a human being lived in the place. I peered into the adjoining kitchen. Not a single dish in view. He probably ate out, avoiding the whole kitchen area completely.

"Nice place," I said, trying to sound like I meant it. I hoped Dee could still hear me.

"I'm not home much," he said. "I sleep, change clothes, and go."

I nodded. "Mind if I see the rest of the place? It's so . . . interesting."

Kyle put his hands on his hips, looking impatient. "Listen, Presley, I didn't drop everything to give you a house tour. I'm beginning to think you're the party planner who cried wolf. What is it you wanted to tell me that supposedly will save my career? I have to get back to the jail and Rob."

"Are they going to release him?"

"I don't know. I'm working on it."

"Okay, but first, do you mind if I use your bathroom? Too much coffee," I said, patting my tummy.

Kyle let out an exasperated breath. "Fine. Down the hall, on the right."

"Thanks. Be right back."

As soon as I reached the bathroom, I closed the door as if I had entered, and instead moved on to Kyle's bedroom.

"Dee?" I whispered into my purse. "Can you still hear me?" I held the purse up to my ear.

"Yes!" she whispered back.

I crossed the room to the closet on the far side of the room and did a quick and quiet search. Kneeling down, I found what I was looking for—his shoes. Specifically, the Ferragamos he'd worn to the party. My shoe-store stint during my college days, combined with my knowledge of ab-psych, had taught me a lot about a person's personality. But this time I wasn't interested in diagnosing Kyle as a sociopath or obsessive-compulsive.

I just wanted to see his sole.

I picked up one of the shoes and turned it over. Pulling out my cell phone, I touched the screen to make the light come on, hoping I didn't accidentally disconnect from Dee, and held it over the sole.

No sparkles. No sign of broken glass on the bottom of his shoes. Just scuff marks.

I put the shoe back in the closet and was about to stand up when I heard, "Hey! Get out of there!"

Kyle stood in the bedroom doorway, his face twisted half in anger, half in disbelief.

"What the hell are you doing?"

I raised my phone and turned it toward him as if it were some kind of weapon.

"What are you going to do with that?" he said, almost laughing. "Phone me to death? You got an app for that?"

"Very funny. As a matter of fact, I have the police on the other end of the phone. I told them if anything happened to me, they'd know exactly where I was and who I was with." I said Kyle's name and gave his address. "They've been listening the whole time."

Kyle lunged for the phone. "Give me that!" he said, snatching it from my hand. "Hello? Who is this?"

I couldn't make out what Dee said, but I hoped it was something like "the Napa Police Department." She was a good actress; she would improvise. I just hoped that high-pitched baby voice didn't give her away.

"Yeah? Well, you don't sound like a cop to me, sweetheart."

With that, he touched the button on the phone, ending the call.

"That was stupid," I said. "The police know I'm with you. They'll be here any minute."

"Really? Well, then I'd advise you to get your ass out of here before they arrest you for breaking and entering."

My jaw went slack. "I didn't break in! You let me in!"

"That's not the way I'm going to tell it."

"But they heard everything on the phone."

He touched another button, looked at the screen, then smiled, those bright white capped teeth nearly glinting in the artificial light. "Your last call wasn't to the Napa Police Department. It was a four-one-five number to someone named Delicia Jackson. Isn't she your party friend—the one who played the wine queen at the party? I think I hit on her."

Busted!

"Give me my phone," I demanded, reaching out a hand.

"What are you after, Presley? You think I killed JoAnne? You're nuts, you know that, right? If I killed off my clients, I wouldn't make any money. Don't you get that?"

I grabbed my phone back and headed for the door.

"Don't worry," I said. "I don't think you killed JoAnne now. But I do think you're a lousy lawyer. And I'll do anything I can to get you disbarred if you don't get Rob out."

I slammed the door behind me, my hands shaking from the emotional confrontation, and took the stairs down, two steps at a time. I couldn't get away from that shyster fast enough.

The phone rang as soon as I got in my MINI. Brad. Thank God.

"Hi," I answered, almost breathlessly.

"I've been calling you! It keeps going to voice mail. What's going on? You okay?"

"Sorry. I've been on the phone with Dee. Any chance you can come back to the Purple Grape soon? I think I'm onto something."

"Did you find out who killed JoAnne?"

"Not exactly, but I think I can find the physical evidence that proves who the killer is. I'd love your help."

"I should be there in a couple of hours. But listen to me, Presley. Do nothing until I get there, understood?"

"Believe me, all I'm going to do is get the evidence. I don't plan on confronting the killer or doing anything stupid. I've learned my lesson."

"Yeah, sure you have," I heard him mumble. Then louder, "Hang tight. I'm serious. I'll see you soon."

"Ten-four," I said, quoting some TV police show.

"Knock it off, Presley. You're not a cop; you're a party planner. Please try to remember that."

I hung up, feeling a whole lot better knowing Brad was on the way. Now all I had to do was one last thing to prove my theory—that Allison had killed JoAnne in order to frame Rob, and then killed Javier because he probably knew too much. I was certain she'd also tried to kill her own sister so she'd inherit the winery.

Unfortunately, that meant if Allison was home, I'd have to get her out of the house and me into her bedroom again.

I punched in the number of the Purple Grape.

"Hello?" It was Allison. Marie was probably still sleeping. At least, I hoped she was only sleeping . . .

"Hey, Allison, this is Presley. I think I know who the killer is, but I need your help. Would you meet me at Kyle's apartment as soon as you can?"

She hesitated, then said, "You know who killed JoAnne?"

"Yes, and I think I can prove it, but I need your help."

"Why do you want to meet at Kyle's? Do you think he's the killer?"

"I don't want to say anything over the phone. Do you know where he lives?"

"Yeah, he has an apartment downtown."

"Good. Hurry."

I hung up, feeling a tingle all over my body. Dee was right—this was exciting! I had Allison running around on a wild-goose chase, giving me the chance to check on Marie and snoop around in her room.

I drove out of Kyle's apartment parking lot charged with adrenaline and headed for the Purple Grape.

In spite of the multiple ribbons of crime scene tape, the winery looked peaceful, belying its recent murderous history. I didn't see Allison's car and figured she had to be nearly at Kyle's by now. She'd probably wait for me there for ten minutes or so, then give up and return home, giving me about half an hour total to find what I was looking for.

As they say in the party biz, piece of cake.

Using the key I still had, I let myself into the house. The place was as quiet as a room full of partiers waiting to yell, "Surprise!" to an unsuspecting guest of honor. I just hoped there were no surprises waiting for me.

My first stop was Rob and Marie's bedroom. I wanted to make sure she was all right. I wouldn't put it past Allison to try to get rid of her sister again, after failing at her first attempt.

I knocked quietly on Marie's door.

No answer. I shuddered, thinking of the possibilities.

Turning the knob, I opened the door and peered into the darkness. The shades were still drawn, the only light coming from the hallway behind me. I moved to the bed and gently put a hand on the rumpled covers.

"Marie?" I said softly, not wanting to startle her.

The covers felt soft. I pressed down harder to give her body a little shake.

My hand met the firmness of the bed.

I threw back the covers.

Marie was gone.

Chapter 25

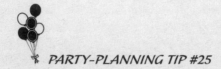

PARTY-PLANNING TIP #25

Overserving your party guests can be a problem at a wine-tasting event. Look for wines with an alcohol content under 14 percent to keep your guests from becoming too intoxicated. Nothing ruins a party faster than a drunken loudmouth or sauced psychopath.

"Marie!" I shouted, starting to panic. I felt tiny beads of perspiration break out on my forehead and down my back. My heart rate went into hyperspeed.

Maybe she's in the bathroom, I thought. I dashed over; the door was open but the room was empty.

Could she have gone with Allison on the wild-goose chase I'd arranged? Or was she wandering the winery again, possibly disoriented? Maybe wounded?

Or even floating in a barrel of wine, like Javier? I shivered at the thought.

I searched the rest of the house, calling her name, but found no sign of her. The only place I hadn't searched was Allison's room. I ran down the hall and tried her door.

Locked.

I tried the knob again. No use. It wasn't going to give just because I tried again. I had to get in there, if not to make sure Marie wasn't inside, then to find the evidence I needed to prove Allison was the killer.

I remembered seeing a sliding glass door that led from the living area of the house to the backyard patio. I raced down the hall, opened the sliding door, and sped outside and over to Allison's room. There were two windows, about three by four feet, that looked out from her room, but they were covered with lavender curtains that prevented me from seeing inside. I remembered seeing a bureau under one of the windows. The left? Or the right?

I looked around for something to stand on and something else to break the window. What was a broken window at this point? If I had to explain, I could always say I was worried Marie was inside and possibly in danger. Locating a stone statue the size of a toddler—of a cherub holding a bunch of grapes—I yanked it up from its spot on the patio and hefted it over to the window. I set it down, then found a wrought-iron chair sitting next to a tiled café table and carried it over.

Stepping carefully onto the chair, I leaned down and hoisted the statue up. Though it was the size of a toddler, the thing weighed a ton. I closed my eyes, turned my head, and swung the statue into the window. Glass went flying, reminding me instantly of the smashed display case. This wasn't the first time glass had been shattered recently at the Purple Grape. And shattered glass was the main reason I was now breaking into Allison's room. Literally.

I dropped the statue, removed my Mary Jane and used the bottom to scrape off any broken glass that remained on the windowsill. After slipping the shoe back on, I lifted my leg over the sill as gingerly as I could, pushing aside the curtains as if they were heavy cobwebs. I climbed through and stepped onto the top of the bureau, then brought in my other leg. Squatting down, I swiped off the broken glass from the bureau with my shoe. Moments later I was standing on the floor in Allison's room.

No Marie.

I zipped over to the closet where I'd hidden myself earlier. No Marie there either.

Kneeling down, I shuffled through all the shoes that rested in boxes on the floor. Coming up empty, I pulled down the boxes from the top of the closet and examined them. No party shoes here either.

I was about to check the last box when a shaft of light came from the bedroom door.

The door was open.

I started and whirled around.

Allison stood in the doorway. She was staring at the broken window, the pieces of glass on the floor around the bureau, her face livid with rage.

Then she looked at me.

"What the hell are you doing in my room!" she screamed. In her hand, something silver glinted.

Caught off guard, I tried to think of a good excuse for breaking her window, climbing in, and going through her closet.

Yeah, right.

"Uh . . . ," was all I could manage. My heart was beating faster than a ticking time bomb. Finally I said, "I was looking for Marie . . . She's missing . . ."

"And you thought she might be in my closet?" She

stared at me in disbelief, one hand on her hip, the other tightly gripping the shiny object. A corkscrew? A small knife? A glass shard? Just about anything could be used as a weapon in the wrong hands.

I grabbed one of the stiletto shoes from the box I still held and gripped it like a hammer. A single black Prada with a three-inch heel was all I had to defend myself. I might have been able to kill a spider with it, but not much else.

Then it dawned on me. The shoe in my hand belonged to the pair that Allison had worn to the party.

"I panicked when I couldn't find her," I said, stalling. I flipped the shoe over and checked the sole.

At the same time, Allison took a step forward. Reflexively, I looked down at her shoes.

Plum-colored Kate Spade flats that complemented her pink top and white shorts.

They looked just like the ones Marie had worn to the party. I remembered how perfectly they'd matched Marie's plum outfit.

"You have shoes exactly like Marie's?" I said, puzzled.

Allison frowned as if I'd truly lost my mind.

"Those." I pointed to the ones on her feet and felt the hairs on my arms stand up.

"They're Marie's, not mine. We wear the same size. But what has this got to do with anything? You broke into my room to steal God knows what and you're asking about shoes. I'm calling the police." She tossed the shiny object on her bed.

Her room key. It was attached to one of my wine-opener key chains.

She reached for something in her pocket.

I tensed up again.

She pulled out her cell phone.

"Wait!" I said, dropping the shoe I held in my hand. "I need to see those shoes!"

"What is wrong with you, Presley? I'm beginning to think *you're* the murderer, the way you're behaving!"

"Please, Allison! Just take off your shoes and let me see them."

Without releasing her cell phone, she kicked off one of the flats.

I reached down and retrieved it, then turned it over. The sole sparkled in the light coming through the doorway.

Not exactly diamonds on the soles of her shoes.

More like bits of broken glass.

Before I could say the name out loud, a shadow suddenly blocked the shaft of light.

My mouth went dry. My heart thudded against my chest.

Marie stood in the doorway.

She held a bottle of wine over her head.

Chapter 26

❦ PARTY-PLANNING TIP #26

Believe it or not, a wine bottle is specially designed to preserve wine. See the dimples (punts) on the bottom, remnants of the glass-blowing days? They help collect sediments, strengthen and make the bottle sturdy, and make the volume look bigger to impress (or fool?) the purchaser. In other words, "The wine in this bottle may appear to be more than it really is . . ."

Before I could react, Marie brought down the heavy wine bottle, striking Allison's head. Allison slumped to the ground like a marionette cut from its strings.

"Marie! What are you doing?" I screamed. Deep down, I knew exactly what she was doing—trying to kill her sister.

And I was next.

So it was Marie who had murdered JoAnne Douglas and Javier Montoya. The pieces of glass on the bottom of her shoes—the shoes Allison wore today and the ones Marie wore to the party—meant Marie was the one who'd broken the protective glass panel, taken the corkscrew, and stabbed JoAnne. I didn't know why exactly—to get even with her cheating husband by framing him for the murder?

Marie looked down at Allison's body, then up at me. She had such a calm, pleased look on her face, I almost didn't believe what she'd just done.

"Marie, you're ill," I said, trying to sound sympathetic instead of totally panicked, which was how I actually felt. "You need to rest. This has all been very traumatic for you. Let me call your doctor."

"Don't worry, Presley. I'm not ill or tired or suicidal. I just want to put an end to all this and get on with my life. And you've done a lot to help me reach that goal by suspecting Allison of murdering JoAnne."

I didn't move, not wanting to provoke her. The most important thing I'd learned in the field of abnormal psychology was to let people talk. Not only would it keep me alive awhile longer, but it would allow Marie to vent. Maybe that would be enough to dissipate her rage.

"Why, Marie? Why did you kill JoAnne Douglas? Because she was threatening your vineyard?"

She held the wine bottle with both hands as she spoke. "That was part of the reason. JoAnne was such a pest to everyone in the county, not just us. But God, I hated that woman. She was always threatening the Purple Grape, trying to close it down, get rid of us. I'm sure she was jealous of all that I had. And then when I found out that she had gotten Allison to sell our wines online at a cheap price—that was the final straw. Dammit, I worked hard to make the winery a success. She just inherited her winery. The wine community needed to be rid of her. And killing her also gave me the opportunity to get even with Rob"—tears sprang to her eyes—"for cheating on the sanctity of our marriage."

I wondered if she knew about the letter I'd found in Allison's shoe box.

"With my own sister," she continued. "So when I accidentally discovered JoAnne hiding under the party table, ready to ruin our special event by throwing green paint at our guests, I got the idea to kill one bird—JoAnne the wine pest—and destroy the other—Rob the cheating husband."

"So you planted the corkscrew at the scene," I said, confirming what I'd guessed.

She nodded. "I broke the glass on his collection with one of your corkscrews, Presley, then got that antique screw with the big handle from the case and replaced it with yours so it would look like Rob did it. When I got back to the pouring table, I grabbed a bottle"—she hefted the one in her hands—"ducked down, and hit her over the head. While she lay there unconscious, I tried to stab her with the corkscrew, but it wouldn't go in, so I grabbed a cheese knife. That did the trick. Then I jabbed in the corkscrew to make a point, wiped both clean, and went back to pouring wine as if nothing had happened."

Recalling Rob's letter to Allison, I said, "But Rob loved you. If he cheated on you, I'm sure he regrets it."

"Maybe. But I couldn't forgive him. Neither of them. I took in my sister when she needed a place to live and gave her a job, and that's how she repaid me—by sleeping with my husband, not to mention nearly every other man in the county. She's always been jealous of me and what I have, but when she took something I loved and ruined it, I'd had enough."

"But you didn't frame her. You framed your own husband," I said, while glancing out of the corner of my eye for something to defend myself with. No doubt Marie had used a wine bottle to hit Javier over the head too, before she drowned him. Unlike on TV, where bottles seem to shatter easily, this one was as solid and dangerous as a rock.

"Oh, but I didn't want to kill Rob. That would have been too quick and easy. I wanted him to suffer for years in jail. After he was arrested, I planned to get Allison arrested for the murder of Javier and for trying to kill me."

Still puzzled, I frowned, all the while alert to her every move. "But how?"

"My suicide attempt? I made it look like someone actually tried to kill me. And Allison was the most obvious suspect. But everyone seemed to miss the clues, in spite of the fact that I tried to make it clear. So I had to come up with a new plan." She glanced at Allison lying lifeless on the floor. "The way I see it now, you broke into Allison's room . . . she attacked you . . . and you hit her over the head with the wine bottle."

"Like you did Javier?"

"Poor Javier. He saw me cleaning the broken glass from the hallway that night. And that was fine, except later, he caught me putting my medication in Allison's medicine cabinet to frame her for attempting to murder me. I told him to keep his mouth shut, but I didn't trust him. So I called him into the storage building and asked him to retrieve my ring, which had 'fallen' into the wine vat. While he was leaning in, I hit him over the head with a wine bottle and pushed him under so he'd drown. Then I dropped the ring in so it would look like he'd been caught with some of my jewelry."

I sensed my time was about up. I thought about trying to make a run for it, but Marie stood between me and the door—and she held a mean-looking bottle of merlot in her hands. Plus, I didn't see any way to defend myself if she came at me, other than a good old-fashioned catfight.

Marie's eyes narrowed. She raised the bottle, ready to pounce like a panther.

Just as she started to lunge, she suddenly screamed. Twisting around, she lost her balance and fell to the floor. The bottle dropped from her hand and onto the tile floor, where it burst and shattered, flooding the area with purple liquid.

I looked down in horror, trying to figure out what had happened.

Allison, her eyes wide but still lying on the floor, had Marie by the ankle and was digging her sharp, fashionable nails into her sister's leg.

Marie screamed again as she tried to shake her leg free of Allison's clawed grip. The two struggled, Marie on top of Allison, biting and scratching and pulling her hair. A regular girl fight. I ran around the scuffle to Allison's bed, yanked off the wine-themed coverlet, threw it over both of them, and fell on top of it.

Allison's head poked out at the side of the coverlet. I rolled a little, focusing my weight on Marie's body, allowing Allison to slither out. She pushed herself to a wobbly standing position.

"Grab some belts or something!" I yelled.

Allison went to her closet and returned with two belts, while Marie continued to flail and scream beneath the cover.

"Help me roll her up!"

Allison knelt down on one side and tucked the coverlet under Marie, while I slid off and began rolling her body up like a mummy. The kicking subsided and the screaming became muffled.

"The belts!" I said, lying on top of the encased Marie.

She took one and cinched it around Marie's legs, then did the same at the top of Marie's head.

I sat up on the floor next to Marie, puffing, exhausted from trying to hold her down. I could hear Marie sobbing quietly from under the cover, no longer struggling.

"Hand me my phone," I said breathlessly. While Allison sat down and rubbed the back of her head, I called 911. She probably had a concussion and would need medical attention. While waiting for the Napa police, I called Brad. I heard a phone ringing in the distance.

"Brad?" I yelled, pulling the phone from my ear.

"Presley?" he hollered back.

"Down here!" I headed for the door. "In Allison's room."

Brad appeared in the hallway in his jeans and a blue T-shirt, then entered the room and took in the scene. He glanced first at me, then spotted Allison on the bed, and finally saw the burrito-wrapped body of Marie.

"What's going on?"

"Long story," I said, collapsing on the bed next to Allison.

"Who's in the cocoon?"

"Marie."

"You're kidding me."

"Afraid not."

"But I thought . . . ," he started to say.

Allison looked at me. "You thought it was me, didn't you, Presley?"

I pressed my lips together. "Sort of. I mean, you were the one who seemed jealous of Marie, not the other way around. But apparently she found out about your little dalliance with her husband and couldn't handle it."

"So she killed JoAnne?" Allison said, the pieces coming together for her.

I told her what Marie had confessed a few minutes before Allison regained consciousness and grabbed Marie's ankle.

"Wow," Allison said, her body deflating like a balloon. "I never knew she hated me that much. And I never told her about Rob and me . . . I wonder how she found out."

I heard sirens.

Moments later someone called, "Police!"

"Down here!" I called back.

Detective Kelly appeared at the door with three officers.

He surveyed the room and nodded toward the form on the floor. She looked like a giant party popper. "What have we here?"

"Your murderer," I said.

"Really? Who's in there?" he asked.

"Marie Christopher. She killed JoAnne and Javier and tried to kill Allison. I was next on her list. But thanks to Allison . . ." I shot her a thank-you look. She nodded.

Detective Kelly signaled the other officers to take over. While two officers unrolled Marie, a third stood ready with cuffs and a Taser. EMTs arrived moments later to check on Allison. It wasn't long before Marie was taken into custody, read her rights, and led out of the room. As she passed by me, her head down, her hands behind her back, she looked like a broken woman.

Meanwhile Allison was placed on a gurney. She was covered in bites, scratches, and bruises and had a lump on the back of her head.

"Wait!" I said as the EMTs started to wheel her away to the ambulance. "Allison?"

She looked up at me, tired and depressed, not like the perky, flirtatious woman she usually was.

She sighed. "Yeah?"

"Thanks."

"For what?"

"You saved my life back there."

"Hey, I saved my own life. I'm sure she would have finished the job if she'd known I'd come to."

As the paramedics pushed Allison down the hall, I wondered if this would be a new beginning for her. Or would she continue to lie, cheat, and steal, as she had for so many years? No doubt she'd be leaving the Purple Grape, now that her sister was headed for prison and her brother-in-law was returning. But she still had her bingo games and her sugar-daddy connections at the hall. I had a feeling she'd bounce back quickly.

After one of the EMTs checked a couple of minor

cuts on my ankle from when the wine bottle shattered, Brad, Detective Kelly, and I went to the kitchen, where the detective took my statement. I explained how the shoes led to the killer—that when Marie had broken the glass and taken the corkscrew, she'd picked up pieces of broken glass on the soles of her shoes. Her attack on Allison would pretty much cinch it for her.

"Will you be releasing Rob now?" I asked, wondering how he would take the news that his wife was a murderer.

"Soon," the detective said. "Good thing, since he would have needed a new lawyer."

"What?"

"Kyle Bennett quit. Didn't give a reason, just said something about 'conflict of interest.' But Rob doesn't really need a lawyer at this point. I'm sure he'll be free by the end of the day. His wife, however, is going to need legal representation."

"What's going to happen to JoAnne's winery?"

"I hear it's going up for sale. You in the market?"

I laughed and shook my head.

"Too bad. Napology will probably absorb it."

"Maybe Rob can take it over," I suggested. "He's been wanting to expand. But talk about irony . . ."

"Well," Detective Kelly said, "the next time you're up in the wine country for a tasting, give me a ring so I can call all my off-duty guys as backup."

"Very funny," I said.

The detective shook hands with Brad and me, then drove off, leaving us alone at the Purple Grape.

"You all right?" Brad asked, looking me over carefully.

I nodded, glad he was there. On our way out, I dropped the house key on the table—I wouldn't be needing it again—and we made our way to the front garden, where all the trouble had begun. I took Brad's hand as we walked and thought about how the wine country was supposed to be so mellow, like a glass of hearty merlot. Instead, it had fizzed like a shaken bottle of champagne, about to blow its top.

"I suppose it's too early in the day for a glass of wine," I said.

"Tell you what," Brad said. "Let's head back to civilization, catch up on work, then I'll take you out for a nice romantic dinner and you can tell me all the details I missed. How does that sound?"

I kissed him my answer. Amazingly, his lips tasted like sweet wine.

Chapter 27

PARTY-PLANNING TIP #27

Want an alternative to wine tasting? How about a beer-tasting party? Provide a variety of microbrews or beers from other countries, or serve ales versus lagers, bottled versus on tap, and even kegs, and then hoist a few with beer-loving friends.

I followed Brad's SUV to Treasure Island, parked, then walked with him to my office. Dee was out at an interview, according to the "In/Out" board, and had left me a stack of party-related notes. It would take me all afternoon to catch up, but I welcomed the distraction from the murder investigation. Brad took a call on his cell and left for his office—another crime scene request—so I took a minute to call my mother and see how she was doing.

"Presley, I was just talking about you to my friends here. I told them about our lovely wine-tasting party and now they want to have one! Isn't that exciting? We can't have alcohol, of course, but I was thinking, instead of wine, maybe we could make it a chocolate-tasting party, with a chocolate fountain and do-it-yourself chocolate bonbons and . . ."

I half listened as she took me through the entire party plan. By the time she finished, I was exhausted just thinking about it, but she had given me some great ideas for the chocoholic party I'd been asked to host at the annual Chocolate Festival in Ghirardelli Square. After I promised to get back to her on the idea, I hung up and promptly ate two See's chocolates I'd stored in my top desk drawer.

The afternoon passed quickly as I brainstormed ideas for several other parties Dee had collected for me. Around four I headed home, taking my work with me, then spent some quality time with my cats, throwing mousies, rubbing tummies, and dangling crepe-paper streamers. When we were all pooped, I fed the cats and hopped in the shower to get ready for my dinner date with Brad. By the time he called for me at six, I was dressed in a short, sexy, strapless black dress I'd bought on sale and had been saving for a special occasion. I hoped it would distract him from the huge meal I planned to order. I'd been starving myself all day—aside from the chocolates.

"Wow," he said, eyeing me when I opened the door.

"Too much?" I asked, glancing at his more casual attire—black jeans and a blue power shirt. "I didn't know how to dress, since you wouldn't tell me where we're going."

"You look perfect," he said. "Shall we?"

I grabbed my purse, told my kitties to behave, and left them with a new stuffed mouse to play with.

"You're still not going to tell me where we're

headed?" I asked, locking the door behind me. I hoped my growling stomach didn't deafen him.

"Nope. It's a surprise," he said, stealing another look at my dress as he escorted me to the carport.

"Not sure I can handle any more surprises today," I said. I spotted Brad's crime scene SUV in the carport and made a face.

He shrugged. "It was this or the bike," he said, referring to his Harley.

"Let's take my car." I handed him the keys.

We chatted about the murder case as we drove over the Bay Bridge to the city. Brad had talked with Detective Kelly again and learned that Rob had indeed been released. That was good news. I wondered how he was doing, after learning that his wife was a murderer. Hopefully he had Gina and Rocco to comfort him.

We pulled up to McAllister Street at the corner of Gough, just off Van Ness. A valet opened my door and helped me out, then took the keys from Brad. I glanced up at the restaurant sign: "Opaque: A Journey for the Senses." Intriguing name, to say the least. We entered through the unmarked door and Brad checked in with the hostess. The waiting room was small but held comfy-looking chairs and cocktail tables.

"Have you been here before?" the young woman at the front desk asked. She had a sly grin on her face, as if she had a special secret.

I shook my head and looked around for the dining area. All I saw was a tiny waiting room.

"First, please turn off your cell phones and check your purse with me."

Frowning at Brad, I reluctantly turned over my purse.

"Now, have a seat in the cocktail lounge and your waiter will be with you soon."

Brad escorted me into the softly lit lounge, where we made our choices for our three-course meal. Unusual, I thought, selecting our meals before we were even seated, but I went ahead and chose the grilled filet mignon, while Brad opted for the seared sea bass. Meanwhile we enjoyed a "specialty drink." Having had my fill of wine lately, I ordered a margarita, and Brad had a rum and Coke. As soon as we finished our drinks, a waitress appeared and called Brad's name. By then my curiosity was as piqued as my appetite.

I waved to signal her as we stood, but she made no move to greet us. She just stared pleasantly into the lounge area.

"Right here," Brad called to her.

The waitress turned in the direction of his voice and her smile grew.

"Hello, I'm Beverly, your waitress," she said without making eye contact. "Will you follow me, please?"

That's when I realized she was blind.

I glanced at Brad to see his reaction, but he obviously knew. He took my arm and we followed Beverly to the door I'd noticed earlier. She opened it and led us downstairs to another room, me holding on to her shoulder, Brad holding on to mine.

The room was pitch-black.

I slid my hand down into Brad's and squeezed it. "What's going on?" I whispered, bumping into something at my side. The waitress guided me to a chair, then seated Brad, talking to us as she helped us orient ourselves in the darkness. She explained how to locate our utensils and reminded us to take in the savory aromas that filled the room.

And then she left us alone.

In complete darkness.

"Oh my God!" I whispered, aware of the diners nearby from hearing their voices, yet still unable to see them. "This is incredible!"

"I thought you might like it," Brad said. I suddenly noticed how deep and resonant his voice was when I wasn't distracted by his good looks. "It's kind of like investigating a mystery."

I giggled. "How so?"

"Well, you were completely in the dark about who the killer was—just like you're completely in the dark here."

I smiled, then realized he couldn't see my reaction. I squeezed his hand again and felt the heat of it. I hadn't let go since we'd been seated.

We chatted a few minutes, mostly about all the twists and turns this murder investigation had taken. "I still don't know if the Briens and Madeiras were having affairs with one another, but that was only a distraction," I said into the blackness. "None of my business anyway."

"That's never stopped you before," Brad said.

I squeezed his hand a little too hard.

The server brought the bread and butter. Never had I done anything so challenging as spreading that butter on the bread. My fingers were covered by the time I was done. While we dined in the dark, I won-

dered aloud what would happen to the rest of the suspects.

"I suppose Allison is out on her butt," I said to
Brad after wiping butter on my napkin—or was it my
dress?

"No doubt. I don't think Rob will forgive her for
selling his wine behind his back. But I don't think you
need to worry. She'll get some sugar daddy to take care
of her."

"Do you think Rob will keep the winery going?"

"After all that work he put into it? Yeah. Although
the memories may be too much for him and he may sell
it after all. Not to Angus McLaughlin, though."

"I suppose nothing will happen to McLaughlin, unless residents get fed up and stop selling to him before
he completely takes over Napa County."

"The publicity for this murder case might help slow
him down a bit," Brad said. "People may wise up."

"And what about Kyle Bennett?" I asked. "Do you
think he'll still practice law in Napa? He's such a slime-
ball."

"Good question," Brad said. "Maybe he'll hook up
with Allison and together they can wreak havoc. Did
they have a thing going?"

"I'm not sure, but I have a feeling Allison tries to
have a 'thing' with every guy she meets."

"Speaking of a 'thing,'" Brad said, "how's your
mom? She still seeing that Larry guy?"

"No. I talked to her earlier and she said it's over. She
didn't feel they could maintain a 'long-distance' relationship."

Brad laughed. "He's only an hour or so away!"

"Actually, that's Mom-speak for 'he just didn't do it for me,'" I explained.

"Hey, I'm just learning Presley-speak, and now I have to learn Mom-speak?"

"You catch on fast," I said. "Don't worry. After all, you knew I'd love this place."

"You like it?" he asked.

I felt around for my water glass with my free hand, praying I didn't knock it over. "Are you kidding? This would be a great idea for a party!"

I thought about taking off my clothes but chickened out. Instead I slipped off my shoes and began playing footsie with Brad under the table. Who knew where that would lead?

Didn't matter. I was ready for anything Brad had to offer.

Wine- and Cheese-Tasting Party

As if you need an excuse to drink wine, here's one any-way. Host a Wine- and Cheese-Tasting Party, where you have to guess what kind of wine you're drinking, then vote on the best of the lot. By the time the party is over, no one will care which one is the best—just that it was the best time they've ever had!

Invitations

Create fun invitations by making your own wine labels, using the computer, a fancy font, and some clip art of grapes or wine bottles. Write the name of the party and add the details. Ask the guests to bring an assigned bottle of red—cabernet, merlot, chianti, pinot noir—or white—chardonnay, pinot grigio, sauvignon blanc, Riesling—or one of each. Have them wrap the bottles in plain brown paper bags to obscure the labels for a game later.

What to Wear

Ask your guests to dress in wine colors. Or get iron-on decals of wine bottles or glasses for T-shirts, and send them to guests to wear at the party. Or give them a pin featuring a bunch of grapes, a scarf with a wine design, or socks that feature wineglasses and bottles.

Decorations

Cover your tasting table with a paper tablecloth in a wine design (so you don't have to worry about spills on your good tablecloth). Decorate the table with plastic grapes, wineglass decorations, and other wine-related décor. Add wine-colored candles and sprinkle the table with wine bottle labels.

Games and Activities

Test your wine-drinking acumen with a few sips from your favorite bottles—and learn some new wine terms.

Wine and Cheese Tasting

The Preparation

Set out glasses for each guest, with identification labels so everyone knows which glass is his or hers. Write up a numbered list, with spaces for each bottle. Include a rating system from 1 to 10 next to each bottle, 10 being "Superb," 1 being "Swill." Add a space for guests to estimate the price of the wine, and include other aspects of the wine to judge, such as appearance, aroma, flavor, and so on, if you like.

The Tasting

Pour the first glass of wine, preferably white if you're serving both red and white wines, but don't peek at the label. Ask the guests to taste the wine, try to guess what kind it is, and give it a rating. Offer a variety of cheeses and snacks with the wine.

Wine Characteristics

Quiz the guests on their wine acumen, using the following terms. Have them take turns giving definitions—real or made up.

Attractive (easy to drink)
Big (full-bodied)
Flabby (lacking acidity)
Robust (intense)
Supple (well balanced with tannins and fruit)
Green (like unripe fruit)
Heady (high in alcohol)
Barnyardy (smells like farm animals)

Cheese Tasting

Serve a different cheese with each pouring of wine, and have the tasters rate the cheeses, much like they do the wines. Have them guess what kind of cheese it is, how much it costs, and whether it goes well with the wine.

Chocolate and Wine

Surprisingly, chocolate and wine go perfectly together, so have a chocolate and wine tasting by pairing various chocolates—bittersweet, dark, milk, and white—with a variety of wines, such as merlot, cabernet, pinot noir, and so on.

Refreshments

To balance the intake of wine, offer a variety of cheeses, along with French bread or crackers. For the white wines, serve Swiss, Gouda, or baked Brie. For red wine, try Gruyère, Muenster, or blue cheese. Serve cheesecake for dessert, with a nice dessert wine, such as muscat. Other good appetizers include goat cheese, shrimp cocktail, olive oil dip and bread, hummus, and pâté.

Favors, Prizes, and Gifts

Give the tasters a bottle of wine to take home, along with a hunk of cheese and a box of gourmet crackers. Let them keep their wine-decorated T-shirts and other wine accessories. Give them a book on wines.

Party Plus

Take the tasters to a wine bar or tasting room and learn about the different wines as you sample them.

And check out my book *Ladies' Night* for more fun party ideas!

Penny Warner

The Party-Planning Mystery Series

A sparkling mystery series featuring
Presley Parker, a party planner and
sleuth supreme in San Francisco

How to Party with a Killer Vampire
How to Survive a Killer Seance
How to Crash a Killer Bash
How to Host a Killer Party

"A party you don't want to miss."
—*New York Times* bestselling author
Denise Swanson

Available wherever books are sold or at
penguin.com

facebook.com/TheCrimeSceneBooks